APPRAISAL
FOR
MURDER

Elaine Orr

APPRAISAL FOR MURDER

by Elaine Orr

Discover all books in the Jolie Gentil Series
Appraisal for Murder
Rekindling Motives
When the Carny Comes to Town
Any Port in a Storm
Trouble on the Doorstep
Behind the Walls
Vague Images
Ground to a Halt

www.elaineorr.blogspot.com
www.elaineorr.com

Dedication

With love and thanks to my husband, Jim Larkin, for his support, and thanks to my good friend Leigh Michaels for her many suggestions and strong friendship.

CHAPTER ONE

THE ONLY REASON I DIDN'T SHOOT Robby was because I couldn't think of how to do it without getting caught. About two weeks later I found out that in addition to embezzling from his bank my husband also stole money from our joint IRA. I should have thought harder.

It all happened pretty fast. I like to think that if Robby had blown the money over more than a couple months I would have wised up to it. Or, maybe not. The only bank statement I ever looked at was my separate checking account. After all, my husband was Mr. Commercial Banker. That's how I met him. I was Ms. Commercial Real Estate.

But, not any more. I did not exactly flee Lakewood. I quit my job and left. There's a difference. And now I need a job.

I walked faster, hearing the thunk of my footsteps on the nearly deserted boardwalk. Three months ago I could not have imagined leaving my deluxe condo in Lakewood, New Jersey and moving into Aunt Madge's Cozy Corner B&B in Ocean Alley. Three months ago I didn't know my husband had been gambling away our assets in New Jersey casinos on evenings I thought he was at Rotary or Lions or one of his other clubs.

My memories of Ocean Alley are mixed. As a kid I especially liked the beach. It wasn't because of the boardwalk, cotton candy, or suntanned lifeguards, but because Aunt Madge was a lot less strict than my parents. She also fell asleep pretty early, so I essentially had the run of the boardwalk after she tucked me in at eight-thirty.

My parents also trusted me to Aunt Madge the year they were 'working out issues' in their marriage, so I spent my junior year of high school with her in Ocean Alley. I was mad at everyone about being there, including my sister, who was in graduate school and thus able to retain some control over her life. I did a lot of roaming by myself. I had few friends, and didn't like the way half the boys teased me about my name. Those memories are one reason that I didn't keep up with anyone. I visited Aunt Madge many times through the years, but when I came to see her I didn't stroll through town that much.

Right now, I'm especially glad I kept my own name when Robby and I married. Jolie Gentil. It's pronounced Zho-Lee Zhan-tee. The "J" is soft, which distinguishes my name from a southern moniker, such as Bobbi Lee. It's rare than anyone gets it right on the first try. As a child I did not like this one bit. Now I consider it a useful way to recognize telemarketers.

My father is of French descent, as he will tell anyone within shouting distance if he gets the chance. Jolie means pretty in French, and Gentil means nice. Clearly, my parents were not thinking straight when they named me. I attribute the name to the twenty-two hours my mother was in labor, something she does not hesitate to mention.

I shivered. It was cool for October, even for the shore. I had a hooded windbreaker over my loose-knit yellow turtleneck, which I thought went well with my dark brown hair with its blonde highlights, the latter courtesy of whatever brand had been on sale two weeks ago when I decided to leave Robby. I stood by him when he had his probable cause hearing, and was greatly relieved that he later decided to plead guilty to the embezzlement charge. I didn't think I could take sitting behind him during a trial looking like the loyal wife. He was barely willing to talk to me about what he had done. He acted as if this was just a slight financial setback – as if his 401(k) account had gone down a little – rather than a federal crime.

Since Robby hadn't had a chance to steal much from his bank and he had no prior record, his lawyer is encouraging about no jail time if he pleads guilty and makes restitution. I don't figure he'll get that fortunate. He's lucky I'm not suing his ass for forging my name to steal from our IRA. My father advised me that I would spend a lot in legal fees and the amount I would recover, since Robby is broke, might not be worth the time and trouble. Fortunately, I was able to talk my parents out of coming up from Florida for Robby's hearing. My mother would have made me nervous. And my father might have hit Robby.

I checked out the ocean as I quickened my pace. I know that it won't go anyplace, but it amazes me how different it can look from one day to another. Today the breakers were foamier than yesterday and there was a gray cast to the sky, making the water seem darker. The wind was from the land, so the smell of saltwater and brine did not reach the boardwalk.

I determinedly pushed thoughts of Robby out of my mind as I entered Java Jolt, one of the few boardwalk businesses open year round. The year I lived in Ocean Alley it had been an arcade, and I had spent a lot of time trying to make the highest score in a video game called "Screw the Bunny." Every time you could make the male and female bunnies run into each other there were suddenly six more bunnies. However, if you made two females or males collide, four vanished. I regret to say that I sometimes fed my bunny addiction with quarters that guests left as tips on Aunt Madge's small breakfast tables.

Java Jolt owner Joe Regan nodded at me as I slipped off my jacket and draped it over a chair. Although he only moved to Ocean Alley about five years ago, you'd think he had lived here forever. He has the lean good looks of a strong surfer. All he's missing is the sun-enhanced blonde hair, his being brown with a hint of red.

I'm not into designer coffee, so I helped myself to the regular brew that sits on the counter in large thermoses. Once the tourist season is over, Joe leaves an oversized sugar bowl on the counter and you pay for your coffee on the honor system. I eyed the pastries longingly. I had no reason to eat any; Aunt Madge has a well-stocked breakfast nook. I reached for a chocolate chip muffin, chastising myself even before I took the first bite.

"The usual, I see," came Joe Regan's voice. He has a way of smirking with words that can be annoying.

"I wish you'd keep the chocolate chip ones behind the counter so I'd have to ask for them. Then I wouldn't be so tempted."

"That'd be good for sales." He grinned as I turned my back on him and moved toward the two computers that sit against the window. The Cozy Corner B&B does not have Internet service, so I do a lot of my job hunting with Joe's open access computers.

I settled into my email inbox, where I had offers to order products as diverse as Viagra, cappuccino recipes, and Bibles. You could buy all three and stay up all night reading scripture. I started to giggle when the door to the coffee house opened with more vigor than usual. The man who entered looked to be in his late twenties, and I wondered idly if he had been at Ocean Alley High when I was. The voice confirmed it.

"Black, large, extra strong," he said to Joe. No pleasantries here. Michael Riordan had run for senior class president at the end of junior year. He got his butt kicked. To an outsider, this might have seemed hard to believe, given his good looks and dark blue convertible. However, he tended to date girls for a few months and then drop them. Thus, he was not the candidate of the girls I heard talking about him in the bathroom in between classes. This had not been discussed much prior to the election, in case he won.

I had my own reasons not to remember him too fondly. We were in -the same homeroom, and he came up to me the first day of eleventh grade. At lunch that day, he sat with me and introduced me to a number of other classmates who stopped by the table. Nearly tongue-tied in his presence, I rehearsed a couple of lame jokes and tried them at lunch the second day. By the third day, it was as if he didn't know me. Didn't say hello in homeroom and sat with a couple of cheerleaders at lunch.

In the grand scheme of life it was not a big deal. At the time, stinging from what I saw as my parents' rejection and mad at being away from my own friends, it really hurt. I spent a couple of days wondering what he was saying about me to others, and the rest of the school year practicing rude comments in case he talked to me again. No worries there. Now, I can ruefully acknowledge he probably felt as awkward as I did – what do you say to a new kid who doesn't seem able to talk in your presence?

As I returned my gaze to the computer screen Michael turned slightly to his left and I could feel him look at me. I wasn't up for pleasantries any more than he seemed to be, so I didn't acknowledge his vaguely quizzical expression. I'd seen it a number of times in the ten days since I'd moved in with Aunt Madge. The do-I-know-her look. I ignored him.

My attention went to the Internet classifieds, and I searched job listings for the area. Pickings are slim unless you want to work in a hotel or restaurant or maintain an office computer network. This was also the sixth day in a row I had read the listing for an exciting career in the trucking industry ("short hauls only, no overnights"), but I wasn't up for regular tours of Jersey and Manhattan. Since I didn't know what I was looking for, I didn't spend a lot of time at the site. Despite my hopes, there just isn't going to be something interesting, well paying, and fun with my name on it.

The door banged again as Michael Riordan left, and I turned to meet Joe Regan's glance. He held up a five dollar bill. "Not exactly Mr. Personality, but he tips well." He grinned.

"I guess so. That's what he gave you for a cup of coffee?"

"Yep. I hear he did real well in some job in the oil industry." Joe pocketed the bill.

"Not in Jersey, I take it."

Joe laughed. "Nah. Texas, I think."

"He just back here visiting?"

Joe's expression grew serious. "Mother's dying. Cancer."

"That's too bad." Not sure what else to say, I turned back to the computer. I hadn't seen the guy for ten years and couldn't recall meeting his mother, though I thought she was a friend of Aunt Madge's.

I went back to the job listings, expanding my search to towns as far as twenty miles north or south of Ocean Alley. A sidebar offered advice for job seekers. "Define your best skills and look for jobs that use them." That qualifies as remedial job seekers' advice. I define my best skill as persistence, although others tend to label this as my stubborn streak.

After a few minutes, I logged off, refilled my coffee cup and started a slower walk back to Aunt Madge's. She lives three blocks back from the ocean, which she says gives her the illusion of being safe from hurricane damage. Ocean Alley is almost two miles long but only twelve blocks deep, with each street that is parallel to the ocean named for a letter of the alphabet. I've heard that when Ocean Alley incorporated there was a move to change the names of all the streets and arrange them alphabetically, but the City Council could never agree on the names so they just used letters. However, the alphabet starts with 'B.' The Great Atlantic Hurricane removed the old boardwalk and most of 'A' Street in 1944. It's the main reason Aunt Madge won't live any closer to the ocean.

At the corner of C and Main I entered the Purple Cow, Ocean Alley's small office supply store. If I was going to get serious about looking for a job, I probably needed some bond paper for my resume. Of course, I had to figure out what 'career objective' to write on the paper. Near the door was a white board on which someone had written, "It does not take much strength to do things, but it requires great strength to decide on what to do." Elbert Hubbard.

I realized the sales clerk was staring at me. What, did I dribble coffee again?

"Didn't you go to high school here?" she asked.

"Yes, I did, but just for one year." Her face was familiar. I didn't have any negative memories, so I held out my hand. "Jolie Gentil. I was here for eleventh grade, but that was more than ten years ago."

She had wide eyes, which gave her the appearance of perpetual amazement, accented by large, octagonal glasses. Thin blonde hair fell to nearly the middle of her back, and was pulled back from her face in a large clip. She was almost four inches taller than my 5'2" and looked as if she enjoyed the fashion of the 1970s. More important, her smile was friendly.

"I'm Ramona Argrow. We had geometry together. You did a lot better than I did." Her voice had a kind of dreamy quality, so I was surprised that her handshake was firm. "Where did you go?"

Her name sounded familiar, as if it should mean more than just geometry class. "Go..?"

"Why didn't you come back to senior year?"

It was such a simple question I had not followed her logic. "My parents lived in Lakewood. I was just down here for a year with my aunt while they sorted some stuff out." In eleventh grade, I had said they were on a long trip through Europe.

"That's right; your aunt has the B&B. I like her. She buys her nameplates here."

Aunt Madge makes small little signs that she inserts in a four-by-six picture frame affixed to the wall outside each of the guest rooms. On it she puts the name of the guests, ostensibly so they don't wander into the wrong rooms. One couple was quite put out by it, said they didn't care to advertise their whereabouts to the world. In retrospect, I suppose they were lovers out for a jaunt. Aunt Madge still makes the signs, but now she asks each guest if they want to place one by their door.

"She's terrific," I agreed. Now what? All I could remember about

Ramona was that she always had a faraway look and probably took art class, since she often carried a portfolio with her. I had tripped over it once in geometry class. "You, uh, still paint?"

She shook her head. "Just pen and ink now. In the summer, I do caricatures of people on the boardwalk. Pays better than here."

"So, you never left?" As soon as I asked I regretted it. Probably sounded as if I was implying that she should have.

"Nope. I like the beach." She gestured in the direction of the ocean. "I walk two miles on the sand every day."

No wonder she was so slim. I automatically sucked in my small tummy. I always tell myself that tomorrow I'll eat less and lose five pounds within a month. Never happens. "Could you, uh, help me find some bond paper?"

"Sure." She moved toward the back of the store and I followed. "We have regular white and ivory bond, and a couple pastel colors. The colors are more expensive."

I could feel her eyes on me as I looked at the paper. I hadn't planned on an audience, and it made me nervous. In general, I don't give a tinker's damn what anyone thinks or if they stare at me for an hour, but after the last couple months, I feel as if everyone is looking at me as the wife of Robby Marcos, embezzler. I grabbed a small box of the ivory bond. "This'll do."

Ramona took it and walked toward the front. "Most people use this for resumes."

I felt like saying I wasn't 'most people,' but in this case, I was. "Yeah. I'm thinking of recareering. Decided to have my mid-life crisis early."

She smiled as she scanned the paper. "I'm not that far along yet." As she reached for a small bag, her eyes met mine. "I'm sorry about your husband's stuff."

"Oh. Thanks." I didn't realize she would know, and I didn't like it. I could feel my face burning and I dropped my purse as I reached in for money.

"I guess I shouldn't have said anything. I just..."

"It's okay. I appreciate the sentiment." I handed her my money. "Um, do you mind if I ask how you heard?" I knew it wouldn't be Aunt Madge.

"Local busybody, Elmira Washington." She put my resume paper in the small shopping bag. "Nobody pays much attention to her, and she doesn't talk much to people our age. I have to listen to her when she comes in here." She handed me the bag. "What was your first career?"

"I've been in real estate."

"Ooh. You can make a lot of money with that here. My uncle does it."

That's why her name sounded familiar. Lester Argrow's photo was plastered on a billboard on the south side of town. "Sure. I remember his sign now. Where's his office?"

"It's a small one, above First Bank. He usually meets his clients in their houses or at the Burger King. It's easy for his clients to park at Burger King."

Sounded as if Lester Argrow had made some conscious decisions about not becoming a major force in the real estate industry. All I said was, "I know where First Bank is."

"If you want some advice about getting into real estate here, just tell him you talked to me." She smiled again as she handed me my bag. "There's a group planning the ten-year reunion. I think they're going to do it Thanksgiving weekend, because a lot of people will be home. Even if you didn't graduate with us you could come."

I thanked her, made no promises about the reunion, and stepped back into the brisk October air. I wasn't up for seeing a lot of people until I had my wits more about me. Aunt Madge says I'm still in the "reeling stage," though I think I'm close to moving to what I have decided to call a "slow spin." I am definitely feeling better about life now that I've put most of my stuff in a storage locker and left the town where people greeted me with either words of encouragement or a sad smile.

AUNT MADGE LIVES ON the corner of D Street and Seashore. Her three-story Victorian has three turrets and a wrap-around porch that is populated with an array of comfortable chairs and a porch swing. She has the house repainted every three years, white with blue trim. She repairs porch boards herself when they start to rot, though she no longer saws her own lumber. When I was little, my sister Renée would read picture books to me as we sat on the porch swing. She took her role as big sister very seriously, and unless she was trying to make me do something I didn't want to, I mostly appreciated her attention.

Aunt Madge is technically my mother's aunt. Madge's sister, Alva, was my late grandmother. They grew up in Ocean Ally in what old-timers at the diner just off the beach call the 'glory days' of World War II. Aunt Madge is a woman who knows her own mind. She does not often feel a need to tell it to you, but when you look at her it's clear she is reflecting on what's going on around her.

Where my grandmother left her hair at its natural white, Aunt Madge says white hair makes her face look like it belongs in a casket, and she tries different colors. Today it is a very light red; or was when I left the house, anyway. She tried deep auburn but she said it made her look like an old lady trying to pass. As a younger one, I suppose; I didn't ask. She doesn't use permanent color, so after twenty or thirty washes she's close to white and can try another look. My father still laughs about the time she tried deep black, leaving a dashing white streak straight back from her widow's peak. He told her she looked like a skunk and she washed her hair thirty times in one night to get it out.

I was still smiling about her 'skunk hair' as I climbed the front steps. Even on the porch I could smell Aunt Madge's cheddar cheese bread. She bakes it and a loaf of wheat every day, and puts them out with coffee, tea and ice water at four p.m. She is the only one of the four B&Bs in Ocean Alley that provides an afternoon snack. She says she does it so she can charge more and keep the riff-raff out, but I think she does it so she has a reason to talk to her guests. She is a lot more outgoing than I, though you never hear a word of gossip pass her lips. I admire her for this, but it has always made it tough to get any town news out of her.

I could hear her two dogs barking from the small back yard, which is unusual; she usually has them in the back of the house with her. Behind the large guest breakfast room is her enclave—her huge kitchen with an old oak table, which adjoins what home magazines today call a great room (and she calls her sitting room), her bedroom, and a large bath. At the back of the great room is a set of back stairs, originally the servants' stairs according to Aunt Madge, who has none. I put my package at the foot of the main set of stairs so I would remember to take it to my room, and made my way to her.

Aunt Madge was taking the breakfast dishes out of the dishwasher.

Like my grandmother and mother, she is tall and thin and stands and sits very straight. If you don't know her, you expect a rigid person who purses her lips a lot. As I smiled in her direction, she turned to me and puckered her lips for an across-the-room air kiss and motioned to a chair at the kitchen table. "Enjoy your coffee?"

"Yep." I tossed the empty paper cup in her trash.

"Any luck?" she asked.

"Not unless I want to drive short-haul trucks or tend bar." I settled in a chair at her large oak table. "Or computers. Every office needs computer geeks."

I caught sight of the larger of Aunt Madge's two shelter-adopted mutts, Mister Rogers, who had his nose pressed against the pane of the sliding glass door. He wagged his part-retriever tail as he looked at me. "Want me to let the guys in?"

"Heavens no." She turned to glare at him. "The dogs have been in the prunes again. They have to stay outside until they do their business." She checked the oven knob to be sure it was off.

She has to be making this up. "Prunes. Your dogs eat prunes?"

"Whenever they can. I store them in plastic bowls now, but if I leave the pantry open, they go in after them and chew through the bowls." She shut the oven door. "I may have to stop making my prune Danishes."

"That would be a loss."

She glanced at me. "Too healthy for you?"

Mister Rogers suddenly dove off the porch and squatted in the small garden. His co-conspirator, Miss Piggy—also part Retriever but with even more mixed parentage—looked down at him and then peered in at me, wagging her tail. "I think you may be able to let Mister Rogers in."

"Oh no, he'll be busy for a while."

Since she was so serious I tried not to laugh. "I ran into someone who knows you. Ramona Argrow, at the office supply store."

She nodded. "Nice girl. In your class, as I recall." She sat at the table with me, bringing with her a stack of cloth napkins that she started to fold into triangles. I grabbed a few and began folding. She studied me for a moment. "So, if no luck on the coffee shop computer do you want me to ask around town?"

"Nope. I'm seriously thinking I should go into bartending." She looked at me with interest, and then realized I was kidding. We watched Miss Piggy run down the steps and Mister Rogers took her place at the door.

"You don't want to try real estate here? Your license would still be good, wouldn't it?" she asked.

"Yeah, but there's not much of a commercial market, and I don't see me schlepping families with kids from beach house to beach house."

"You did appraisal work first, what about that?" She finished her stack and reached over to turn the knob on the electric kettle. She drinks about ten cups of hot tea every day. When it's really cold she adds amaretto to her evening cups.

"Maybe, but you have to know the local market and land values really well. I'm not sure Stenner and Stenner would be interested in me now. Old man Stenner's retired anyway, hasn't he?"

"Yes, but his daughter took over. You may remember her; she was a class ahead of you."

Jennifer Stenner. Of course. One of the cheerleaders Michael Riordan had dumped, now that I thought of it. "My class, if she's who I think. Tall, light brown hair, lots of white teeth?" Jennifer was something of a snob, to boot.

"That's her. Of course, she has competition now, you know."

This interested me. "Who?"

"Older man, Harry Steele." She poured tea into a mug. "His grandparents lived here and he spent summers here for probably twenty years. He retired from someplace near Boston and came here and opened Steele Appraisers."

She was concentrating very hard on draining excess water from her teabag. "His wife died after he retired, and he wanted something to do besides play golf and visit grandchildren. He bought the house his grandparents owned at G and Ferry and turned the first floor into an office."

"Sounds like your kind of guy."

She smiled. "He goes to First Presbyterian, too. All the women of a certain age," her eyes showed her amusement, "invite him to Sunday dinner."

"Have you?" I tried to keep my tone casual. As far as I knew, she had not been interested in anyone since Uncle Gordon died.

"Didn't your mother teach you not to chase the boys?"

I laughed. "I don't remember that. She was a lot younger than you. I think it was OK to at least call them when she was dating." I passed her my small pile of napkins. She would probably refold them, but at least I hadn't just watched her work.

She sipped her tea. "You could call Harry. Use my name."

That was the second time today someone had told me that. A good sign, perhaps. I glanced at the dogs, now sitting calmly on the porch. "They may have worn themselves out."

She turned and looked at them. "You can let them in now, but watch where you step in the garden until I go out there with the hose."

I decided to take this sage advice, and to think about calling Harry.

CHAPTER TWO

I UNLOCKED THE DOOR to my room (Aunt Madge insists I lock it, despite her belief that she keeps the riff-raff out) and Jazz greeted me. I've had the tiny black cat for three years, and she was often my sole comfort the last couple of months I lived in Lakewood. Not that others didn't try, but they needed me to tell them that I was OK, and Jazz did not require any such lies. She just assumed I was fine and issued her usual commands for food, scratches, and trips outside.

Her prior owner had declawed her, something I did not believe in, but it meant she was no danger to Aunt Madge's furniture. When she wanted to go out she stood on her hind legs and pawed relentlessly on the door. At the moment, she was in the mood for a scratch.

I obliged, and sat in the small rocker thinking about my next move. If I kept to my current routine of chatting with Aunt Madge, getting coffee and muffins at Joe's place, and scratching Jazz I would be broke and five pounds heavier in short order. It was time to get back to my usual spontaneous behavior. I stood and Jazz jumped to the floor, meowing to let me know she was put out at being dumped so quickly.

I was going to go see Harry Steele. The only question was, should I tell Aunt Madge before or after? *Manners, Jolie.* I mentioned it to her on the way out.

I drove along G Street to Harry's, slowing every now and then to see how a house I'd been in during high school had changed. My good friend Margo had lived in a small blue bungalow, and I thought I'd missed it until I realized it now had a second story and yellow vinyl siding. Ocean Alley, town of transitions.

Harry Steele's place also looked as if it had been built in the Victorian period, but it had not been kept up as well as Aunt Madge's.

Paint was in early stages of peeling and a gutter dangled from the right side.

The house looked as if he was working on it. The front porch, with its rails and intricate lattice work, had some new boards and was partially painted. It looked as if he was going to go with what I think of as a gingerbread house design. The rails themselves were a dark green, the latticework beneath them was yellow, and trim on the windows on the porch was a lighter green. I never understand why people make painting so complicated.

I rang the old-fashioned bell and heard a deep bong inside the house. Hurried footsteps brought an older man to the door and he greeted me as if he'd known me for years. "Madge Richards' niece. What an honor. Do come in."

"I take it Aunt Madge called." I should have figured.

He laughed, showing a full set of teeth. He was quite a bit taller than I, but then, who isn't? He had a red face and hair that was auburn mixed with white. Though you wouldn't call him exceptionally fit, he was in pretty good shape for a man I judged to be in his mid-sixties, not much younger than Aunt Madge. Despite his Anglo-Saxon name I pegged him for someone with a lot of Irish blood, which I also have, through my mother's side of the family.

I murmured something polite and followed him into the room on the right. It had once been the formal drawing room, but had at some point been divided in two. He had taken out the partitions that had split the room and replaced the wood in the floor that had been damaged by the two-by-fours that had held the partition wallboard.

There was an ornate fireplace at one end, a huge pie safe in a corner, and a large, old-fashioned desk. Under the windows near his desk was a table similar to Aunt Madge's kitchen table, and on it were piled stacks of file folders. The only truly modern thing in the room (besides his computer) was his desk chair, which looked very ergonomically correct.

I glanced at him, and realized he was watching me survey the room. "I was just admiring your progress at renovation," I felt myself flush under his gaze.

"It's a labor of love, I tell you. Madge has been advising me on where to get wood that comes close to matching the old trim in this room. She's quite a lady. Did she tell you that my grandparents owned the house for thirty years?" He spoke fast, almost as if he was nervous.

"She said you enjoyed your time here." I tried to imagine a five-year old Harry in a wet swimsuit, tracking sand into this house.

"Boy did I. My kids think I'm nuts to be renovating it, but if you don't do something crazy in your life, why bother living?" He gestured that I should sit in one of two chairs in front of his desk, and he sat next to me.

I liked this man immediately. "My mother thinks I'm crazy to come here to live, so we're even."

He smiled. "And you might be interested in doing some appraisal work?"

"I'm thinking about it. I've kept my appraisal credentials in order, but I haven't used them in more than six years. I've been doing commercial real estate work in Lakewood." I hesitated. "Did Aunt Madge tell you why I came back?"

"Nope, but do you know Elmira Washington? She did." His eyes looked kind.

"I keep trying to remember that compulsive gambling is an illness. He's in some kind of treatment program, and he goes to a lot of meetings." I didn't add that I figured with the extent Robby avoided talking about his compulsion he'd be stuck for five years on step one, admitting he had a problem.

"Good attitude." He grew businesslike. "I don't have a lot of business yet. Truth be told, I spend more than half my time renovating this place." He waved his hands toward the hallway. "I'm doing a lot myself. The rest of the house doesn't look nearly as good as this room." As his eyes met mine he continued, "I'd be willing to talk to you about some part-time work, pay you on a case-by-case basis. I could use a colleague who has a better feel for the town's neighborhoods than I do at this point."

I almost told him I hadn't spent much time here the last few years, and then remembered I was supposed to be selling myself, not selling myself short. "I've never thought of Ocean Alley as having neighborhoods, but I guess it does." My humor returned. "Do you appraise much near the bowling alley?" "Best Bowl" is on the far southern end of town, and the area around it has houses in various stages of repair. A few years ago, someone painted theirs a garish chartreuse and since then nearly every repainting job has entailed an equally prominent color.

"More people than you think want those popsicle houses. That neighborhood has the only real bargains left in Ocean Alley."

That stopped my jokes. I really was out of date. "I figure you'll want me to spend some time going over your recent appraisals, and I'd be happy to do that on my own time." I decided I wanted to work with this man, and needed to demonstrate some level of personal commitment.

"Sure. There are only seven though. I'm just starting to get serious about the business."

"Seven? That's serious?" I winced at my own lack of tact.

"I do need to do some marketing. You can help," he said, easily.

We talked about his family for a few minutes and I side-stepped most discussion of mine, except for Aunt Madge. When we shook hands as I was leaving, he said he would have some cards printed for me, and that I could feel free to pass them out at local real estate offices.

INSTEAD OF DRIVING straight back to Aunt Madge's I drove the few blocks to the boardwalk and walked along it. I was restless and anxious, two emotions I don't usually have, and wanted to walk. More than half of the boardwalk stores had closed for the season, and the few that were open had huge sale signs as they tried to get a little more business before shuttering for the winter, which they would do after Thanksgiving weekend. It had not been a good tourist season for Ocean Alley. It was cool and rainy on Memorial Day weekend, and that set the tone for a cooler-than-normal summer. Threats of the remnants of a hurricane, which had not materialized, kept Labor Day traffic light, too.

I turned toward the ocean and took a deep breath. The wind had shifted, so there was a hint of salt in the cool sea breeze. As I started walking again, I saw Michael Riordan about fifty yards ahead, sitting on a bench facing the ocean. He certainly seemed to have a lot of free time. I should talk. I debated going up to him, and decided that if I was going to let people know what I was doing in Ocean Alley I was going to have to talk to more than Aunt Madge, Jazz, and the dogs. Maybe he wasn't as big a jerk as he was in eleventh grade.

I paused near his bench. "You're Michael Riordan, aren't you?"

He jumped slightly in surprise. He must have been concentrating very hard on something. "Yes." He stood. "I saw you this morning. You look familiar." He had a very direct way of looking you in the eye as he held out his hand, which I took.

"We didn't know each other well. I spent a lot of summer time here, and went to high school at OAH for eleventh grade. Jolie Gentil." He was quite tall, maybe 6'2" and there were a few flecks of gray in his dark brown hair. Oil business in Texas must be pretty stressful.

He nodded in recognition and started to say something, then seemed to change his mind. He gestured to the bench. "Would you like to join me in the view?" he asked.

His attitude was one of perfunctory politeness, but I sat anyway. "I've decided to move here. I'm staying with my Aunt Madge. She owns Cozy Corner B&B."

His look was friendlier now. "Sure. She goes to First Presbyterian, same as my mother. Every now and then I see her when I visit Mom."

Church is not part of my life's routine, has not been since I first went to college. I had forgotten that so many of the permanent residents here described one another in terms of the church they, or someone else, attended. "In fact," he continued, "she taught Sunday School for a few years. She threw me out of her class a couple of times."

"You must have really been a bad boy. I didn't know she ever tossed anyone out."

He grinned. "My parents would say I was so bright I was bored, but I just hated to sit in a classroom on a Sunday. Nothing personal to your aunt. Why'd you move back here?"

The abruptness jolted me, but it was a logical question. "Left my husband, wanted a change of pace."

His expression became somber. "There's a lot of that going around." He resumed looking at the ocean.

"I'm sorry. I heard your mom is sick, too. Tough times."

"Yeah. It's all enough to make you drink."

I must have stiffened, because he half turned his head to look at me, and his look softened somewhat. "Sorry," he said. "I guess I'm a little self-absorbed at the moment."

A little? I figured his mother had the bigger problem. I struggled for something to say. "I'm sure your mother's glad you're here."

At that he gave a half-smile. "She loves it when I visit. Older parents of only children tend to be that way." His expression darkened again. "I just wish I could do something that would really help her. She helps everybody else."

"Being here is the best thing you can do," I volunteered.

"Yeah, right." His sarcasm hung heavy, and I shifted my weight, ready to stand up.

He looked at me again, and crumpled the coffee cup that had been sitting by his feet. "I can be an asshole, sometimes."

"There's a lot of that going around, too."

He gave a genuine smile and held out his hand. "Does the high school have your address? The ten-year reunion is at Thanksgiving."

"Ramona told me, I might..."

"Ramona," he interrupted me. "Talk about someone stuck in a time warp."

Just when I had started to cut him a little slack. I returned his handshake and was surprised that he held my hand a couple seconds more than a customary shake requires. "You look really good," he said, looking at me very directly.

"Thanks," I withdrew my hand as I blushed.

He grinned and turned to walk north on the boardwalk, tossing me a look over his shoulder. "I'll give you a call at Madge's."

His friendliness surprised me, and I hadn't liked his comment about Ramona. You could use a friend. I told myself he was going through a bad time because his mother was dying. Maybe he was less critical of people when he wasn't dealing with something that tough. I decided it would be okay if he called, though I certainly wasn't looking to date anyone. The ink was barely dry on my separation agreement.

Feeling directionless, I walked into one of the few tourist traps still open and stood looking at the conch shells lining a display. If anyone ever finds one of those on the beach in Ocean Alley, I'll eat cat food. As I glanced up, a man in what could only be described as a very loud golf outfit—lime green shirt and pants with a small green plaid—looked away. I was sure he had been staring at me, then remembered the time a woman on the New York subway had hit me with her umbrella because she was certain I'd been eyeballing her, when all I was doing was studying the subway map above her head.

I walked up and down aisles of useless knick knacks, ashtrays, and magnets. I soon tired of wondering how small a person's fingers had to be to make miniature crabs out of shells and left the store. After standing idly for a second I turned, to walk north on the boardwalk, and almost walked into the loud golfer. He jumped almost as high as I did.

"Sorry," he said.

"No problem," I felt my heart pound.

As I started to pass him, he spoke again. "Umm, are you Jolie Gentil?"

Since he knew how to pronounce may name correctly, I must have known him, but he looked a good ten years older than I am. "Yes. Are you my personal bodyguard?"

He smiled sheepishly. "I'm Joe Pedone. Can I buy you a cup of coffee?"

"No thanks." I didn't mean to be unfriendly, but the more I looked at him, black patent shoes and well-coiffed hair, I didn't think I recognized him. "Do I know you?"

"No, but I know your husband." He studied me as he backed up half a step, apparently trying to ascertain if knowing Robby would make me slug him.

"I've learned there were a lot of people who knew him who didn't know me. And it'll be former husband as soon as my lawyer makes it legal."

He cleared his throat. "I'm really sorry about what you've been through." He gestured to a bench. "Could we sit for a minute? My bunion's killing me."

I hesitated, then figured the boardwalk was as good a place as any to talk to a stranger. "Sure." We walked to a bench, one facing the boardwalk rather than the ocean.

He cleared his throat again. "Sinus," he said.

The man is a walking calamity.

"The thing is," he continued, "your husband owed some money to some people."

"I'd be top on that list, I think. He raided all our joint assets, even my personal retirement account. And his bank is more than a little irritated at him."

"Yeah, I read about that." He cleared his throat again. I was tempted to tell him just to have a good spit in the sand, but I didn't. "See, my boss lent him some money, to kind of help him out."

"Your boss was a fool."

"Well, he don't like to be put in that position, you see." He looked sideways toward the ocean, and then back to me. "He wants me to talk to you about paying some of that debt."

My laugh was so harsh and loud that two seagulls squawked and flew off the bench next to us. "I don't think so."

"You see…" he began.

"My lawyer said that since I saw no benefit from the money I'm not responsible for any gambling debts Robby incurred on his own, or for money he embezzled. The law firm published some notice to that effect in the newspaper."

"Yeah," he said, "we saw it."

"Who's we?" I was growing more than a little tired of these illusions to a boss I figured might not exist. This guy is trying to con me.

He slipped off one of the narrow black patent loafers and began massaging his foot. "You could say that my boss lends money to people down on their luck, especially when they frequent certain casinos in Atlantic City."

Suddenly, I felt chilled all over. Am I in some sort of mob movie or is this real? "I don't like casinos. Too much cigarette smoke." I stood. "I need to go now."

"Please," he shoved his foot back in his shoe and stood. Despite his seeming friendliness, I felt nervous. "The next request, it might not be so nice."

"Are you threatening me?"

"No, I'm really not. It's just how things are."

I turned and walked away quickly, without looking back.

CHAPTER THREE

I SPENT THE NEXT TWO DAYS trying to put Joe Pedone out of my mind. This was easier than it would have been a few days ago because I was driving around Ocean Alley looking at the houses Harry Steele had appraised and the prior sales that he listed as comparably priced to each one he was working on. I had thought of Ocean Alley as a place to relax rather than in terms of its real estate values. I was going to have to spend a lot of time looking at past sales.

I spent several hours researching a bunch of other prior sales in the Miller County Court House. It was built in the early 1920s, the previous one having been severely damaged by fire. Uncle Gordon's mother was the county elections clerk at the time. She heard the fire engines and ran to the building in her bath robe to try to save records. When the firefighters refused to let her in, she snuck in the back and closed several of the heavy interior oak doors, thus keeping the fire from spreading into several offices. Every time someone told that story when I was young my mother would add that while her actions had saved a lot of valuable records, no one should ever run into a burning building. This was not a lesson she really needed to reiterate, but I suppose she felt obliged to stress this.

This court house was built on the site of its predecessor, and includes several of the old oak doors and some other fixtures that survived the prior court house's fire. It sits in the center of town. As I entered the building, I detected what I always think of as the smell of history. It's a mix of musty books, worn hardwood floors, and the stacks of files that sit atop old filing cabinets.

As I looked through the records for the homes Harry had appraised, I said a silent thank you to Uncle Gordon's mother. While none of the seven houses were built in the early 20th century, many other houses in town are that old. If Uncle Gordon's mother hadn't shut those old oak doors, it would have made title searches tough for those properties. Unclear titles can reduce prices and thus agent commissions. *You idiot, you aren't selling real estate now.*

I concentrated harder on what I was doing. Harry Steele had supported the prices of six of the seven homes, so I paid special attention to that seventh sale. He had believed the sales contract was for more than the house was worth, and he seemed to have the comps to prove it. There were a couple of really nasty faxes in his file from the real estate agent, none other than Lester Argrow. "If you'd spent more than 20 minutes in this town you'd know the Marino's house is worth a helluva lot more than $228,000."

When Harry stuck to his guns, with a much more polite reply, Argrow had fired back, "Next time I'll get a professional appraiser. You don't know your ass from your elbow." Perhaps that is what passes for professional real estate talk in Ocean Alley.

In the end, the sellers had come down $15,000 in price, since no bank would write a mortgage for more than a house is worth. This reduced Lester's commission. Probably there had been no other offers and the sellers realized Harry was right. They appeared to have a better grasp of anatomy than Lester did.

Now that I was working, even though I had not been paid yet, I felt better about life. I had a reason to get up in the morning other than to feed Jazz or respond to my own hunger pangs. I even considered an evening run along the boardwalk. It would be fifty degrees at about seven o'clock, and since Jersey was still on daylight savings time, it would not be pitch dark.

I try not to be unreasonably concerned about safety stuff, but I'm not stupid, despite not having wondered about the amount of time my husband said he spent with clubs or clients when he was actually in casinos.

I STOPPED BACK AT Harry's to drop off the three files I'd reviewed that day. It had taken me the better part of the day because of the time I'd spent at the courthouse to look at some more sales that were similar to the house Harry had found was overvalued. I wanted to form my own opinion, and it was that Harry was right to stick to his guns.

Harry was applying extra coats of paint to the new porch boards, apparently trying to get them to look the same color as the repainted older boards. Would never happen. "Hey, you still at it?"

Duh.

"Getting ready to close the old paint can for the day," he said. "What did you think?" He nodded toward the files I was carrying.

He must have figured I would really dig into the Marino's house sale. "I think Lester Argrow won't bring you any more business, but if you let people know that, you might get some from other agents."

He laughed. "I won't call him again, that's for sure. You can, if you want, of course," he said, genially.

Since I wasn't up for turning away any business, I thought I might use Ramona's name to get my foot in the door with him. What did I care if he called me names?

He stuck his paint brush in an old can that held turpentine or some other foul-smelling stuff. "I got a call today about another house. Thought you might want to tackle it."

Who would have thought I'd get an adrenalin rush from the chance to appraise a house, I who had negotiated top-dollar deals in Lakewood. "You ready to trust me?"

"More than willing to let you take the first stab at it. We'll go over your results together, of course."

"Of course." That was fine with me. I figured him for a gentle tutor rather than a 'see-what-you-did-wrong' kind of guy. "I can get started tomorrow."

"You know Mrs. Riordan?" he asked.

The surprise must have shown in my face, because he gave me a quizzical look. "I don't think I know her, but I know her son Michael a little. I talked to him a couple of days ago on the boardwalk."

"Small world," he said. "I asked him how he got my name, and all he said was that he didn't want to go to Stenner's."

I grunted, with half a laugh. "He dumped Jennifer Stenner in high school. He probably doesn't want to deal with her."

"You are going to be useful to have around."

"I don't really know either of them well, just girls' bathroom talk from eleventh grade."

"Either way we, I should say you, have a nine a.m. appointment tomorrow." He placed all his painting paraphernalia in a small plastic tub and started for the door. "You won't need a key. Someone will be there." This simplified things. I wouldn't have to fuss with picking up the key at the realtor's office and returning it after I did the appraisal.

I stepped in front of him to open the door for him. "You sure it's OK if I go alone?"

"How else will I find out if you're worth what I plan to pay you?" He winked.

That night, Jazz drank from the glass of ice water I fixed for myself after my run, and I didn't even care.

THE NEXT MORNING, I got up at six a.m., full of energy. I set the table in the breakfast room for Aunt Madge's two sets of guests and turned on the coffee pot, which she always leaves ready the night before.

I love Aunt Madge's kitchen, probably because I helped her redesign it. A few years ago I received a large commission for convincing a developer that the site of the old bowling alley in Lakewood would be perfect for luxury condos, and he bought the lot for half a million dollars. My half of the six percent commission might not seem large by New York City standards, but it was the most money I'd ever made for about four hours of work.

Robby and I toyed, yet again, with buying a house, but we didn't want to be bothered with shoveling sidewalks and trying to decide whether to use pesticides on a lawn. Since he probably would have done a second mortgage on a house behind my back, this turns out to have been a particularly good decision.

In any event, I told Aunt Madge I was going to buy her a really big present, so she might as well pick it out, and she surprised me by saying her kitchen counter tops were getting a bit old. This was an understatement. Even oak will show its age after several thousand loaves of bread are punched into shape on its surface.

Aunt Madge did not have in mind anything as elaborate as I did, and we had to do it in the winter, so she wouldn't have to turn away many guests. I convinced her that her cabinets were falling apart, which was nearly true, and even talked her into a garbage disposal, dishwasher, and a stackable washer and dryer, so she would not have to go down to the cellar so often. She drew the line at a double sink, which she deemed impractical in case you had a really big turkey to stuff.

The pecan cabinetry with butcher-block countertops looks new but blends well with her oak table and antique ice box. Aunt Madge is quite pleased with the lazy susan in the corner cabinet, and I'm partial to the trash compactor, since it means less garbage for me to take out.

I was alone in the kitchen, reading the paper, when Aunt Madge came in about six-thirty. Breakfast is not until seven, unless someone asks for an early one. "Aren't you the early bird," she offered, as she glanced at the coffee pot, which had finished brewing.

"I have paying work today. Who would have thought I'd get so excited about that?"

She smiled, "Good for the soul." She bustled about, taking the batter she mixed the night before from the fridge and placing it in paper-lined muffin tins. I had known better than to do this for her. She has precise ideas about how much dough makes the perfect muffin.

"I meant to ask you last night if you knew how sick Mrs. Riordan is. I'm wondering what to expect when I get there."

She didn't answer right away, and I looked up. She was holding a spoon with dough poised over the muffin tin. "Aunt Madge?"

"Oh, yes. Ruth's not too bad, yet. I mean," she took a little dough out of one muffin cup and put it in another, "it's terminal, unfortunately, but she was in church Sunday looking quite good. She's taking chemo, but she's on a break."

"Why's she taking chemo if she's not going to make it?"

Aunt Madge shot me what novelists call a withering look. "It could buy her considerable time, months or a year, not weeks."

"Of course," I was appropriately chastened. "You know her pretty well, right?"

"Yes. We've known each other through church, of course. Since she and her husband divorced we've done quite a bit together outside of church." She smiled at me. "We've even gone to bingo at St. Anthony's a couple of times."

"Did you win?"

"Good heavens, no. It's just money down the drain, but it's kind of fun." She smiled at me but her smile faded as my face must have shown I knew all about money going down the drain.

To change the subject, I took her electric kettle to the sink and dumped out yesterday's leftover water and began to fill it. "Is this what you use to fill the hot water thermos in the dining room?"

She gestured toward the stove. "You can fill the tea kettle on the stove for that. And don't ask me why I do it that way, I don't know." Miss Piggy ambled into the room from Aunt Madge's bedroom and sniffed. "Not for you, dear," Aunt Madge addressed her. "Would you let her out, Jolie? Mister Rogers is already out there somewhere."

I opened the door and Miss Piggy went out, still sniffing. In a moment she had spotted Mister Rogers and leaped down the steps. From the amount of nose-to-brick sniffing going on out there, I figured the rabbits had been out the night before. "I saw Mrs. Riordan's son on the boardwalk and talked to him for a minute a couple days ago. He seemed a bit...distracted."

Aunt Madge glanced at me as she put the muffins in the oven. "I hear he has a lot on his mind."

"OK, it's not gossip unless you embellish it," I wanted to know more.

"Well, in addition to Ruth dying, his wife left him a few weeks ago, and I hear he's had a falling-out with some business partners."

"Wow." That is a lot.

"I suppose the up-side of it is that he's able to spend some time with his mother. Ruth was forty when she got pregnant; she was more than a bit surprised, I can tell you. Anyway, since Ruth and Larry divorced several years ago, she's really wanted to spend more time with Michael."

She set the timer for twenty minutes and continued. "Ruth also has a lot to talk to him about. I think she wanted to do it in person."

"About her illness?" I asked.

"About the house." She took jars of jam from the fridge and began spooning some into small bowls. "Ruth isn't going to sell the house, she..."

"Why am I doing an appraisal then?" Aunt Madge's look was enough to silence me and I made a zipping gesture across my lips.

"She wants to give it to the local Arts Council to use for shows for area artists and for poetry readings and such. They can use the downstairs for that and have their offices upstairs. They're crammed into a tiny space in the library. The appraisal is largely to establish the worth of the property for tax purposes."

I gave a low whistle. "That's one heck of a gift."

She nodded. "Since Michael is her only heir, she wanted to be sure he didn't mind. She's concerned that," she paused as she put the jam and some butter on a tray, "he may somehow feel cheated."

"Maybe all that's why he seems a bit...moody."

She waved a hand as she sat down next to me to wait for the muffins to cook. "He's always been like that. Although, his mother says he's mellowed a bit the last year." She seemed about to say more, and stopped.

"I didn't really know him at school." I started to say he didn't want to know me, but instead I stood and kissed her cheek. "I'm going upstairs to shower. I didn't want to wake anyone earlier."

I took more time than usual getting ready. Scrubbed and dressed in a light wool, tan pantsuit with a hunter green turtleneck and earrings that matched the suit, I appeared in the kitchen for Aunt Madge's compliments. With her encouraging words in my ears, I walked out to my Toyota to drive to the Riordan's. Why does my car look lopsided?

"Damn." The right front tire was flat. I must have driven over a nail. It just reinforced my current opinion that anything with tires or testicles was trouble. I looked closer. The back one was equally deflated. For some reason, Joe Pedone's face flashed to my mind. I glanced at my watch. Nothing to do but tell Aunt Madge I had a flat (and hope she didn't notice two) and borrow her car. It was too far to walk. Double damn.

I made my way to the Riordans' large home on the north edge of town, the neighborhood of two and three-story homes built from the 1890s to early 1940s. Many of the newer ones were brick or had brick facades, not too common at the beach. The older homes are Victorian and much larger than Aunt Madge's. Several have guest cottages behind the main house. It is easily the priciest area of Ocean Alley.

I had tried to look up prior sales for the Riordan's home, but it was pointless. Her parents had bought it more than fifty years ago, and they left it to her. At least the appraisal when Ruth's parents bought it (for all of $21,500) listed the size of all the rooms and showed the appraiser's hand-drawn layout. Jennifer Stenner's grandfather had had a steady hand. "Third-generation family business," as their ads said.

I was about to push the doorbell to the Riordans' when Michael opened the door and said, "Don't ring the bell."

I almost stumbled into the house. "It's just such a handy way to let people know you want to come in." Probably not the reaction Harry Steele would have. I had to remember I was working for him.

"Sorry," he said, grudgingly. "My mother's still asleep. Late for her, so she must need it." His tone was protective.

"I'm glad you caught me before I rang." I looked around the elaborate foyer, with its faux-marble floor (or maybe it was real?) and elegant crown molding. "Will you be showing me around, then?"

"No. I have some business in town. You can find your way around, can't you?" He was pulling on a light suede jacket.

"Of course. Since I have to measure every room and closet, I'll probably be here awhile. Will your mother mind getting up to a stranger in the house?" My mother certainly would.

"I told her you're Madge's niece. She's looking forward to seeing you. If she's not up, just go in her room."

"Oh, I could come back…"

"No," he said with his hand on the door, "Go on in. She has a meeting of the church's Social Services Committee at eleven, and I doubt she has her alarm set."

"I'll, uh, knock first." I said this to his back as he walked out and he didn't reply. What a turd, I thought. Thou shalt not call clients turds. I decided I didn't care about his promise to call me at Aunt Madge's.

The house was set up in a common style for center-hall colonials. On the left was a huge living room, with a twelve-foot ceiling, more elegant crown molding, and beautiful hardwood floors. It was surprisingly stylish, with bright white paint for the molding and window trim and a deep tan on the walls. The furniture had a mix of tan and burgundy tones, and I liked it immediately. Anything wood was antique oak.

I chastised myself about admiring the furniture, which has nothing to do with a house's value, and set about measuring the room and checking the windows.

The room to the right of the foyer was a truly formal dining room, with a stunning color scheme of bright yellow walls and naturally finished chair rail and molding. As with the living room, there were hardwood floors and very expensive area rugs, these in a light brown that accented the molding. A large oak hutch and antique ice box were along one wall, matched perfectly to an oak table. Oak seemed to be the preference for the over-sixty Ocean Alley crowd. This room was almost twenty by forty feet, and the table seated twelve. I wondered idly if Michael Riordan had children who spilled orange juice on the rugs.

The kitchen was behind the dining room and had newer windows in three adjoining sections, with the middle one somewhat wider and taller than the two side sections. They were natural wood, perhaps oak, and matched the thoroughly modern cabinetry.

I hurried my measurements, anxious to get to the large family room across from the kitchen and the upstairs. The family room was clearly where Mrs. Riordan spent most of her time, though it was still House and Garden quality. Furnishings were more modern, almost contemporary, except for what I took to be Mrs. Riordan's favorite spot. There was a tall rocker with comfortable-looking cushions and a foot stool. A small table next to it held a basket of needlework and a small stack of books. Not a television in sight.

I finished the measurements and hurried up the open stairway to the top floor. I tried to imagine what the master bedroom would look like; it probably had a four poster with a canopy. I paused, counting doors. Four were wide enough to be bedroom doors, and were shut. A bathroom door stood open, and there were two smaller doors I took to be linen closets. I glanced at my watch. Ten o'clock. Surely Mrs. Riordan would want to be up by now. I would knock on her door and call out that I was Madge Richards' niece. I hoped that would not startle her too much.

I assumed she would sleep in the master bedroom, and guessed it was the one at the end of the hall. I knocked lightly, then harder. "Mrs. Riordan? It's Jolie, Madge's niece, the appraiser." No answer.

I opened the door slightly. The room was still dark, shades drawn. I pushed the door open a little more to let some light into the room. Mrs. Riordan was on the left side of her bed, with open eyes staring at the ceiling.

CHAPTER FOUR

I SAT ON A LOW BRICK WALL that encircled a raised garden, just outside the Riordan front door, sipping a can of soda that a policewoman had placed in my hand. She had escorted me out so they could "secure the scene." I'd watched enough TV to know she meant they didn't want me in the way while they looked around, but I vaguely wondered why someone had called a police photographer to take pictures of an elderly woman who died in her bed.

I had never seen a dead person outside of a casket, and was quite shaken. There had been no real logic to my immediate decisions. I called Harry rather than an ambulance, and sat on the floor in Mrs. Riordan's room until an ambulance crew and the police arrived, thanks to Harry's call to them. It didn't seem right to leave her.

The EMS staff didn't need more than a quick look to tell Mrs. Riordan really was dead, and then one of them turned his attention to me. He said something about me being in shock. I didn't think I really was, though never having been in shock, how would I know? I do know that I can't say "kick the bucket" again. It now seems very disrespectful.

An older police officer walked out of the house and asked me if I knew where "the son" was, making him the third one to ask about Michael Riordan. I repeated his "business in town" comment, and was tempted to remind him that 'town' was so small they should be able to find him easily. "He does buy coffee at Java Jolt." I wished I had thought to say this earlier.

"Yeah, we knew that."

The officer was probably in his mid-forties, but he dressed like someone in their seventies – polyester pants and a tie with a pattern that

30

had been in fashion about the time I was born. Only his shoes could be called modern, a dark-colored athletic shoe that I knew sold for well more than twice as much as I spend for my jogging shoes. I supposed he was on his feet a lot, so he acquiesced to comfort over cost.

His badge said 'Sgt. Morehouse.' "Why are there so many police here?" I gestured with the soda can to the three cars, which I figured were a good portion of Ocean Alley's force.

"Unattended death. We have to investigate." He waved to what looked to be a hearse.

I realized it said "County Coroner" on the side. It seemed the investigation meant poor Mrs. Riordan was not going directly to the funeral home, not that it would matter to her either way. Still sitting, I touched Morehouse's elbow. "But she was sick."

"Yeah, but not that sick."

I drew a quick breath and his tone grew kinder. "We just have to document the cause of death. Probably a heart attack or something." He turned his attention to the coroner's staff. "You can take her in about twenty minutes. We're almost finished dusting."

For prints? All I could think of was the beautiful paint and woodwork. Before I could ask him why they were looking at fingerprints when it looked like a heart attack, a silver Mercedes pulled up and Michael Riordan got out. It must have been in the garage, I would have noticed that car in the driveway.

"Where is she, what happened?" he demanded of Morehouse, and tried to follow the coroner staff into the house.

"Whoa. Just hang on a minute," Morehouse said. "I'll explain…"

Riordan turned on the man. "Explain now!" His face was reddening fast and I sensed that if Morehouse hadn't had a badge pinned to his sport coat Michael would have shaken him.

That ought to endear him to the police. I glanced back to Michael and realized his gaze had shifted to me. "I'm sorry Michael, she seems to have passed away."

"That's not possible," he said, as if there was simply no option for that. "She was fine when I left."

"I thought she hadn't been up," Morehouse said, quickly.

"No, but I looked in on her a couple of times. She was breathing and…everything." His voice trailed off, and he suddenly looked a lot less arrogant. I held out my soda can. "No thanks," he said, and turned to Morehouse. "When can I go in?"

"It won't be too long. Why don't you have a seat with the young lady," Morehouse gestured to me, "and I'll come get you soon." He went back in the house.

"They throw you out?" he asked, looking at me.

"They brought me out. I needed some fresh air." I wasn't sure what to say. "I sat with her, until the ambulance people came."

"I appreciate that." He turned his gaze from me and looked straight ahead, so I studied his profile for a moment. His angular face was taut. After a moment I could tell his thoughts had gone elsewhere. It was a relief for me not to feel I had to comfort him. I was still kind of jittery myself.

I began to reflect on the last hour. I had gone upstairs and called to her, and Mrs. Riordan didn't answer. Since I hadn't heard her moving around, I'd opened the door and looked in, and there she was. There was nothing more to it than that. Nothing suspicious, like a loud thump before I went upstairs.

The female police officer, who was quite a bit younger than Sgt. Morehouse, walked toward Michael and me and addressed her question to me. "Ms…" she glanced at her small notebook, "um, Gentle."

She pronounced it way most people did when they first tried out my name. I corrected her. "The "L" is silent. It's pronounced Zhan-tee, it's French." I have this memorized.

"Oh, okay. Mind if I sit down?" She moved closer to me, on the opposite side of Michael.

"Sure." I glanced at her name badge. "Corporal Johnson. Did you meet Michael Riordan?"

He nodded at her but did not extend a hand. Instead, he stood up and walked a few feet away from us.

"Tough day for him," I was not at all sure why I was making excuses for him.

"I'm sure it is. I have a couple of questions for you, if you feel calmer now." Michael cast a glance at me, and then moved farther away. When I didn't object, she continued. "Exactly what did you see when you went into the bedroom?"

I told her what I'd seen, which did not require a detailed

explanation. She took notes, and only interrupted me once. "Her eyes were definitely open, then?" I assured her they were. I wouldn't forget that expression for a good while.

As she stood to go back into the house, Harry Steele's car pulled up and Aunt Madge got out of it faster than I'd seen her move since the time I fell down her front porch steps. But, she didn't come to me; she went straight to Michael. I saw her take one of his hands in both of hers, and then she gave him a hug. I also noticed her hair was now blonde.

Harry walked toward me. "Are you all right? I wanted to come sooner, but I thought I should bring your aunt, and one of her guests said she had walked to the grocery store. I missed her there, and then went back to her house, and…"

I smiled at him, and he stopped. "I'm okay. It was just a bit of a shock. I'm really sorry if I scared you, calling like that." I couldn't resist. "You didn't mention anything like this in any of your other appraisal reports."

He looked dumbfounded at first, then shook his head slightly. "I guess your aunt knew what she was talking about when she said you'd be okay. She was much more worried about him." He glanced toward them, and Michael and Aunt Madge were walking toward us.

Aunt Madge looked to me. "Won't you tell Michael how many extra rooms I have? I want him to know he can stay with us if he wants to."

I almost gulped at the thought. "She does, really. But if you would rather stay here, if you'll stop by for muffins, she'll feel better."

Michael almost smiled. He looked at Aunt Madge. "I'll probably stay here, but I promise if I'm lonely I'll come find you. I know you would be glad to have me."

I didn't realize he could be that gracious, but then remembered he said she'd been his Sunday school teacher.

I was introducing Harry when Sgt. Morehouse came back out. "Would you folks like to come into the house? I didn't mean you should all wait out here." He nodded to Aunt Madge.

I found his words odd, as he had definitely wanted us outside. We followed him in and he offered condolences to Michael. "If you'd like to go upstairs and see her now, that would be okay. I have to ask you not to touch anything." He led Michael upstairs, and I heard him repeating his explanation of how the police had to handle an unattended death.

Aunt Madge slapped her hand against her thigh in frustration. "Such a shame she had not registered for hospice yet." In response to my questioning look she added, "If you're in hospice, they don't treat unattended deaths this way."

This must be one of the things you learn when you get to be her age. Corporal Johnson came up to us. "You can go now, Ms. Gentil." She pronounced it correctly. "I know how to contact you if we have any more questions."

She walked away, and Aunt Madge looked upstairs. "I think we should wait for Michael."

Harry and I looked at each other. "We could…" I began.

Harry gently cut me off and spoke to Aunt Madge. "My sense was that he would call you if he needed to."

"I suppose you're right. I just hate to think of him all alone," she said.

"He must have friends here." I was anxious to get home and give Jazz a good hug.

"Not so many," she said, as we turned to leave.

AS SOON AS WE GOT HOME, I called the local garage and asked them to come put two tires on my car. I said I'd be down to pay them later, and that the car key would be under the driver's side floor mat. There are such advantages to small towns.

I didn't realize how tired I was until I hung up the phone. Harry declined Aunt Madge's offer of lunch. I, never known for declining a meal, said I wanted to take a short nap. Aunt Madge was certain it was because of the shock of finding Mrs. Riordan, while I attributed it to getting up at six a.m. Whatever the reason, I was asleep by eleven-thirty and didn't wake up until almost one-thirty. I might have slept longer, but Jazz was pawing on the door. She had had enough of this afternoon nap stuff.

When I couldn't deter her by saying "Here kitty, kitty," I finally got up. I slung her over my shoulder and headed downstairs. I was trying to get her used to the dogs so she could have the run of Aunt Madge's living area; so far, she would have none of them. She sat on top of the refrigerator (reached by jumping from floor to counter top to flour canister to fridge), and hissed at the dogs, who were most anxious to meet her.

The dogs were outside and Aunt Madge was nowhere to be found. I stepped into the small backyard and spent the obligatory half-minute scratching the dogs before wandering back to the garage, where Aunt Madge kept Uncle Gordon's small boat and her gardening tools. The garage was so small there was barely room to walk around the boat, a flat-bottomed dory that Uncle Gordon used to launch into the ocean from the surf. Aunt Madge often comments about how he loved to fish. I peered in, not really expecting to see Aunt Madge, and saw that the boat had a fairly fresh coat of paint. Since she never takes it out, I was surprised.

Turning to go back to the house I saw Aunt Madge's car was in her small parking area, next to a guest's, so I went back into the house. It was then that I noticed her half-empty tea mug on the oak table, with a piece of paper beside it. The small note said, "Be back in a couple hours." Since I didn't know when she left, I could not guess when she'd be back. It struck me as odd, since by now she would usually be working on her bread. I peered in a large bowl that was covered with a kitchen towel, and saw it had been rising too long and had deflated.

The tire guy was still working on the flats, so I walked the short distance to the in-town grocery store. Aunt Madge's guests would expect their afternoon snack, and I was fully familiar with the loaves of bread you could buy in the frozen food section. However, I could not remember how long it took to thaw or cook them. It turned out there would be just enough time to do both and have the small loaves ready by four p.m. No cheddar bread, but it would still be good.

The dogs paced the kitchen as I put the preformed loaves on cookie sheets. This was not my usual job, and they seemed to want to supervise. I had just put the loaves in the oven and reached up to take Jazz off the fridge when the front door opened and I heard Aunt Madge's deliberate footsteps approaching the kitchen. Thank goodness. I had no idea how to make small talk to guests I'd never met.

The dogs raced to the kitchen door and sat expectantly in front of it. She gave them an absent pat as she entered and stopped when she saw me and the empty loaf bags, which were on the table. "Oh, good. I knew there was no way to save the bread dough; I thought I was going to have to make muffins, and people don't like surprises." She took off her coat and poked a few stray hairs into her blonde French twist.

"I've had enough for one day myself." Jazz had gotten onto my shoulder from the top of the fridge and was now trying to climb to the top of my head. Aunt Madge took her from me and gave me a kiss, then reached into a small canister and took out two large dog treats. "Outside, you two." They slobbered as she led them to the door.

"What, no prunes?"

She returned Jazz to my outstretched arms, and turned the warmer on her electric kettle to make her tea. "Very funny." But, she didn't look amused.

"Where were you?" I sat Jazz on the floor, took a fresh tea bag from the tiny basket next to the kettle and dropped it in a clean mug for her.

"At the funeral home with Michael Riordan."

"You're kidding."

She raised one eyebrow. "He showed up at the front door and said he'd like some company while he made arrangements. I didn't mind, of course."

I was astounded. "Why you? Isn't there family, or something?"

She shook her head. "He knows I was good friends with his mother. His father moved to Atlanta after the divorce. Apparently he met some young woman at one of those resort things in the Bahamas, and he moved to where she lived."

"No shit." I thought that stuff only happened to rich people. Wait, the Riordans were wealthy.

Aunt Madge ignored what she had once referred to as my "shit slip" and continued. "Ruth has a sister, but she's in Phoenix. And," she hesitated, "Michael isn't too popular around here."

"What do you know that I don't?"

"Quite a bit," she said, dryly, pouring the water into her mug.

"Let me rephrase that. Would you like to let me in on any of it?"

"Since anyone who lives here knows, I guess it isn't gossip." She ignored my rolling eyes. "When Michael married, the wedding was here, because his bride's parents were supposedly unable to host the event. Ruth and Larry went all out, even though they'd been divorced for a year. They could not have been more gracious to her, never a word about arranging, and paying, for everything."

"Dad would have liked that."

"Your father always jokes a lot about the costs of your and Renée's weddings, but you know how proud he is of you."

I nodded, mildly chagrined.

She continued, "Within two months, it was as if Ruth and Larry were Michael's wife's worst enemies. She wouldn't come to visit and she didn't want Michael to. No one ever knew what happened, but I can't believe either of them did anything so awful. Anyway, if one of them did, why would she have been mad at both of them? They were divorced."

I thought about this for a minute. "So, how does that translate to Michael not having anyone else to ask to go to the funeral home with him?"

"It was very hard on Ruth. Larry had remarried and I guess she felt pretty alone. People thought Michael should have been here more often. He did come occasionally, maybe once a year. By himself, of course."

It seemed to me to fall in the 'nobody's business' category, but Ocean Alley is a small town. There is a collective mindset about some things, like "tourism is good" and "the ocean never really warms up until July," but it seemed in this case it had been applied to Michael Riordan. Sort of a town perspective on gratitude, or lack of it.

Later I helped Aunt Madge put out margarine and jam with the warm bread, but excused myself and Jazz before the two couples came in to eat. I thought I would take a slow jog on the boardwalk before supper, maybe even try to talk Aunt Madge into letting me take her out for dinner, my treat. After all, she'd had a hard day, too.

NEWHART'S DINER IS SMALL and always crowded for dinner, a reflection of the great price for the off-season blue plate special. Today it was meatloaf, green beans, mashed potatoes made from real potatoes, gelatin salad, and chocolate cake. In the summer, the menu is largely fish, including sushi, which owner Arnie Newhart sells to the tourists for pretty high prices. From October to April, Arnie and his wife Marguerite take it easy, as he puts it, and they scale back the menu and add the blue plate special. I had been willing to splurge and take Aunt Madge to a more formal restaurant, but she wanted Newhart's.

We were seated at a booth near the door, and three people had already stopped by to say hello to Aunt Madge. She introduced me each time, and I would make appropriate comments and turn my attention back to the walls, which are lined with photos, framed newspaper articles, and various Ocean Alley memorabilia.

When I was here during high school, the collection was displayed in a helter-skelter fashion. Now, each news article is matted in a thin wood frame that is painted the same color as the booths. Aunt Madge told me on the short drive to the restaurant that Arnie's aunt had left the couple $30,000 a few years ago and they put half of it into redecorating the diner.

Arnie served us himself. "How do you like my new photo?" he asked. He pointed to a framed head shot above the door. "Bob Newhart. And he autographed it, too."

I looked more closely and could see the words but could not make them out. "What's it say?"

"It says 'To my favorite cousin.'" Arnie laughed.

Aunt Madge looked skeptical. "I didn't know you were related to him."

"We aren't. I got him to sign it that way, for a joke." He looked quite pleased with himself.

"Why put it up so high?" I asked.

He frowned. "Some jerk would take it, wouldn't you know?"

"Hey, Arnie." A food server looked out from the kitchen. "When's the next batch of meat loaf done?"

We turned our attention to our dinners. We had both gotten the special, and what the food lacked in glamour it made up in volume. I figured we'd be asking for doggie bags.

Aunt Madge had just started on her salad when she frowned. I turned to follow her gaze and saw an older woman in a blue wool coat, which kind of matched her hair. She had her coat on and money in her hand, making her way to the cash register by the door. "Who is she?" I asked.

"Elmira Washington." She frowned.

"Ignore her," I turned back to my food.

"I don't like to be rude, but she's the one who's been letting people know why you moved here."

"I heard. She's a jerk. I don't care what she says." I pushed my dinner plate toward the edge of the table and pulled the cake toward me. "Is this as good as it looks?"

"Better," said Aunt Madge, as she looked directly at her plate. I took this as a sign that Elmira was approaching.

"Good evening, Madge!" Her voice was loud and had a sing-song quality. I didn't think I'd ever met her, but her voice alone was enough to make me want to stay far away from her.

"Evening, Elmira," Aunt Madge said. She gave the woman a brief nod and continued eating, even after Elmira paused at our table.

"So," Elmira said, "this is your niece."

I gave her one of my best smiles. "Yes, the one you've been talking to folks about."

Aunt Madge reached for her water glass, but she didn't fool me. I could tell she was trying not to laugh.

Elmira stiffened. "Talking about you? I never…"

"Come on, Elmira. There's no point in being a gossip if you don't want to own up to it." I continued to smile pleasantly.

"Really, Jolie." She looked to Aunt Madge, as if she expected her to reprimand me.

"How are you this evening, Elmira?" Aunt Madge asked her, as she patted her mouth with her napkin.

"Very well, thank you," she replied stiffly. "I was going to ask how you two are, what with Ruth's death."

Suddenly, my stomach roiled. For a few minutes I'd forgotten about Ruth Riordan. "We're fine." I almost snapped the response.

Elmira ignored me and looked at Aunt Madge as she spoke. "Just a few days ago Ruth and Michael were in here for dinner."

"I'm sure you're glad you had a chance to see her," Aunt Madge replied, evenly.

"Oh, I didn't talk to them. It looked like they were having a pretty heated discussion."

I resented how pleased Elmira looked. She wanted to sound as if she was somehow in the know about Ruth and her son. I could only imagine what she would say about me finding the body.

"I'll see you at church Sunday." Aunt Madge's nod was curt. Elmira probably couldn't tell that the look on Aunt Madge's face was pain, but I could.

Elmira didn't reply, but continued her walk to the cash register. I'd never seen Aunt Madge rebuff anyone. I leaned over and touched her hand. "I'm sorry. Do you want to go?"

She shook her head. "She makes me so mad. She knows Ruth and I were friends. She didn't even say she was sorry about her."

"She's a witch," I was trying to be sympathetic.

"There's no need to follow her example," Aunt Madge said, as she reached for her cup of tea.

NEEDLESS TO SAY, I did not get up at six a.m. the next day. Although I wanted to finish the appraisal, I thought it unlikely to be rescheduled until after Ruth Riordan's funeral. I planned to stop by Harry's office mid-morning. He had fixed up a small workspace for me and said that after we did a few more appraisals he would buy a second computer. I offered to bring my laptop to the office, but he said not to bother, I could use his whenever I needed it.

I took my time showering and blow-drying my hair. There was no urgency to the day, and I felt disappointed at that. Jazz, unaware that I was out of sorts, or perhaps ignoring this, was impatient with my slow pace. She walked across the small dressing table as I applied make-up and raced toward the bedroom door every time I stood up.

When Jazz and I went downstairs about nine-thirty, I first looked out the window to check on my car. All four tires were inflated. I was surprised to see the newspaper on the kitchen table. Aunt Madge usually left it in the dining room for guests to look at throughout the day. No sign of her. After Jazz had some dry food and a small saucer of milk, I carried her back to my room, then scribbled a note to Aunt Madge and struck out for Java Jolt.

The air was damp, though not too cold. I inhaled the smell of seaweed and ocean breeze and climbed up to the boardwalk. I had only gone a few steps when I saw a man sitting on a bench, carefully applying duct tape to his worn sneakers. Next to him was a bag from the local dollar store.

Something about him seemed familiar, but I didn't think I knew anyone who had to tape their shoes. The man had an open knapsack on the ground beside him, and it was crammed. Sticking out of the top were a bottle of water and a couple of books. Homeless people were rare in

Ocean Alley at this time of year. A small number appeared each summer, but most had left by now, heading for a warmer winter climate.

He must have been aware that I slowed my pace, and he lifted his head and looked at me. "Son of a bitch, if it isn't Jolie Gentil."

His greeting took me by surprise. I looked at him more closely and saw that his jeans had a small tear on the left knee and his brown hair hung to his shoulders; it was clean, but uncombed. The bangs that reached his eyebrows and full beard made it difficult to discern his features. "I'm sorry, sir, but I'm afraid I don't remember you."

"Sir!" His laugh revealed teeth that were white and straight, a sharp contrast to his ragged appearance. "Is that what you call the only person who had a higher score than you did in 'Screw the Bunny?'"

"Scoobie? That's you?" For the life of me I couldn't think of his real first name. Scoobie and I had hung around a lot in eleventh grade. I wasn't sure why he was allowed to stay out so late, but I had been glad of the company.

"Yep, it's me. I saw you were back." He grinned. "You look almost the same, except for the preppy clothes."

I automatically looked down at my blue Dockers and cotton sweater of blue and yellow that showed under my unzipped jacket. "This is not preppy, it's...stylish."

"Stylish, preppy, take your pick. You look good."

It was a simple compliment, and I felt myself flush. It seemed almost wrong that I lived in comfort and he couldn't afford new shoes. "Gee, Scoobie." I wasn't sure what to say. "I'm going to Java Jolt. You want to join me and get caught up?"

His hesitation was brief. "You get it, and bring it outside. It's warm enough." He turned and waited for me to walk the few paces to him and we fell into step.

We walked in a fairly comfortable silence, but my thoughts were anything comfortable. Where had Scoobie been the last ten years? How did he end up with what looked like all his possessions in a knapsack? When we had traversed the hundred yards or so to Java Jolt, I turned to him. "What's your pastry preference?"

"I like their blueberry muffins." When I started to push the door to enter, he added, "Decaf with cream, no sugar." This was a change. In high school, Scoobie had lived on high-voltage soft drinks.

As I approached the counter I was conscious that Joe Regan was looking at me very directly. "You know him?" he asked.

"We went to high school together. I haven't seen him since then." I busied myself fixing the two cups of coffee and ordered two blueberry muffins.

Joe continued. "He's been in and out of rehab. Be careful."

I felt annoyed at the advice, but tried not to show it. "Thanks." I paid for our food, and added, "I never thought of Scoobie as dangerous."

Joe shrugged. "Probably not. As far as I know, his only arrests have been for using and selling pot." He grinned as he gave me my change. "I hear it was good stuff."

Swell. I slipped the handle of the small plastic bag of muffins over my wrist and picked up the coffees. "Not that you'd know," I threw over my shoulder.

Scoobie opened the door for me and took the paper coffee cups. "Thanks. Let's go to a bench over there." We walked on the boardwalk for about half a block and settled on a bench across from the small store I'd browsed in just before meeting Pedone.

"So, did Regan tell me to keep away from me?" he asked as I indicated which coffee was decaf.

"Not exactly. He said to be careful."

Scoobie peeled the paper off a muffin and took a huge bite. He chewed and swallowed quickly. "Probably not the worst advice you'll ever get, but I don't think you'll need it." He grinned. "I'm reformed. In fact, it's rare that you'll see me raiding garbage cans these days."

"I didn't know you needed to. Reform, I mean." I watched as he continued to eat, noting that even though his appearance was ragged his nails and hands were clean. "We used to goof around, but we never did anything really bad." He said nothing as he tried to peel the plastic tab off the small opening on the coffee lid so he could take a drink.

I sipped my coffee and regarded him. "You could have stabbed me under the boardwalk any number of times, but you didn't." I smiled at him.

He grew somber. "You were a good friend. Don't you remember, hardly anyone would talk to me in school?"

"You know, I don't remember that. I guess, gee, I guess I was too busy thinking of my own problems."

He nodded. "You've just defined adolescence—the certainty that your own problems put you at the center of the universe."

I peeled my muffin paper, wondering when Scoobie had become a walking psychologist. "Sounds like me back then. My life did get better though." I took a bite, much smaller than his. "My parents got back together and had actually worked things out, and I liked college."

"Me too, but my major was marijuana manufacturing, so I never graduated."

"Do you, uh, still…?"

"Nah. I might have stopped anyway, but I've been arrested a few times for possession and once for selling. For that I spent several months boarding with the county." He grinned. "I'm eventually trainable. Now I spend my evenings in Narcotics Anonymous meetings."

"And your days here?" I asked, gesturing to the beach and boardwalk.

"A lot, unless it's below freezing. Then you can find me in the library or Java Jolt." He probably sensed my next question. "I have a room in a sort of permanent half-way house. It's warm, but not where you want to spend a lot of time."

Talk about different roads traveled. I tried to think of something witty to say, but was fresh out.

He continued. "So, when did you get into the appraisal stuff?"

"Gee, what are you, the town crier?"

"No, I saw the article in the paper. The one that said you found the old lady murdered."

I spit out a sip of coffee, narrowly missing him. "She wasn't murdered! She was just dead, in her bed, even."

"Huh. Maybe I read the paper wrong." He stared at me as he drank his coffee.

I smacked my forehead with the palm of my hand. "That's why Aunt Madge left the paper in the kitchen." I picked up my muffin. "I gotta go. I'll look for you again."

He said nothing as I turned to half jog back to Aunt Madge's.

I sat at the table and picked up the paper. "Police Investigate Suspicious Death of Prominent Resident." The article was brief, noting that while she had cancer, Mrs. Riordan had looked and acted better in the last few weeks than she had in months.

I scanned quickly, wishing not to see my name, and was of course disappointed. Though it appeared near the end of the article, I was referred to as the "woman who found the body, Jolie Gentil, of Steele Appraisals." Oh well, they say even negative publicity is a good thing. Maybe Harry would get some new business. If anyone remembered me from eleventh grade, they'd know I was back and what I was doing. Instantly, I felt as if I'd trodden on a grave, not that I really know what that feels like.

There was also mention that Michael had been staying in the house, but that he was not home when I "discovered" the body. As if I'd been looking for buried treasure. When I reread the article, all it really said was that the cause of death was not yet determined, but suspicious. I couldn't understand why the paper made such a big deal out of it; and on the front page, yet.

I pushed it aside and tackled the rest of the blueberry muffin. Miss Piggy came out of Aunt Madge's bedroom and stretched. "This is not for you." She immediately plopped on the floor and put her paws over her ears. This was a trick she had learned before coming to Aunt Madge, and it must have earned her doggie treats in her prior home, because she always removed her paws and wagged her tail expectantly.

"You're impossible." I tossed her a piece of muffin.

"Don't do that," Aunt Madge said as she came through the swinging kitchen door with a small sack of groceries.

"Yes ma'am." Feeling reduced to age twelve, I jumped up and opened the door to the fridge as she took a half-gallon of milk out of her bag.

"Aunt Madge, I ran into Scoobie today…" I began.

"Adam, dear, Adam." She spoke absently as she took a small box of artificial sweeteners from her bag.

"That's it. I couldn't…"

The phone rang and I answered it, annoyed that my thought about Scoobie was interrupted. "Miss Gentle?" a man's voice asked. Obviously not someone I knew well.

"That's 'Zhan-tee.' What can I do for you?"

"I'm George Winters at the Ocean Alley Press."

Not being fond of the media at the moment, I let his words hang there. "Did you want something?" I finally asked.

"I wondered if you had any comments about the cause of Mrs. Riordan's death."

"Comments? Of course not." I really wanted to hang up, but I was in Aunt Madge's house, not mine, so I couldn't.

"Have you heard?" he asked.

"Heard what?" I held the phone away from my ear, aware that Aunt Madge was now standing next to me. The blonde color was already fading; I had a fleeting though that she must have used a cheaper brand of color.

"That the coroner has ruled that the cause of death was due to suffocation or strangulation. Hard to tell just yet."

I said nothing. I couldn't. It was impossible.

"Miss Gentil?"

"I really don't have any comment. I'm sure you can get any information from the police." I hung up and looked at Aunt Madge. "That means she was murdered." This isn't how it is supposed to be. Wealthy old ladies die in their sleep.

Suddenly, I started to shake and sat down quickly. "I was...whoever did it...might have..." Absurdly, I couldn't finish the thought. Not out loud anyway. Whoever killed her could have been in the house when I was.

Aunt Madge sat down across from me and held onto the edge of her chair as she stared past me. "Poor Ruth. How can this be happening?"

I realized Aunt Madge had just lost a close friend and went to her chair and leaned over and gave her a hug. "They have to be wrong."

She let me rest my head on her shoulder for a second, and I could almost feel her sag an inch. I kissed her on the cheek. At that, she straightened. "I'm going down to the police station and find out what's really going on."

I took my hand off her shoulder and looked at her. My aunt, the no-gossip woman.

She picked up her purse and glanced at me. "Are you coming?"

I wouldn't miss it for anything. Next thing I knew, they'd be accusing me.

CHAPTER FIVE

THE PANELED WALLS and hard plastic chairs of the police station's small waiting area did not provide a welcoming atmosphere. Fortunately, the uniformed officer behind the counter said she didn't think we'd have long to wait.

I'd only been in here once, in eleventh grade when I got picked up for smoking on the boardwalk. I didn't realize it wasn't a crime or I wouldn't have gone with the cop, a guy in his early forties named Sgt. Tortino. He knew Aunt Madge and wanted to scare me straight or something. I was far more scared of her than him, of course. She hauled me home and wouldn't let me watch TV for two weeks. Since I had only smoked a few times, to be cool, I decided to quit rather than fight.

As luck would have it, a now-older Lieutenant Tortino came out when the front desk clerk called back, and he escorted Aunt Madge and me to his small office. He'd gone from light brown to a mix of brown and gray hair and put on about twenty pounds since I'd seen him. He still had the same firm walk I remembered when he was parading me down the boardwalk to his car.

We sat down facing him, and I thought I detected a look of amusement when he glanced at me. "I promise, I quit smoking that night."

"Was that before or after you finished cussing me out?" He grinned.

Aunt Madge turned to me. "You didn't."

"Um, of course not." I tried to glare at Tortino without her noticing.

"So, what on earth is this business of Ruth being murdered?" she asked him.

He was somber. "It's definite. Someone applied pressure to her windpipe." He paused. "There are some other indications, but it wouldn't be appropriate for me to give a lot of details."

"But, she looked so...peaceful." OK, her eyes were staring straight up, but that was sort of normal for a dead person, at least in all the mystery books I'd read. "I guess I didn't look real close..."

Tortino looked at me now. "I read your statement after your aunt called. I can see why you'd think she looked peaceful."

"But," I persisted, "if you strangle someone, they would like, fight with you wouldn't they? Her bed wasn't messed up at all."

"They would resist, probably. Unless someone had drugged them. We're waiting for toxicology reports." He paused. "I'd appreciate if you wouldn't mention that to anyone."

"A reporter called me this morning. I told him to call you guys."

Tortino was interested. "I'll pass that on to Sgt. Morehouse in the Detective Division. Who was it?"

I glanced at Aunt Madge.

"George Winters," she said.

He sighed. "He's young. Always trying to get a big story."

"Sounds as if he's got one," I said, glumly.

"Where's Michael?" Aunt Madge asked. "Does he know?"

"Uh, yeah," said Tortino. He sounded like a kid trying to hide something. I could relate to that.

He stood. "Listen, Jolie, they're going to ask you for your fingerprints." The shock must have shown in my face. "Not because anyone suspects you, because we'll have to compare the fingerprints we lifted to those of people who were supposed to be in the house."

I nodded, and he continued, "If you think of anything else, call Sgt. Morehouse, okay?"

So, we were done. Aunt Madge continued to talk to him as we walked out. "I feel terrible for Michael. Ruth said they were so enjoying their time together the last two weeks."

"Were they?" he asked. "That's nice."

When we got to the small waiting area Tortino left us. Aunt Madge seemed not to want to leave, as if she hadn't gotten what she wanted. She gave her head a slow sideways shake. "Ruth would hate this." I started to say Ruth didn't have to worry about that or anything else, but stopped myself.

As we stood there for a few seconds, there was a loud slam of a door behind us, and we both jumped. Michael Riordan stormed into view. He was walking rapidly toward the back door that leads to the parking lot, and didn't notice us. He tried to slam that door, too, but it was hydraulic, so he couldn't.

Aunt Madge looked after him and then at me. "I was afraid of that."

"Of what?"

"They think he killed her."

"That doesn't make sense." I didn't quite know why. He certainly knew how to demonstrate a temper.

"You know what the police shows say, he had motive, means, and opportunity."

I had to stifle a laugh. "Aunt Madge, are you saying he knows how to drug people and then strangle them?"

"No, of course not, but it will look that way. You mark my words." She led the way out, and I followed, not certain when my aunt had started watching police shows on TV. Last I knew she was into the reality shows that masquerade as talent contests.

I TRIED TO TALK AUNT MADGE into getting coffee at Newhart's or Java Jolt, but she wanted to get home. "The dogs will need to go out."

Aunt Madge's hands were in her lap. Usually, when I drive she leans her head against the seat, but today she sat slightly forward and held her purse tightly to her. I'd rarely seen her look so tense. "They went out right before we left. It's been a rough morning, you could use a break."

She shook her head. "I'm better when I'm busy. Besides," she glanced at her watch, "I still have one room to make up."

"Will you let me help, for a change?"

I took a quick glance and saw the beginning of a smile play around her lips. "You can run the vac in the upstairs hall."

So I don't do hospital corners when I make a bed. I've never understood the big deal about making a bed a certain way. "The vac it is."

I STOPPED BY HARRY'S after lunch to see if he had any more

work (preferably without dead bodies) or if he knew when we would finish the Riordan house. It occurred to me that if Michael was Ruth's heir, he might not want to give it to the Arts Council and would put it on the market. If he did that, he probably would not want me to finish the appraisal now. He'd wait and let a prospective buyer pay for it.

But, Harry said that Michael had called that morning to say he would get in touch again after the funeral. His father and his wife were coming into town this afternoon, and he had invited them to stay at the house. He didn't want a lot of other activity. I was surprised he'd had the presence of mind to call. Had to be before his scene at the station.

No other work, but Harry had had what he termed get-acquainted calls from three agents that morning. He tried not to look too pleased, since we both knew it was probably because of the mention of me and his firm in Mrs. Riordan's article. "I'm not sure that everyone is as pleased with Stenner's as they once were," he said, trying to appear tactful.

"I bet they told you more than that." I was fishing for info.

He shrugged. "Jennifer's very competent, but I hear she can be a little brusque."

Gee, she and Michael could get together. I left his office headed for the boardwalk, and walked a couple blocks looking for Scoobie. The boardwalk had a forlorn air about it, as if it missed having hordes of visitors and the smell of fries and cotton candy. The benches, which were usually not repainted until spring, showed the effects of a summer of wet bathing suits and many had the usual hearts with names of teen lovers. When there was black paint over a few inches of bench I knew that meant those carved words were less polite.

No Scoobie, so I headed for the Purple Cow. I was confident that I didn't need to do a resume, at least in the short term, but I was thinking of getting a new business card case. Mine was gold-plated and had the seal of my old real estate firm on it.

As I drove to the Purple Cow, I tried to memorize every street name. It seemed an appraiser should know where each street is, at least in a town the size of Ocean Alley. The blocks of the very long alphabet streets are intersected many times with cross streets with names like Seaside, Fairweather and Conch Shell.

There are a number of large Victorian homes that probably had at least a half-acre of land around them when they were built. However, the wealthy city folks who built those homes are long gone, and before Ocean Alley instituted its current lot size requirements people built as many as two or three bungalows or summer cottages between them, more on the streets closest to the water. Some of them started as two-room cottages with no indoor plumbing and now have a small concrete addition in the back. Here and there are small tool sheds that were outhouses in a prior life. Although it's a hodge-podge, I find the lack of order appealing.

I drove through the center of Ocean Alley. While not a town square in the true sense, the block that houses the court house also has the post office, police station, library, and small in-town grocery, so it is as close to a downtown as a small beach town can get. I parallel parked in front of The Purple Cow and locked the car, wondering as I did so if I would ever live in a place where I didn't think to lock my car. Not if people murder elderly women in their beds.

Today, the store's white board said, "All beginnings are somewhat strange; but we must have patience, and, little by little, we shall find things, which at first were obscure, becoming clear." Vincent de Paul. It took up all the room on the board. Clearly, someone at the Purple Cow was into life changes. It was a little too kvetchy for me. I pushed open the door and waited a few seconds for my eyes to adjust to light that was dimmer than the brilliant sunshine.

Ramona, her long hair held back with a dark purple bow, greeted me with more than mild curiosity. "I saw you in the paper. That must have been terrible."

She didn't know the half of it. "It was a more than a little unnerving."

She nodded. "George Winters was in here this morning. He said she was murdered." Her always-wide eyes looked owlish. "Did it look like it?"

Death can bring out the tactless in some of us. "Not to me. Looked like she just died in her sleep." Before she could ask me another question, I mentioned why I was there, and she led me to the business card holders.

"Do you like working for Mr. Steele?" she asked, as she took several card holders from a case that held small leather goods and expensive pens.

"Harry seems real nice." For some reason wanting to make it clear that in the adult world we call people by first names. *Stop thinking like a bitch, Jolie.*

"Jennifer was really mad that someone else got into that business in town."

"That's not very realistic. You'd think she'd even like it, with interest rates so low." I realized she did not get this, so I added, "There's almost too much work for appraisers. Everyone's trying to refinance their houses."

This did not interest her. "The paper said Michael wasn't home."

"Yes, I saw that." She must think I hadn't read it, or maybe she wasn't connecting on the fact that I had actually been there.

"He could have been, you know. It's a big house." Ramona looked away as she spoke.

"Ramona!" I stared at her, half amused, half irritated. "You're starting a rumor."

She shrugged. "I never liked him. He always called me 'Monaramona.' He knew I didn't like it."

"That doesn't mean he murdered his mother." I paused. "Maybe he was teasing you because he liked you." Given his comment about her, I doubted it, but that's what my mother always said when boys teased me.

"People think he wanted her money." She gazed at me directly. "I heard his business is bad."

"But you don't know any of this, Ramona." I was irritated with her, but didn't want to show it too much. I might want to know what else she heard later. At least as it pertained to me.

I paid for my business card case – burgundy leather, very cool – and left the store. Yesterday I had been so purposeful, but today I felt very much at loose ends. I decided to go back to Aunt Madge's and take Jazz outside. I wanted her to get to know the area a little, in case she accidentally got out.

My plans were waylaid by the sight of a silver Mercedes in Aunt Madge's small parking lot. *What does he want with me?* Then I remembered that he was more likely to be here to see Aunt Madge. She greeted me at the door, with a sort of odd expression. Michael was right behind her.

"They act like they think I killed her." He was very upset. I hoped Aunt Madge's guests were out. "How can they think that?" He paced to the window and back to the foyer and faced me.

"They're probably just fishing around" I tried to sound reassuring.

"Do you think I did it?"

"No. I can't prove you didn't, of course, but I don't think you did." It was true, for some reason I didn't believe he killed her. Not that I would have said I thought the police were right, even if I did, in his state of mind.

"Good," was all he said.

"Let's go back to the kitchen," Aunt Madge said, quietly. My guess was that he was a lot calmer now than he had been when he first arrived.

Aunt Madge turned up the warmer on her tea kettle and offered us both a cup. He shook his head, but she fixed him one anyway, with honey. Aunt Madge is convinced that tea calms anyone.

"They can't have any real reason to suspect you." I was trying to ask a question without framing it that way.

"The police don't tell you what they think," he said bitterly. He took a sip of the tea. "You know I left, right?"

"I saw you leave. Where did you go?"

"You mean do I have an alibi?" He gave a harsh laugh. "I was mostly at the beach, just walking. I sent a fax from the Purple Cow before I parked my car by the beach."

"Someone must have seen you. Or at least your car."

He smiled grimly at that. "Not after I left the Purple Cow. I parked the car in the municipal lot, but it's too chilly for most people to be on the beach. I don't recall seeing anyone, anyway. I was…thinking." He looked away from me, then back. "I suppose I could have walked by people and not noticed."

"As Jolie said," Aunt Madge put in, "people will remember the car."

"Yes," he was fuming again, "but this is a small town. Our house may be at the edge of it, but it's only a fifteen-minute walk." He took another sip of the unwanted tea. "Someone will say I could have parked the car, gone home, killed her, and walked back." He paused, teacup in midair. "Or they'll say I killed her just before you got there."

"But, you didn't," Aunt Madge said.

"No, but I can tell they think I did." He splashed tea as he set the cup down hard.

"They have to have a reason to think that." I remembered that Elmira Washington said he seemed to be arguing with his mother in Newhart's a few days ago, but that hardly seemed like a reason for the police to suspect him of murder. "You, uh, didn't go around town bad-mouthing your mom, did you?"

He waved his hand dismissively. "Of course not." He sighed. "I'm her sole beneficiary, except for her plans for the house, plus my business is not doing as well as it was. And," he gave a forced smile, "some people think I'm an asshole."

"But surely not everyone on the police force," I said.

He half laughed, but Aunt Madge said, "For heaven's sake!"

He grew immediately somber again. "They already called my partners in Houston. A lot of people know I'm here because we had a major falling-out."

"That doesn't sound like a motive for murdering your mother. Your partners, maybe," I said.

He looked at me directly, "I'm not going to walk away from the business with much cash. We have a clause in our partnership agreement that says if one person voluntarily leaves the firm they only take what they brought with them plus a portion of last year's profit." He paused. "It was not our best year."

I was dying to ask him why he was leaving the firm, but I caught Aunt Madge's eye and decided not to. "Sorry, Michael, still no motive."

"OK, here's one. My wife is divorcing me, and I'll probably need a lot of cash for the settlement."

"Yeah, okay. But your mom was going to die anyway. What's the rush?"

Aunt Madge sat up straighter, but didn't say anything.

Michael looked at me as if he had never seen me. "I'm known to be somewhat impatient," he said, dryly.

"So, an impatient asshole." I saw Aunt Madge flinch. "That could relate to state of mind, but not motive."

This time he really laughed. "I don't remember you being funny in school."

"The only time you talked to me was the first couple days of school and when you were running for class president and you wanted my vote."

"That's probably true," he said, almost amiably.

"To be honest, I didn't vote for you." Am I flirting with him?

Aunt Madge interrupted. "When does your father arrive?"

He glanced at his watch. "In about an hour at Newark. I need to get on the road." He stood. "Thanks for the tea." He looked at me with an expression I could not interpret.

"On TV, they usually don't arrest family suspects until after the funeral." I said.

"Thanks for that nugget." He bent over and kissed Aunt Madge's cheek.

CHAPTER SIX

JAZZ AND I WERE ON THE FRONT PORCH sweeping sawdust from Aunt Madge's latest carpentry project into a dustpan when Sgt. Morehouse came by in the late afternoon. He glanced at the dustpan. "What's she working on now?"

"She's putting crown molding in one of the upstairs bathrooms."

"A bathroom? Isn't that kind of fancy?"

I shrugged, and looked at him more closely. He looked as if he hadn't slept much, and I figured there probably weren't too many murders in Ocean Alley. Although he was not wearing the same clothes that he had worn yesterday, today's polyester pants, nondescript blue shirt, and old-fashioned tie were so similar that it was as if he was in uniform.

I invited him to sit and he sank wearily into a wicker chair. Jazz ran to the other end of the porch and jumped on the railing. I could hear the dogs barking in the back yard; they knew someone was out front. "How's it going?" I asked.

"You and your aunt came to the station this morning." So much for him answering my questions. I told him about the call from the reporter, and that Aunt Madge was especially upset by it.

"I hate that guy," he said.

I shrugged. "Isn't he just doing his job?"

"Yeah but he always calls before we're ready for him."

"Then he must be doing his job really well," I said, intentionally needling him.

He grunted. "You sure you told us everything yesterday?"

"Gee, why don't you ask me if I did it?"

"Did you?"

"Of course not." I was offended. "Why would you even ask?"

"You seem pretty friendly with the Riordan kid."

"The 'Riordan kid' and I didn't even socialize in high school. I was just there because I'm doing some work for Harry."

"Yeah, I know." He signed heavily. "You don't have an obvious motive, but I have to ask."

Somewhat mollified, I asked, "Do you have any idea who did?"

"Just theories," he said. As if he'd tell me. "The funeral home said Madge went with him to make arrangements. I kinda need to talk to her."

I led him back to the kitchen and excused myself. Aunt Madge would probably defend Michael, and I wasn't ready to go that far. My instinct said he didn't do it, but I really had no reason for any opinion. On the other hand, Aunt Madge seemed convinced that Michael and his mother were having such a great couple weeks that he couldn't have done it. I can trust her instincts.

Since I'd left Jazz on the porch, I went back there. At first I didn't see her. Then I looked to the sidewalk in front of the house and saw Joe Pedone holding her. "What the hell are you doing? Give me my cat." I was down the steps in two bounces and he handed her to me without comment.

"Did you flatten my tires?"

"Gee, you had a flat? I'm sorry," he said, looking away.

I took in his clothes. No more loud golfer outfit. "You didn't answer my question."

"That's a no," he said, pleasantly, adjusting his obviously expensive tie. I couldn't help but be struck by the contrast between his clothing and Morehouse's. Pedone obviously didn't live on a civil servant's salary.

"You probably had someone do it." I stroked Jazz, who seemed to want to go back to Pedone. I held her tighter.

He didn't reply to that. "Did you give any more thought to repaying your husband's debt?"

"Look, I don't have the money. He cleaned me out. Anyway, Robby owes it, not me."

"But, Robby ain't got it." He said this as if this was the only clarification I should need.

"Do you want to pay my student loan?" I asked him.

He looked puzzled.

"Same logic." I walked back into the house. I didn't want to admit it, but I was shaken. This was not something I wanted to bother Aunt Madge with when she had just lost a good friend, and I wasn't about to bring it up in front of Morehouse. I could call the lawyer who had advised me on my rights as the wife of an embezzler, but what would that accomplish? Just a huge bill, probably.

At least Pedone hadn't threatened to break my legs. I pondered whether I would mind if they did this to Robby, and tried to remind myself that his compulsive gambling was supposed to be an illness. I pushed Joe Pedone out of my mind with the vigor I usually attached to eating chocolate ice cream, and went upstairs with Jazz.

WE DIDN'T SEE MICHAEL all weekend. I figured he had his hands full with his father and stepmother and funeral planning. I spent a good part of the weekend trying to put together an easy-to-assemble computer desk I had bought at Wal-Mart. There were some really nice ones at the Purple Cow, but with very limited funds in my bank account the $29.99 price at Wal-Mart was more in line with my checkbook. When I had six screws left over and it wobbled, Aunt Madge took pity on me and suggested that there must be another piece to brace the back. I found it wrapped in paper at the bottom of the box. Not amused at my swearing, Aunt Madge lent me her electric screwdriver but did not help with the disassembly and reassembly.

I hauled the box, empty except for Jazz, downstairs and placed it on the sitting room floor. It was long and thin, which meant Jazz could crawl in easily but all the dogs could do was insert a nose or paw. It took less than thirty seconds for this to become a popular game. Jazz would dive for Mister Rogers' paw. She let go each time he pulled it out.

Aunt Madge came into the room as Miss Piggy was inserting her nose into the box and Mr. Rogers was head-butting her in the midsection so he could have another turn. "I see you're enjoying yourself," she said, somewhat curtly.

"You want us kids to play outside?" I asked.

"No." She sat next to me on the couch. "I'm sorry if I'm short. I just can't believe the police would consider Michael a suspect. Ruth would be so upset."

I squeezed her knee, not sure what to say. "I trust your instincts, Aunt Madge, but…"

"But what?" she bristled.

"What makes you so certain? I mean," I saw the protest coming. "You've hardly seen him for years, have you?"

She answered immediately. "It isn't just that Ruth said they were enjoying each other's company. They talked about how he would help her through the next few months or year, and he was going to go with her to the assisted living place to help her pick out an apartment there. You just don't talk about those kinds of things and then off your mother."

"Off your mother?" I couldn't hide my smile.

"Oh, you know what I mean. It just doesn't make sense. None of it makes sense." Her voice cracked and she put her hand to her mouth to keep from crying. I leaned over and put a hand on her wrist. Mr. Rogers came over and put his head in her lap. "You're a good boy." She spoke softly, petting him.

Miss Piggy pulled her nose out of the box and gave a soft grunt before loping over and trying to move Mr. Rogers' head from Aunt Madge's lap and insert her own. She laughed and stood. "I don't know what I'd do without these dogs." She pointed to the door. "Come on, out you go."

I watched as she slid the sliding glass door so they could bound into the back yard. I would do anything to help Aunt Madge feel better, if only I knew where to start.

WHEN SHE CAME HOME FROM CHURCH the next day Aunt Madge said she had seen Michael's father in church, but he sat alone and left before she could talk to him. "You know who was there," she added, "Your friend Adam. It was almost forty degrees. We generally don't see him unless it's much colder."

"Scoobie goes to church?" I was more than a little surprised.

"The library doesn't open on Sundays until one o'clock. Our service is one of the shorter ones." She slipped off her pumps and sat them on her long oak table. "And we always have coffee and donuts or cookies afterwards."

I sat at the table and turned up her electric kettle. "Just before that reporter called, I started to ask you about him. Then I forgot. What happened to him? Where is his family?"

Aunt Madge actually made a tsk-ing sound. "He's better off without them. Didn't you ever wonder why he was the only other child out late on the boardwalk with you?"

I stared at her and could swear she almost smirked. "You knew where I was?"

"As I've heard you say, Ocean Alley is a very small town." She poured her tea. "I decided that as long as so many people were keeping track of you on the boardwalk, I'd let well enough alone."

I continued to stare at her, saying nothing. All these years I thought I'd been so smart to thwart her rules.

She glanced at me. "If I had confronted you, you would have started going to someplace more remote than the boardwalk. I didn't want that." She strained her teabag and placed it on a saucer. "And I certainly didn't want to have to stay up until you went to bed. I'm no night owl."

I decided to take the focus off me. She was enjoying this too much. "What did you mean that Scoobie is better off without his parents?"

"His mother drank a lot. His father tried to ignore it. When he couldn't, he left. Adam seemed to almost raise himself." She leaned over to turn the temperature up on her electric kettle. "Think how angry you were that your parents paid more attention to themselves than you in eleventh grade, and imagine what Adam must have felt."

"I can't." I took a moment to get Jazz out of her box, and then went upstairs. I lie on top of the bed, staring at the ceiling. All the time Scoobie and I had spent together, I had thought he didn't have a care in the world. I hadn't known him at all.

IT SEEMED THAT HALF THE TOWN attended Ruth Riordan's funeral on Monday. Larry Riordan and his wife, who looked to be all of thirty-five, sat in the front row with Michael. I thought that was pretty tacky, not so much that Larry Riordan was there, but the new wife. Ruth's sister from Phoenix sat on Michael's other side. Aunt Madge and I had gone to the funeral home the night before and I'd noticed Ruth's sister had studiously avoided talking to Mrs. #2.

When the minister asked if anyone wanted to say anything about Ruth Riordan, Aunt Madge surprised me by getting to her feet at once. She walked purposely to the front of the congregation and up to the pulpit. However, once at the microphone, she hesitated, then seemed to collect herself and began to speak. "Ruth Riordan was one of the kindest women I've known. She could have spent her time playing bridge or traveling, but you were more likely to see her helping at the food pantry or fixing food for an after-funeral meal here at the church."

She paused, and I thought for a minute she would cry, something I've never seen her do. "She was an intensely private person who would never burden a friend with her troubles, and if you trusted her with yours, you could be sure she would never repeat your confidence." At the front of the church someone blew his nose loudly.

"She was quiet but she had a great sense of humor. Not everyone got to see that side of her. If you didn't, it was your loss." She stopped again. "And she loved her son, with all her heart."

When she sat down next to me, Aunt Madge stared straight ahead. I touched her on the arm and was surprised to see a tear leaving each eye.

We moved as lemmings from the church to the cemetery, where I saw Sgt. Morehouse at the edge of the group of mourners. It was pure cop TV. After that, we went to the Riordan's house. I might have skipped that, but Aunt Madge had made three loaves of cheddar cheese bread and insisted on taking them. This was a much smaller group, as tends to be the case.

The house looked nothing short of elegant with the well-dressed crowd moving around the dining room sampling the plates of canapés. A maid in a black uniform and white apron served white wine from a silver tray. She looked either very sad or very tired, and I wondered if she'd been hired for the day or had known Mrs. Riordan well. If she had, it must be tough to have to serve food while everyone else could take the time to grieve.

I saw Jennifer Stenner on the other side of the room. Her blue suit struck the appropriate conservative tone of a funeral, but the white blouse afforded a good view of her firm cleavage, which I guessed was helped by an underwire bra. This I do not normally associate with proper mourning attire.

I had wanted Harry to come because it would be a good place to meet a lot of folks, but he had demurred. Since the only time he had seen Michael was the day his mother died, Harry thought his presence would be a reminder of a difficult day. Such a gentleman. Not good for business.

As I stood filling a plate with assorted goodies, Jennifer approached me. "Jolie. I wouldn't have recognized you." This was an unkind reference to the fact that I looked much better these days than I had in the camouflage pants I wore half the time in eleventh grade. In retrospect, the bangs in my eyes hadn't helped, either.

"You look about the same. Same blonde Jennifer." This was my revenge. The blonde had to come from a bottle as her hair had been brown in high school.

"I hear we're competitors," she continued.

"Technically, you and Harry are. I just freelance for him."

"I'm amazed you didn't come to see me first."

I was tempted to say something about the fact that she only spoke to me in high school if she bumped into me, but settled for, "Harry is a friend of my Aunt Madge's. I've really grown to like him."

"You certainly had a tough first day"

I nodded. "Tougher on Michael, though."

She agreed and moved on to a group of women dressed as sleekly as she. She seemed to pay particular attention to a woman in a black silk suit that looked as if it might have cost a thousand dollars. I probably had gone to school with some of the women, but didn't recognize them. None of the few friends I'd had lived here anymore, except Scoobie, of course. None of the women introduced themselves to me. I found that odd, but didn't really care.

A short, older woman with loosely-permed white hair introduced herself as head of the First Presbyterian Social Services Committee. She said her name was Mrs. Henriette Jasper – "that's Henriette dear, no 'A' at the end." Her eyes were red-rimmed, and her two-piece dress of navy blue with white trim made me think of a sailor. She said that Ruth Riordan was the church member most devoted to helping the needy. "Your aunt's remarks were wonderful. I wanted to say something, but I was just too choked up to speak."

As she began to tell me how many truly needy people there were in Ocean Alley, Aunt Madge walked up and asked me to help clear away some dishes. She whispered that I would have "been there all day" otherwise, since Henriette tended to talk a great deal about her work with the church. I said this sounded like gossip, and Aunt Madge said it was a fact.

I helped Aunt Madge clear away empty paper plates that had

accumulated around the living room, and wished we could leave. As I carried a pile of plates into the kitchen, I stumbled into a little girl who ran around a corner, straight into me. Red gelatin salad spilled down the front of my blouse, and I was barely able to stop myself from swearing loudly or knocking over a woman using a walker. Instead, after I steadied the fortunately good-natured woman, I assured the little girl's mother that the blouse was washable and refused her offer to have it cleaned. It was pure silk, and the dry cleaner would have no more luck with red food color than I. One for the waste basket.

I hurried to the kitchen sink, where the maid handed me a wet paper towel, saying nothing as she did so. "Oh, dear, that's too bad." Jennifer appeared at my side, daintily holding a glass of white wine.

"Yes, well, accidents happen." I blotted at the stain with the paper towel. Useless. Plus, the wet blouse now offered a great outline of my right nipple.

I went back to the dining room and looked for Aunt Madge. She was talking to Larry Riordan. Not a lot of Ruth's friends had sought him out. Aunt Madge saw me and beckoned. "Jolie, did you ever know Mr. Riordan?"

"Larry," he said, extending his hand.

"I don't think so. Sorry to meet you under these circumstances." What else could I say? How's life with the young honey? Just then, she walked up. Though her clothes were clearly expensive, the lines were not those of classic tailoring. Rather than an A-line fashion, the skirt of her rust-colored suit had a ruffle at the hem and the jacket had large buttons in a tiger-eye design. A person would only buy such an outfit if there were twenty others in the closet and she didn't have to wear it one day with a yellow blouse and another day with tan.

"Jolie, this is my wife, Honey Riordan."

Thank goodness I didn't have anything in my mouth. I sputtered a vague hello.

"Isn't this a lovely home?" she gushed.

Could she be more tactless? Maybe she would ask Michael for some of the furniture. "Yes, it is." As she turned to look at some crystal figurines on a shelf, I turned to Aunt Madge. "I'd kind of like to change." I gestured to my shirt. "Would you like me to come back for you?"

"No, I can leave now. I'll just collect my bread board and butter plate." We said goodbye to Larry and Honey (whose name I would certainly never forget) and headed for the kitchen.

Michael came up to us as Aunt Madge loaded the bread board into her carrying bag. "Sorry about the blouse," he said, with a look of mischief.

I gave him a look I hoped would discourage further comment. "I probably did that to someone when I was her age."

"More than once," said Aunt Madge, absently.

"They say payback is a bi..bear." He hesitated. "I wanted to thank you both for being so supportive. I know I'm not the easiest person to be around."

"I'm sure you've said that more than once." I found myself smiling at him.

"Jolie!" Yet again I'd embarrassed Aunt Madge.

"Mostly it's said about me," he said, with a smile.

Jennifer came up and took him by the arm in a very possessive fashion. "Dear Michael. I just wanted to say good-bye and to let you know to call anytime."

I have to admit, I was pleased that he did not look happy about the interruption. What do you care? I don't. Or, I don't think I do.

SURE ENOUGH, the next day the police arrested Michael just as he returned to town from dropping his father and Honey at the airport. The next day's paper said the bail hearing had been held two hours after he was arrested, and implied that not everyone would get this courtesy. However, the Ocean Alley Press did not detail the county prosecuting attorney's basis for filing the charges. It said the prosecuting attorney was "not releasing all of the evidence at this time." I resisted the temptation to call George Winters, who might know more. He would only turn the call into an interview.

CHAPTER SEVEN

I DID AN APPRAISAL A DAY for the next three days, often looking over my shoulder for Joe Pedone. It seemed he had forgotten me and returned to whatever hole he'd crawled out of. I figured if he was going to bug me again he would have already been back. I began to relax.

Harry was very happy with my work, and was teaching me to use the computer-aided appraisal software. Years ago I had done my drawings by hand.

Three days after the funeral Michael called and asked that I return to finish the appraisal. He told Harry that, given all the stuff going on, he would stay at the house while I worked. I was glad to hear that, since I wasn't looking forward to measuring Mrs. Riordan's bedroom. Plus, I might also be able to talk to him about his mother's death. Aunt Madge would be so relieved if he wasn't guilty. And how about me? *I would like that, too.*

I drove to the house on a Friday morning and parked my Toyota in the driveway next to his Mercedes. This time he let me ring the bell, and opened the door without comment. Things looked pretty much as they did little more than a week ago. I glanced up at him. "How are you holding up?"

"I think the traditional reply is 'as well as can be expected,' but I'm still really ticked off." He was wearing gray sweats and an old pair of running shoes, and didn't look anything like the successful Texas oil executive.

"I would think sad, too." I fished a tape measure out of my purse.

"Yeah," he led me upstairs, "I am, but the arrest is so frustrating I mostly think about that."

We didn't talk as I measured and made notes. Fortunately, he had opened all the curtains in the master bedroom, so it looked nothing as it did the day I found his mother in ultimate repose. The upstairs was in the same immaculate condition as the first floor. Someone had done a good job cleaning up the fingerprint dust, which impressed me given how long it had taken me to clean the ink off my own hands.

One of the bedrooms had been turned into a den of sorts, complete with a large-screen TV and computer, which was housed in a very expensive wall unit that looked like solid maple. *That must have been a bear to get up the steps.*

I stopped at the threshold, taking in the green walls, maple crown molding, and rich brown carpet. A man's room if there ever was one. I glanced at Michael and he was smiling at me. "Yes, she decorated it with me in mind."

I must have flushed because his smile broadened. Since I could think of no smart comeback, I said, "It's lovely," and got to work.

As we walked downstairs I asked him if he needed help with anything. "Mother's friend, Mrs. Jasper, keeps calling to see if I want help going through mother's things. It seems a bit early to do that." He sighed. "I know she's just trying to help, and mother really admired how much she did for First Prez."

"I met her briefly at the house after the funeral." I hesitated and then told him Aunt Madge's assessment of her talkativeness, trying to make it sound funny. I failed.

"Yeah, Mother didn't have an answering machine, but I bought one to screen calls and I don't answer when it's her anymore."

"How about Sgt. Morehouse's calls?" I realized this was a mistake as soon as I said it.

"That bastard doesn't have the nerve to call." He had led me to the kitchen and gestured to some mugs on the counter near a coffee pot. He helped himself and I did the same. "It's still not clear what they have other than the firm belief that I wanted my mother's money sooner rather than later."

"Surely they have to tell you."

"Eventually. My lawyer says we'll learn some at the probable cause hearing, where the judge hears information so he can decide if the case will go to trial." He frowned as he took a drink of coffee. "And if he rules I do go to trial, my attorney and I will learn a lot more during discovery."

From crime novels, I recalled that this was the process through which the two sides shared a lot of information prior to the trial. "Maybe it won't even get that far." I tried to be encouraging. "Maybe they'll find the real killer."

"Thanks, but I don't think they're looking."

"There must be a way," I was thinking out loud, "to plant a seed of doubt about you. As far as killing your mom goes, I mean."

His smile was genuine. "What are you, girl detective?"

"I used to sniff out some pretty good real estate deals. For all the good it did me." I was starting to get letters from all kinds of creditors I'd never heard of. I simply forwarded them to my lawyer, and was resigned to paying him a lot of money to handle it and having a really lousy credit rating for a decade.

"Sorry you came here?" he asked.

"Not at all. Sorry about the mess my ex-husband left in Lakewood."

"Did you meet my ex at the funeral?" he asked.

My surprise was so evident I didn't need to say no.

"She hung around with Jennifer a lot," he said. "Black silk suit. Would be good as a burial outfit."

"I did see her, but I didn't know who she was. It was, uh, kind of her to come."

He snorted. "She's not kind. She wants me to think she is so I don't fight so hard about the size of her settlement, now that I've come into Mom's money."

"Sooo, maybe that gives her a motive."

"How do you figure that?" I had his interest.

"If your mom lived until after your divorce, it would be all your money when she died, right?"

"Sure, but geez, I don't think Darla would kill someone, even my mother."

I realized I had not known her name. I plowed ahead. "Aunt Madge said she, Darla I mean, wasn't too fond of your mom."

He sighed. "She was jealous. It had the same effect of dislike. She tried to drive a wedge between me and my parents, especially my mother."

"Why should she care? I would think, given what you stood to inherit, that she'd want to be on their good side."

"There's no figuring Darla. Took me awhile to figure that out." He studied me for a moment. "You probably thought you knew your husband pretty well, but there were some things you really didn't know."

I grimaced. "You can say that again."

"What I found out was that Darla has a hard time maintaining relationships with very many people." He stood and poured himself another cup of coffee. "She was even estranged from her parents when we were married. At the time, I thought it was her parents with the problem. Wrong."

"Maybe you could talk to Sgt. Morehouse about what Darla has to gain…"

"I'm not talking to anyone but my lawyer." He was quite firm on that.

"What if I…"

"Give it a rest, Jolie," he said shortly.

I sat stiffly, stung by the tone he used to reject my offer to help.

He ran his fingers through his hair. "Look, I'm sorry. It's just that I'm paying this lawyer a lot of money, and I figure she has people who work on stuff like this." He smiled. "I'll pass your idea to her."

I smiled in return, though in truth I thought he should be more aggressive about his own defense.

THAT NIGHT I SAT IN BED and tried to think of ways to test my theory on Sgt. Morehouse. More specifically, ways to test it without Michael figuring out I had done so. I told myself I was doing this because Aunt Madge would hate to see Michael in prison, but I can rarely totally fool myself. This was something I could dig into in a way I hadn't wanted to dig into anything in the last few months. Since learning about Robby's crimes I'd alternated between wanting to hibernate and figuring out how to leave Lakewood. And it seemed Michael was growing on me. Maybe I even liked him a bit. *So what if I do?*

Any good lawyer would probably consider that Darla had a lot to gain if Mrs. Riordan died while Darla was married to Michael. Plus, unless the police knew a lot more than they were letting on, it seemed unfair to accuse him. Of course, I didn't know him well. He could be a serial ax murderer in Houston. Though if he were, the Ocean Alley police would probably have matched his fingerprints to some left at a crime there. *Unless he wore gloves...*

I stopped my train of thought and frowned as I played absently with Jazz, who was trying to attack my toes which, fortunately, were under the covers. Even a cat without claws has teeth. "Why do you do that?" I asked her. "You have no motive to maim me, I feed you." I picked her up and held her under the front of her belly, with her face facing mine. She tried to swat me. "Nice," I put her down.

I examined my interest further. There was a great deal I didn't know about Michael. Maybe the split with his partners was actually because he was hard to work with or was lax about business procedures. There was a lot more to find out before I stuck my neck out. Right now, I was relying on Aunt Madge's and my own instincts. Hers might be good but, hell, I never figured out Robby was draining our bank accounts. How good were my instincts? *Maybe he did kill his mother.* I pushed that thought aside.

I WAS MORE RELAXED THAN I had been in a long time, and spent the weekend walking on the beach, reading a Sue Grafton novel and trying to convince Jazz that Mister Rogers and Miss Piggy only wanted to smell her, not eat her. Aunt Madge suggested that I simply leave Jazz alone, perhaps sitting on the bookcase, and she would get used to the guys. I was convinced that I needed to protect Jazz until she had her confidence about the relationships. One of the best things about Aunt Madge is that she only makes her suggestions once.

Every time I went out I looked for Scoobie. I thought of going to the library, but reasoned that it would be invading his space. Who am I kidding? We had been good friends for one school year, but was there a reason to strike up that friendship again? We had had a lot of fun, though. I decided that's what I was looking for, something fun to do. I debated calling Michael, but decided even though I thought he was innocent it bordered on nuts to invite a possible murderer to lunch. If I hadn't found anyone to hang out with besides Aunt Madge by next weekend, I'd visit my sister and do some shopping at the Mall in Lakewood.

On Monday I went to Java Jolt before I stopped at Harry's to see if he had more work. I had thought of a way to learn more about Michael. I didn't even know the name of Michael's firm, but I figured if I Googled "Riordan + Houston + oil" I'd get something. Sure enough, Michael Riordan was still listed as vice-president for operations of USA Energy Distributors. The company web site said the firm distributed "home-grown Texas oil" throughout the western United States. *Home-grown? These guys could use a botany class.*

I found a Houston newspaper on line and a brief article said Michael would be stepping down at a date to be determined, but it was only a short note on the business page. I scanned the business section and saw an article by Joel Kenner about the drop in home heating oil prices because OPEC had lowered the per-barrel price. Maybe Mr. Kenner would know more about the circumstances behind Michael's departure. I went to switchboard.com and found the phone number for the paper and jotted it down.

Thank goodness for mobile phones. Mine is programmed not to give out my name or number on anyone's caller ID. I wasn't sure I'd be exactly honest with Mr. Kenner about who I was. I went out to the boardwalk and sat on a bench. Kenner took my call and listened as I explained I was a reporter for the *Ocean Alley Press* and was looking into Riordan's background in conjunction with a piece I was doing on him. When he asked, I hesitated a second and then said my name was Georgine Winters. *Damn, that was dumb.*

Good reporter that he was he wanted to know more about the story I was working on. The murder accusation was public information, so I started to give brief background when he stopped me. "You're telling me Michael Riordan has been accused of murder? Let me get my pen." My heart almost stopped. *This is not good.*

I spent a couple minutes telling him that I was one of a number of people who thought the police evidence against Riordan seemed flimsy, and that's why I was doing the story. He wanted a lot of particulars, so I told him he should consult the paper's web page, as I had not done the prior articles. That stopped him, and I was able to ask my questions.

"All I could find in your paper was a brief piece saying Riordan was stepping down as VP for operations at USA Energy Distributors, but a couple folks here have said he had a falling out with his partners. Do you know any more about that?"

"I don't know a lot yet, though I'll be doing some more digging now." I winced and he continued. "There's been talk about some accounting irregularities, and accounting's under him, or was. I heard the concerns don't seem to rise to the level of Securities and Exchange Commission violations, but investors are really squeamish these days, you know what I mean?"

I said I did, and asked if he knew why Riordan had not resigned outright. He didn't know about that, and mentioned it seemed to be a "gentleman's agreement" that he resign. He was, after all, one of the partners, not just an employee.

"Listen," he continued, "you've been a big help. How about I get back to you later today or tomorrow?" I told him I was going to be moving around a lot and would call him, and hung up. Probably not what a good reporter would do, but it got me off the phone. I was furious with myself. If Kenner thought I'd been a big help that was probably not good for Michael. When would I learn that my persistence was not, as my mother had often told me, always a virtue?

I folded my mobile phone and stuck it in the pocket of my jacket. *How stupid can you be?* As I turned to face the ocean, I stared into Scoobie's face.

"So," he said quietly, "Now you're a reporter."

"Are you going to rat on me?" I asked, in a definitely grouchy tone.

He smiled. "Hell, if I were going to tell on you I'd let your aunt know that you used to sit under the boardwalk and squirt water up at people."

"That was you." I felt myself relax. "I just filled the big squirt gun for you."

"We did some pretty stupid things for kids our age. Better watch that you aren't now." He gave me a half wave and strolled away, knapsack on his back.

WHEN I GOT TO HARRY'S a few minutes later, he had his hands folded on his desk and was listening attentively to Mrs. Jasper, who was seated in front of him and had her handkerchief in her lap. Today she had on an old-fashioned, but designer-looking, suit of pale blue. It gave her a very washed-out look. Harry jumped up as if I was the Publisher's

Clearinghouse prize announcer and introduced me to her.

"Yes, we met after the funeral." I took her hand, and very directly asked if she was going to be selling a home soon and needed an appraiser. I really didn't want to give her time to launch into something I had no interest in. Besides, I sensed she felt sorry for herself, and right now I wasn't up to coddling anyone.

"Oh, no. I'm just visiting new businesses, asking for donations for the church's Social Services Committee. Our food pantry is getting low and, as you know," she dabbed one eye, "I don't have Ruth's help anymore."

"I just told Mrs. Jasper I'd be happy to donate a hundred dollars," Harry said.

"Why don't you grab your checkbook and I'll keep Mrs. Jasper company while you write the check?" He looked at me as if he thought I was very insensitive, and pulled his checkbook out of the bottom drawer.

"You found Ruth." She looked at me intently.

Since I knew this, I was tempted not to comment, but instead said, "Yes, it was quite a shock." Seeing her stiffen, I added, "She looked very peaceful."

She blew her nose. "It doesn't sound as if she died peacefully."

I closed my eyes for a second and tried to remember she was old and had lost a friend. "Ruth's face looked very relaxed, as if she was sleeping." I decided not to mention her staring eyes.

"It's just so awful that everyone thinks Michael did it." She dabbed at her eyes with the other end of the handkerchief.

"I don't happen to think Michael killed her."

Her eyes widened, and I saw Harry look at me, too. "Why not?" she asked.

I shrugged. "Aside from the fact that he seems to have been genuinely fond of his mother, why would he set himself up as the prime suspect? He doesn't strike me as stupid."

"Oh, of course not. His parents were very proud of him." Her eyes narrowed. "But he wasn't very smart about that girl he married, was he?"

That comment hit too close to home. "We all make mistakes." Harry had finished writing the check and torn it from his register, so I picked it up and handed it to her. "I'm so glad we could help the Social Services Committee."

She actually got the hint and rose from her chair. She was surprisingly agile for a woman her age, which I judged to be at least mid-seventies; no need to grip the arms of the chair. "I can't thank you enough," she said to Harry.

He started to say something, but I cut him off. "Let me walk you out. Do you need any help on the stairs?"

"Oh no. I walk the boardwalk every morning."

I made a mental note to be sure to walk in the evenings.

Harry came from behind his desk, and I could tell he wanted to say something, but I moved Mrs. Jasper toward the door. "It's very good of you to do so much for the church," I said.

"It's my life." Her tone changed. "Did you get to finish your work at Ruth's?"

"Just Friday." I opened the front door for her.

"Was everything...in order?" she asked.

At first I wasn't sure what she meant, then I wondered if she wanted to know if the upstairs still looked like a crime scene. Nosy woman. But, Ruth Riordan had apparently been close to Mrs. Jasper. "It was lovely. Ruth had excellent taste."

She brightened. "I helped her redo the den. She wanted a place Michael could relax, and she didn't want a TV downstairs."

We were on the porch now. "I'll let Aunt Madge know I saw you."

"Please do." She walked down the steps without even touching the rail. I shut the door.

When I turned around, Harry was looking at me as if he didn't know me. "She would have been here all afternoon. Ask Aunt Madge. I just couldn't take it today."

"Whatever you say." His tone was reserved, and I could tell he did not like the way I had treated her. I felt bad for a moment, then decided I could take his reservations about me more than I could take an hour with Mrs. Jasper.

"Anything new?" I asked.

He shook his head. "Have you given any more thought to dropping by some of the real estate offices? I did it when I first opened, but it wouldn't hurt for them to see a new face."

OK, so he wanted me out of his sight for a while. "Good idea. It's so nice outside, it's a good day to do it." I picked up a stack of my cards from their holder on his desk and gave him what I deemed a jaunty wave as I left.

TWO HOURS LATER, I'd met some very friendly people. I was smart enough to know that every agent saw me as a potential homebuyer, so I didn't take their sociability too personally. Fortunately, there was no home number on my card, though half of them knew I was Aunt Madge's niece. That's what discovering a dead body does for you.

There are six real estate offices in Ocean Alley, which is a lot for a small town, but most of them also do beach house rentals as well as sales. I'd gone to five of them, and left Lester Argrow for last. Did I really want to find him? No, but I could use Ramona's name, and he could make decisions that would add to my checkbook.

I went into the side entrance of First Bank, which led to the offices housed upstairs. It was a frame building that had been covered in yellow vinyl siding. Though the front had a plate glass window that revealed the small bank, the windows on the side of the building were trimmed in a shade of green clearly meant to resemble the ocean. As I walked up the exterior stairway I was treated to several plastic fish that were fastened to the siding. The interior hallway was well-lit and brightly painted, so you didn't have the feeling of being in a corridor as narrow as it was. Lester's small office was at the end of the hall and the door stood open. The smell of cigars wafted into the hallway, and my heart sank. I hate cigars; they give me a headache.

He had his feet propped on the small desk and was reading the comics. He looked about forty-five, and his balding pate looked as if it had been sunburned many times. So, he smoked and let himself get sunburned. Smart guy. Viewing him in profile, I could see a neatly trimmed mustache. He also had a large mole beside his nose. Definitely a distinctive look.

At my knock, he threw the paper on the desk and rose, stubbing out his cigar as he did so. "Hello," he extended his hand. "Sorry about the smoke, I wasn't expecting anyone." He was very short, and he seemed to buy his suits in a regular size, since the jacket was way too long, even in the sleeves. He did have a friendly smile and firm handshake.

"I can come back…"

"No, of course not. I just meant I wouldn't have been fouling the air

73

for company." He gestured to a chair. "Please sit down."

I introduced myself and he nodded. "Ramona said she told you to stop by. Glad you did." He grinned. "Heard you're working for my favorite appraiser."

I handed him a couple of my cards. "Yes, I read some of your poetry in Harry's files."

He barked a laugh and thumped his fist on the table. "Yeah, my friends say no one should let me near a pen or a phone when I'm pissed."

I had not expected to like him, but found his frankness appealing. "That would probably be good advice for me, too." I grinned back at him. "I thought maybe you might be willing to try Harry's company again. I hear we're twenty-five dollars cheaper than the competition."

"Yeah, that's why I went there. Would you do the work?"

"Yes. But, I have to be honest and tell you I agreed with Harry's appraisal on the Marino house. I reviewed it pretty carefully, and pulled up some other comps."

He screwed up his face as if in pain. "The Marinos seemed to take him at his word, too."

"No other offers on the house?"

"Not right then. Mighta been later, you know." He leaned forward as if trying to convince me.

I nodded. "I just don't want to give the wrong impression. I think I'm pretty flexible, but I have to go with my professional judgment."

He studied me for five seconds, which is a long time if someone is staring at you. "Okay, I hear you." He looked at my card. "I'll call again." His tone changed. "Too bad about Mrs. Riordan."

"Yes," was all I said.

"Ramona said you don't seem to think Michael did it."

I shrugged. "Just my instinct. Aunt Madge's, too."

"I don't either," he said. "He's a straight shooter, Michael. No pun."

"Actually, she was strangled." *What the hell is wrong with me?*

He stared at me before barking another laugh. "You're a pisser." He grew somber. "A lot of people think Michael's big-headed. Maybe he is, but he was always respectful to his parents. I heard his father say that, when the kids graduated from high school."

"Some people seem to think he wasn't so good to them after he married Darla."

He shrugged. "Dames. He came every Thanksgiving, I can tell you that. By himself. That woulda pissed off any of my wives. Shows guts."

Any of his wives? If there'd been only two, he probably would have said both wives. "I see what you mean."

I stood to go and held out my hand. "I hope we get to work together." I meant it.

CHAPTER EIGHT

THE ARTICLE IN THE TUESDAY HOUSTON paper was very one-sided. I knew that because Aunt Madge had a faxed copy, which Michael had left when he stopped by earlier. "I tried to give it back to him before he left, but he said he wanted you to read it."

Uh-oh. I figured that was my guilty conscience reacting, because there was no way he could know I'd talked to Joel Kenner. Kenner's article was long, but he listed only one source by name.

"Some people just have a problem with their tempers," is how Sgt. Morehouse of the Ocean Alley Police characterized Michael Riordan, when asked why he might have murdered his mother, as he is accused of having done earlier this month.

Kenner had not bothered to get quotes from anyone who questioned Michael's arrest or had anything positive to say. He did say he had learned of the murder from a friend of Riordan's. I figured it hadn't taken Kenner long to learn there was no Georgine Winters at the Ocean Alley Press.

Interspersed with the details of the crime were references to the fact that Michael and his partners had "mutually agreed" that he should resign as vice-president for operations for USA Energy Distributors. Again, no mention of why he had not yet acted on that resignation, or even why he was leaving.

I glanced at the top of the fax to see where it had come from. Someone at Michael's firm had sent it, as it bore their name and fax number across the top. This was terrible, and it was all my fault.

When he returned a few minutes later, I could tell that Michael was at least entertaining that possibility. "You up for coffee at Java Jolt?" he asked. He didn't extend the offer to Aunt Madge. Probably wanted to talk to me out of her earshot. He picked up the article from the kitchen table as we left.

"It's too bad about the article." We walked toward the boardwalk.

"Yeah, it is." He glanced at me. "I called Joel Kenner, whom I know pretty well. He said a female reporter called him."

"From here?" I asked, feigning innocence.

"So she said, but she seemed to have her name mixed up."

"Oh?"

"She seemed to think her name was Georgine Winters."

"Is she related to George?" I asked.

"I'll tell you why I think it was you."

His tone was mild, but I sensed he was controlling it.

I said nothing and he continued. "First, you're pretty quick, and if you hadn't done it, you'd be following what I'm saying better, probably jumping in with more than just 'Oh.'"

Gulp.

"Two, you know how to be cagey, so I don't think you're above calling Kenner and using an assumed name. Though that was probably not the brightest one to choose."

He has a point there.

"And, three, the article said he heard about this from a 'friend of mine' and you seem to be one, and to think I'm innocent. Although," he said almost amiably, "I'm not sure that's to my advantage."

I had to smile at that. But, I should have known his seemingly good mood would not last. He stopped and faced me.

"So, I'm telling you for the last time, Jolie. Stay out of my business!" His face was inches from mine. He turned and started to walk away and turned back pointing his finger at me. "And I'll tell you one more thing. My parents told me to be nice to you at school, because you were Madge's niece. I never would've talked to you otherwise."

I TOOK AUNT MADGE TO SUPPER that night. Newhart's was extra busy because the blue plate special was crab cakes, and the ones Arnie Newhart makes taste as if they have more crab than breading. Plus, he always serves pasta with the crab cakes. I needed something to distract me from the acid in my stomach ever since Michael had yelled at me. I kept hearing him say, "I never would've talked to you otherwise." What did I care? The thing was, I did.

We ate in companionable silence for most of the meal. Aunt Madge had the decency not to ask about Michael's article. As well as she knows me, she had probably figured if Kenner had a call from someone in Ocean Alley it was me. Bless her, she would have assumed my motives were good but, like so many other aspects of my life, things had not worked out as I'd planned.

I swore that the only business I would mind from then on was my own. I would emulate Aunt Madge, no gossip, no poking into anyone else's life.

Arnie stopped at our table, picture frame in hand. "What do you think of this?" he asked Aunt Madge.

She took the eight by ten-inch frame and laughed. "Local rumrunner gets his boat back," she read aloud, and passed it to me.

The old photo was dark, but I recognized Uncle Gordon and the small dory that Aunt Madge still keeps in the garage. The photo looked to be a good copy made from the original print, but the small article was a photocopy of one from an old Ocean Alley Press.

I looked at Aunt Madge, who was asking Arnie where he would hang it and following his gaze to a spot not too far from our booth. I turned back to the article. The two paragraphs said only that the local police had confiscated Gordon Richards' boat the day before Prohibition ended and that Mr. Richards had traded the local police chief two bottles of "pure Jamaican rum" to get it back. As Arnie walked away I looked at Aunt Madge. "I thought Dad just called Uncle Gordon a rumrunner for fun."

She shrugged. "I met him much later, of course. You can see how young he was in the photo." I nodded and she continued. "He told me that he helped an uncle if there was a lot of fog. He'd stand on the beach and have a line in as if he was surf fishing, and a very small fire next to him, like he was going to cook what he caught. If he saw any local police or revenuers he'd quickly add to the fire so his uncle wouldn't come in along the cove, he'd go further down."

"I thought all the bootleggers were in the Mafia."

She shook her head decisively. "First, true bootleggers usually made the stuff, and rumrunners just went out to sea a mile or so to bring in cases of liquor. Some of it was really big business." She took a bite of her cooling crab cake and continued. "Your Uncle Gordon's uncle just brought in a few cases at a time, what the local hotel needed for its speakeasy."

"But," I protested, "if it was Prohibition, what was the hotel doing selling it?"

"You don't think that stopped people from drinking, do you?" she asked dryly. "Speakeasies were sort of underground bars. I'm told this one was on the third floor of the hotel. The rooms on that floor were only rented to people who were going to be imbibing."

Aunt Madge kept eating, and her expression reminded me more of Ramona's faraway look than her own practical alertness. When she met my gaze again she was smiling. "It was Uncle Gordon's boat – he had spent two months building it. His uncle's boat had been seized a few weeks before." Her smile faded. "People did what they could to feed their families."

"He's lucky he got it back" I turned to my pasta.

"No luck about it. You remember me telling you about his grandmother, the one who closed the doors in the courthouse during the fire?"

"I thank her every time I visit the Registrar of Deeds."

"Uncle Gordon said she marched into the police chief's office the day after they seized the boat and gave him, if you'll pardon me, hell. Told the chief he only took the boat because he wanted a good fishing boat for himself, and if he didn't give it back to her grandson she'd make sure everyone knew that the chief snuck off to go fishing a lot of Friday afternoons in the summer." She was smiling again, and craned her neck to look at the framed photo, which Arnie had since hung on a nail a short distance from us.

That reminded me about the seemingly fresh coat of paint I'd seen on the boat in her garage. "Who painted the boat for you? Looked as if it was just done."

She waved her spoon dismissively. "I get it painted every couple of years. Salt air will weather it too much if I don't." When I started to ask another question, she added, "I picked up two guests for the weekend. Pretty good for late October."

"Where are they from, or are they from different towns?" I asked.

"Texas. Houston."

Uh oh.

THE NEXT DAY, THE county prosecuting attorney's office called to schedule a time to have his staff talk to me. "But, I don't know anything." I was distressed that I would once again be butting into Michael Riordan's life.

"Then it won't take too long," said the woman, who probably had to listen to all kinds of excuses when she made these calls.

"Do I need a lawyer or something?" I asked.

"Not unless you think you do."

What a stupid answer, I thought, as I drove to Harry's office. I wondered if I should call my divorce lawyer, but he would say I should have someone with me and recommend a lawyer who would probably cost quite a bit of what little money I had in my bank account. I had just bought two tires and made my student loan and a credit card payment – the only card that a bank had not canceled – but Harry was supposed to pay me today. We had agreed on every other week, and I would get $200 of the $400 of each appraisal fee.

I would feel better after I deposited my paycheck in the bank. If I thought of my pay in terms of an hourly wage, it was far lower than I was used to. However, I was able to be with Aunt Madge and had little pressure in my life, other than that I created for myself, that is.

Harry had a house for me, but I couldn't go until tomorrow. Still, I could drive by today, and get a sense of what houses I could use for comps and pull that information. He also had a phone message for me, from George Winters.

The big disadvantage to not having your own place is that you don't have your own phone line. You can't screen calls, and you really can't hang up on people if you are in someone else's house or place of business.

My face must have reflected my lack of enthusiasm for the message, because Harry seemed sympathetic. "You can just say you don't have anything to tell him."

"He already has the general impression that I don't want to talk to him."

I was in a funk as I drove back to Aunt Madge's. I decided to change into jogging clothes and do my half-run-mostly-walk exercise earlier than usual. The day was cool, but there wasn't much breeze, so it wasn't the kind of damp chill that makes you understand why people go to Florida in the winter. I walked slowly toward the boardwalk, stopping every now and then to stretch my calf muscles.

I hadn't counted on seeing Joe Pedone again. He was sitting on a bench outside Java Jolt, reading the paper. It was about forty-five degrees, and he was wearing a winter coat. Not used to October beach weather, I thought.

"What the hell are you doing bothering me again?" I threw at him as he walked over to me.

"Thought I'd give you a few days to think about my offer."

"What offer?"

He smiled, a not especially pleasant expression for him. "It was implied."

I felt a chill. "I may have to talk to the police."

"You have a job now, you can make payments. My boss would go for, say, $1,500 per month."

I felt my chest tighten. "That's not only more than I could make some months, you don't seem to get the point that I'm not repaying any of my husband's gambling debts. They're his."

"I warned you," was all he said, and walked away.

"Who was that?"

I turned sharply. Michael must have just walked out of Java Jolt. "He wants me to pay some of Robby's gambling debts. I don't think they were the kind of loans you get at a bank."

He frowned. "It's against the law to collect on some gambling debts." My face must have brightened, because he added, "Of course, not all the people who lend the money would feel obliged to abide by that." His attitude was decidedly cool.

"Look, I'm really sorry about calling Kenner."

"You should be," he said.

"I said I was." This came out more sharply than I had intended, and I winced.

"Wishing you could take it back? I recognize the expression." He smiled at me.

Maybe he wasn't so mad anymore. Did I really care? Yes.

"I was just thinking…" I began.

"Don't," he said. "It's dangerous for all concerned." He turned and walked away, but I figured he probably wouldn't have hollered if I followed him. Remembering Aunt Madge's axiom about not chasing boys, I began my steady jog, going in the opposite direction.

I knew I needed to talk to the police about Pedone, but I was still reluctant to do it. I kept thinking that if I ignored it he would go away. I have often tried this, and once or twice it has worked. It cannot always be said that I am always a fast learner. Since my talk with the prosecuting attorney's staff was scheduled for the next day, I figured I'd see if Sgt. Morehouse was there and talk to him.

MY APPOINTMENT IN THE OFFICE of the Prosecuting Attorney was scheduled for ten a.m., and I arrived early. I was supposed to appraise a house in what Harry called the popsicle district at eleven-thirty. I figured I had plenty of time to get there.

As I walked slowly down the hall looking for the office to which I'd been told to report – "Trial Team One" – I saw Sgt. Morehouse sitting on the narrow bench outside that office. He greeted me almost coldly, and I wondered if I had somehow managed to offend him. "I thought I'd get a cup of coffee to take in with me. Can I get you one?" I asked. This seemed to relax him a little.

"I'll walk down to the cafeteria with you," he said. He didn't speak until we were by ourselves in the elevator. "Noticed you been gettin' pretty friendly with Riordan."

"I'm not sure I'd say friendly. In fact, he's not really speaking to me at the moment."

"You were on the boardwalk with him yesterday," he countered.

"Are you following me?" I was astounded.

"Nope. Just happened to be up there myself."

What a crock. "Then you would have noticed we only spoke for a minute when he came out of the coffee shop."

"So, he's not your buddy?"

"My buddy," I repeated. Do not mouth off to cops. "He's fond of my aunt. You already know she helped him make funeral arrangements, and he's stopped by to talk to her other times. I do live with her, you know."

"Yeah." The elevator opened and we walked to the coffee machines in the small courthouse cafeteria.

"I'm curious, when do we get to find out why you suspect Michael?" He shot me a quick glance and I continued. "It just seems that he'd be kind of…stupid to have done it. Especially to have done it and had me discover her, when he had just left."

He finished adding cream to his coffee. "No one said murderers are smart."

"If they were, we wouldn't have so many good cop shows and murder mysteries on TV." I gave him what I hoped look like a sincere smile.

"Smart asses never do as well in the world as regular people," was his only reply.

I wasn't going to get anything out of him, so I changed the subject. "I need some advice."

"Get a lawyer," he said, testily.

"Not about this. It's about a guy who's been bothering me."

He grew businesslike. "I can put you in touch with another officer who works almost full-time on stalking cases and domestic violence."

"I'm not sure this would fall into either of those categories." As we made our way back to the prosecuting attorney's suite of offices, I described my experiences with Pedone, including my suspicion that he had flattened my tires.

He was definitely interested. "If he's threatening you, this is very serious. I could have him picked up."

As we again sat down on the bench outside the Trial Team One office, I went over Pedone's language. "When he says stuff like his 'offer was implied' it seems like a threat to me, but maybe he could convince a judge he was kidding, or something."

A woman came out of the office and invited me in. "I'll see if I can find out who he is," Morehouse said, crushing his coffee cup and tossing it into a waste basket. He strode down the hall. I realized he had only been sitting there so he could talk to me, and I didn't like it.

The room in which the staff was questioning me was very small, barely big enough for the tiny desk and three wooden chairs that looked about forty years old. "Annie Milner," said a woman about my age as she extended her hand, "and this is Paul Damon. He's a special investigator in the prosecuting attorney's office." I took that to mean he was not a lawyer. He was even younger, and gave me a slight wave without getting up.

"Do I know you?" I asked Annie.

"We may have been in the same class in high school for the year you lived here." Her eyes met mine. "I looked quite different then."

Noting her tailored clothes and what looked to be an expensive haircut, I figured she could well look better as a lawyer than a high school girl. "Paul will ask most of the questions today." She nodded to him.

At first it seemed to me as if the prosecuting attorney's staff could have asked me the questions over the phone. I told them exactly what I had told the police. After a few minutes of this, the tone of the session changed, at first almost imperceptibly. "How well did you know Michael Riordan prior to the day you first went to his house?" asked Paul.

"I didn't really..." I began.

"Surely you remember him from high school," he interrupted.

"If you had let me finish, you'd have heard that I knew who he was in high school, because he ran for student body president." I wasn't about to say I'd liked him. He nodded as if to acknowledge that he shouldn't have interrupted, and I continued. "I talked to him for a minute on the boardwalk one day not long ago and, frankly, he pi...ticked me off. He mentioned that my aunt had thrown him out of Sunday School class, and I could understand why."

"Sgt. Morehouse said your aunt seems pretty sure Riordan didn't kill his mother. Why is that?"

What an odd question, I thought. "If you want specifics, you'd have to talk to her." I paused, thinking I really didn't want her to have to go through this, and continued. "She's known him a long time, and despite the Sunday School stuff, she just doesn't think he would do it. He was good to his mother." I shrugged. "Aunt Madge knew Ruth Riordan a lot better than Michael, of course."

"She has no definite information, then."

"Of course not." I was starting to get irritated.

"You don't think he's confided in her?"

I was now thoroughly annoyed and, I had to admit, nervous. He was implying Aunt Madge was hiding information about someone he thought to be a murderer. I glanced at Annie Milner and back at him. "Again, you'd have to ask her, but I think their confidences have been limited to discussions about the funeral, the fact that she knew his mother loved him, the kind of stuff people say to someone who's lost a parent."

I stood. "I am happy to answer any questions about what I remember the day I found Mrs. Riordan, but I really can't think of more that I can add."

"Thanks," he said. They didn't get up as I left, but Annie did nod at me.

As I did the appraisal I had an internal debate about how much of the conversation to relay to Aunt Madge. On reflection, I decided to give her full details. I didn't want them surprising her with questions later.

"That's balderdash." She unloaded some towels from the dryer. "Those people are paid to think of all kinds of things; angles, I think they call them."

I took some of the folded towels and put them in the basket she used to carry them upstairs. "Maybe it's not. Maybe they think you're hiding something."

"I'm not," she said, in her usual practical manner. "I don't care what they think."

Miss Piggy barked once, and I opened the door and let her in. I sat on a kitchen chair, and she placed her head in my lap. I bent down to pat her and smelled something distinctly unpleasant. She dropped a mangled piece of what had probably been a bird in my lap. I screeched and jumped up.

"Sorry, dear," Aunt Madge said as she resumed folding. "I should have told you never to let them put their heads in your lap when they first come in. They sometimes bring presents."

CHAPTER NINE

AS MICHAEL HAD TOLD ME EARLIER, you learn what the prosecutor has for evidence at the probable cause hearing. It was scheduled for Monday and would be open to the public; according to George Winters' article, the hearing would be "the first time *Ocean Alley Press* readers learn the facts and issues of the case." Most of the article repeated the circumstances of Mrs. Riordan's death, but this time Winters added that not only had I "discovered" the body soon after I had been with Michael Riordan, but that he and I had gone to high school together.

"He writes as if Michael and I plotted to kill his mother!" I had been pacing around Aunt Madge's kitchen and sitting room as I read the article aloud to her.

"You're reading that into it, dear." She shaped her bread mixture into a loaf.

"And so will anyone else." I threw the paper on the couch.

"No, they won't," she said, more firmly than she usually spoke. "You're upset. Have some tea." She gestured toward the electric kettle.

I avoided telling her tea was not the panacea for major problems by telling her I would take the dogs for a walk and grabbing their leashes. I let myself out the sliding glass door and into the back yard.

WHEN SGT. MOREHOUSE CALLED the Friday before the probable cause hearing, he said that I was not likely to be called as a witness. He would be asked questions about what I had told him. "Now, if you'da seen somebody wielding an ax, they'd have you up there." Cop humor. Not funny.

Before the hearing, I had to get through a weekend in the B&B with two guests from Houston, one of whom was Joel Kenner. It had to be more than a coincidence that they picked Aunt Madge's Cozy Corner. I was sorely tempted to stay in a motel or go visit Renée and her family in Lakewood. I discussed this with Aunt Madge who tactfully told me she thought I considered myself more important to what Mr. Kenner and company were doing than they did. *Point taken.* Plus, Renée and I would shop, and I shouldn't spend money I didn't have.

At least Friday night was Halloween. I put an orange ribbon around Jazz's neck, and she wrestled with herself on the steps trying to get it off. Aunt Madge opened the kitchen door so that the dogs could see through the dining room into the hall. Since she didn't want them bolting to the door every time Trick-or-Treaters appeared on the porch, she put a child barrier across it. They would have had to take a running leap to get over it, and Aunt Madge had learned they couldn't get the proper traction on the tiled floor, so they were safely relegated (from Jazz's point of view) to the kitchen.

To avoid Joel Kenner, I put eyeholes in an old sheet and distributed candy in costume. When a little kid was afraid to come to the door, Aunt Madge would go out to them with raisins or candy. While she was not fond of my 'get-up,' as she called it, she didn't insist I behave like an adult.

Kenner and another man, whose name I did not get since I stood on the front porch as they checked in, arrived about seven-thirty and then went out in search of crab cakes. Avoidance tactic number one had worked, and I had not scared too many children.

SATURDAY MORNING I STOPPED by the Purple Cow, ostensibly to buy envelopes but hoping to see Ramona. She seemed to be a good source for the kind of information Aunt Madge was not willing to hear, or at least pass on.

The message on the white board was, "Change is not merely necessary to life, it is life." Alvin Toffler. I was tired of change, at least the disruptive kind that had characterized my life lately, and asked Ramona who put up the quotes.

"I do." She seemed quite proud of them. "Usually people like them. A couple of times, when I wasn't looking, someone erased my message and put another one." She leaned against a counter and pushed her long hair, which she was wearing down today, behind her ears.

This interested me. "Like what?"

"Last week, I had something up there about making sure you think about what you say so you don't hurt anyone, and someone erased it and wrote 'make sure brain is engaged before marker is in hand.' I thought that was rather rude."

I thought it was funny, but didn't say so.

"Did you decide if you're going to the reunion?" she asked, as she rang up my envelopes.

"I think I will." *As if.*

"Good. People are asking about you." She looked at me. "All the time."

"Swell. Like what?"

"Jennifer wanted to know if you were dating Michael."

I laughed. "Has she forgotten he dumped her in high school?"

Ramona did not laugh. "Oh, I don't think so." She leaned closer to me and lowered her voice. "But he wasn't rich then."

"Is that all you've heard?" I didn't have the patience to hear more about Jennifer's hoped-for love life.

She shrugged. "The other stuff is just rumors, like you said last time."

My words were coming back to haunt me, as usual. I changed the subject a little. "Are you going to the hearing?"

She shook her head. "It's Monday, and I have to work. A lot of people are, though. People liked Mrs. Riordan."

"It just doesn't seem fair," I fumed, "that they seem to have made up their minds on Michael."

"Fairness is not a concept that is innate to humans."

I stared at her. I could never quite figure her out. One minute she seemed like someone stuck in the time-warp Michael mentioned, and the next very insightful. "I suppose you're right." I picked up my envelopes. "See you next week, probably."

As I reached the door, she called. "Jolie. You never answered Jennifer's question."

"Question?"

"About whether you're dating Michael Riordan." She didn't wait for an answer, but turned to walk toward the back of the store.

FOR THE REST OF THE DAY I watched for Joel Kenner, whose picture I had looked up on his newspaper's web site, but he did not come to afternoon tea. Not that I planned to meet him, but I had hoped to hide in the kitchen to eavesdrop on his conversation with whomever he sat with. Aunt Madge had not been too enthused about this.

I waited until past dusk to go for my jog. Since there would be few people on the boardwalk at that time I took Mister Rogers and Miss Piggy. I had them on long leashes, and planned to let them run on the beach a bit, unleashed. They were not very good jogging companions, as they tended to stop a lot to sniff the garbage cans or anything else that required their personal attention. However, they loved the boardwalk and beach, and I was growing very attached to them. Unfortunately, Jazz had still not warmed up to them. I left her in the kitchen with Aunt Madge since 'the guys' would be out.

We ran north first, but there were more restaurants at that end, and Mister Rogers and Miss Piggy thought the doggy bags people carried out were for them. We switched directions and were soon in a less crowded section; not that anything was truly crowded in late October.

I let them off the leash and they ran onto the sand. Miss Piggy immediately ran north and Mister Rogers ran south. "Hey, get your tail down here," I yelled. She stopped, but it had nothing to do with my command. Something in the sand interested her. I'd have to watch what she had in her mouth when she rejoined me. Mister Rogers barked twice, and she ran toward him. So much for remembering who fed her.

They galloped ahead of me, which was what I liked. I could keep an eye on them. In their younger days they ran into the surf a lot, but now they keep away from it. Aunt Madge said they had jumped in one day when there were hordes of jellyfish floating about, and the dogs had not been fond of the experience.

I had gone about two blocks when someone stepped from behind a public phone booth, directly in my path. Joe Pedone. Damn. I realized there was a car with its engine running sitting in a parking space just off the boardwalk. What is this, the movies? I stopped, not wanting to run in the opposite direction because the dogs were far ahead of me.

"Thought you were pretty smart, didn't you, talking to that cop about me?" He did not look remotely friendly anymore. I guessed Morehouse had talked to Pedone and wished he had told me he'd done that.

"It seemed like the thing to do. I can't really afford more tires."

He moved a couple steps closer, and I backed up. "We're way past tires now." He cocked his head toward the car and the door opened and two men got out. Robby stood next to someone who was a good six inches taller than he. However, Robby looked even shorter than his usual 5'10", as he was somewhat stooped.

"What are you doing here?" I called to him.

"He's not here to talk," Pedone said. "He's just a reminder of why you want to make payments."

I was frightened and furious at the same time. How could this happen in Ocean Alley, on the boardwalk at eight-thirty p.m.? "You won't hurt him, or me." I spoke more firmly than I felt.

"Of course not," he said, smoothly. "Or your Aunt Madge, or your cute cat." He let that sink in. "Because you're going to start repaying some of your dear husband's debts."

"I want to be sure Robby's okay. Let him come up here." I really didn't want to set eyes on this man who had ruined major aspects of my life, but I figured it was better to have him up here than down there. Not that I had some sort of plan. This was not the movies.

Pedone nodded and the other man pushed him forward. Robby walked unsteadily up the few steps to the boardwalk. His normally impeccable clothes were wrinkled and he had a bruise on his left cheek. Given the way he walked, I assumed he was stooped over because he'd been punched in the stomach.

"So, you seen him. Go back down, Robby."

I reached over and grabbed his hand. "I think he's better off if he stays with me."

Pedone laughed. "Gee, I'm getting the unhappy couple back together again." He reached for Robby's arm.

"No!" I yelled, and pulled Robby back. The soft padding of numerous paws made me look over Pedone's shoulder. Mister Rogers and Miss Piggy were running toward us on the boardwalk. They had no intentions of jumping anyone, of course, but Pedone didn't know that. "Get him, guys!" I called, and pulled Robby closer to me.

Pedone jumped down a few of the steps. As Mister Rogers stood at the top, tongue panting, he laughed. "They don't look too…"

A window opened on the second level above the shuttered ice cream shop. "Everyone OK down there?" a man's voice called.

"Please call 9-1-1," I yelled.

Pedone looked at me as he backed up. "You just made a really big mistake."

My eyes followed him to the car, and as I turned back toward Robby I saw Scoobie just a few feet behind Robby, holding a good-sized piece of driftwood. He said nothing, but turned to walk away.

TWO HOURS LATER, I was so frustrated with Robby I would have left him if I hadn't already done that. He sat there, his black hair disheveled and Armani shirt untucked, moodily staring at the floor. He had refused to say anything to Sgt. Morehouse, who had now left the room, apparently hoping that I could encourage Robby to change his mind. Obviously, I rarely had a clue of what went on in Robby's mind, so I had no methods to change it.

I sat next to him. "They'll only do it again."

He looked at me, tears welling in his eyes. "I'm so sorry."

I looked away. When I looked back, he again had the floor in his gaze. "I know you are. I'm not mad at you anymore."

He looked up, almost hopeful.

"I'm done with you, but I'm not mad."

He gave me a half smile.

"But these guys will be back if you don't give Morehouse a reason to pick them up."

"They'll be back even if he does, or someone else will. I can't make them any madder than they already are." He looked at his hands and almost whispered. "I like my fingers."

I winced. I could tell Sgt. Morehouse that there was another witness to what happened, but I was pretty sure that Scoobie didn't want to get involved. Why else would he have walked away? Still, I was certain he had been willing to clobber Pedone, and I was grateful.

The door opened and Sgt. Morehouse stood back to let Michael Riordan enter. The sergeant did not look happy. "Your aunt called him," was all he said, and shut the door behind him.

I introduced Robby and Michael, and saw the questions in Robby's eyes. Did I have a lover already?

"Why would Aunt Madge call you?" I asked.

Michael shrugged. "She probably knew I'd come, and Sgt. Morehouse told her she shouldn't be here." This much I knew to be true. Morehouse had personally come to the boardwalk and then driven the dogs home before continuing to the station with Robby and me.

Michael turned to Robby. "Madge and my mother were friends, and she just helped me with my mother's funeral arrangements and such." Robby murmured his sympathy and seemed relieved that Michael had not introduced himself as my beau.

"What are you going to do about all this?" he asked Robby.

"I don't know," he said, floor in his line of vision again.

"*Nothing* isn't an option," Michael's tone was gruff. "They aren't going to leave Jolie alone, and this is a lonely place in winter. She'd be an easy target."

I started to say something about defending myself, thank you very much, but he didn't give me a chance.

"You either roll over on these guys, or you find a way to give them back their money."

Perhaps it was the firmness of his voice, but Robby sat up straighter and looked at him. "They won't stop at me, and I don't have eighty thousand dollars."

I stood up. "Eighty thousand dollars! Who would lend you that much?" Even when I was making my big-time realtor salary, no one would have lent me that much money, unsecured.

He grimaced. "It stared out at forty-six thousand, but these guys have higher interest rates and compound more often."

Michael pressed him. "You must know something about them that would help the police." When Robby didn't answer, he said, "Kidnapping alone carries a pretty stiff sentence. You've got to work with the cops. If they can't get at Jolie they'll go for Madge or other people in your family. They're pissed off now."

"They were before," he said, but something in his tone had changed. He was very fond of Aunt Madge.

Sgt. Morehouse opened the door again. "We don't have time for a pity party."

Robby stood, and he seemed to have new resolve. "I'll tell you what I can, but if you let me walk away from here, they'll kill me for sure if they find out."

Morehouse nodded. "I've been making some calls. The prosecutor in Atlantic County is working on something big on Pedone's boss. Seems like he lends money up and down the coast, and his tactics to get it back are usually a lot rougher than with you. The prosecutor can maybe work with the feds to get you in Witness Protection."

Robby looked doubtful. "Testifying against a couple of guys who lend money to gamblers? That doesn't sound like something that would interest the federal government too much."

"I believe I said something big," said Morehouse, emphasizing his last two words. "If there's more to it than I know about, you can bet there's more to it than you know."

"Great, insult him." Why am I defending Robby?

"I'm trying to help you out here," said Morehouse, yet again irritated at me.

"What about Jolie?" Robby asked.

"If she doesn't know where you are, she can't tell them anything," replied Morehouse, quite curtly.

"I meant what about..."

Morehouse cut him off. "We'll handle it." He opened the door wider, and Robby looked back at me as he walked out. He didn't say anything.

"Party's over. You two can leave." Morehouse left the door open.

I looked up at Michael. "I'm so sorry she..." I began.

"It's okay. I'll drive you home." He gestured that I should walk ahead of him.

We didn't talk, and I stared out the car window as we drove through the familiar streets. The houses and small stores loomed like shadowy guards rather than the well-maintained businesses and homes that they were in daylight. The wind had come up and the brightly colored banners that flew in front of some of the homes whipped smartly. Idly I watched a fast-food bag blow across the street in front of us.

What could Robby have been thinking, borrowing that kind of money? And how little did I know him if he had been so heavily in debt and never spoken to me about it? We'd been doing less together, but I had passed it off on our busy careers. Many nights I showed a property, went to a civic meeting, or had dinner with a potential commercial builder or lessee. But still, we did things with friends every weekend, and we never really fought. What had I missed?

It was a moment before I realized that we had gotten to the Cozy Corner's small parking lot and Michael had shut off the engine and opened his door. "I'll say goodnight to your aunt and be off."

She hadn't heard us drive up and was sitting at the kitchen table, tea mug in front of her, stroking Jazz. She rose quickly and hugged me, looking at Michael as she did so. "Thank you."

I felt like telling her she didn't need to send Robin Hood to rescue Maid Marian, but I resisted. I had to give him credit, however grudgingly, for talking Robby into working with Morehouse. "I'm fine, really. Sit down and finish your tea."

"I'm off," Michael said. "I just wanted to deliver your package and…"

The door to the kitchen swung open and Joel Kenner stood there with another man. "Michael. Good to see you." He held out his hand, but Michael didn't take it. "Sorry about the article," he said, withdrawing his hand. "It's my job, you know."

Aunt Madge broke the awkward silence. "Why don't you all have a seat in the breakfast room, and I'll make some coffee and tea."

"Kenner," Michael said, "you might like to meet Georgine Winters."

IN THE END, Michael had let himself be persuaded to have coffee. I helped Aunt Madge fix it, and she and I joined them. The conversation was stilted, as could be expected given that Kenner and his colleague, a young man named Peter Sellers (really), were there to cover the hearing for their Houston paper. Mostly Kenner told Michael what was going on with people he knew in the oil industry in Houston.

I banished my thoughts about the conversation and rolled over in bed and looked at the sun coming in through the slats in the window. Jazz walked off my pillow and onto my face, and I pushed her to one side. Now that she was sure I was awake, I'd have to get up and feed her. My new strategy was to give her the daily dose of canned food in the kitchen so she'd have a reason to like the room. However, she was no longer allowed to jump on the fridge. Aunt Madge said it was unsanitary.

I showered quickly and Jazz and I went downstairs. The guests were long gone, thank heavens. Kenner had been delighted to meet me; he hadn't had a clue who called him. I think Michael told him so Kenner would pester me. All's fair.

Aunt Madge was at church, so Jazz and I had the run of the house. The guys were outside, anxious to come in because Jazz was visible through the glass door. She was growing bolder. She paraded in front of the sliding glass door and they whined. "You hussy," I told her as I drank my orange juice.

The phone rang, and I answered, wondering if it would be Morehouse telling me what was going on with Robby. Instead, the voice said, "Georgine?"

"Nooo. Who's this?"

"Hi, Jolie. It's George Winters." I could hear the humor in his voice. "I guess you've talked to Joel Kenner."

"Yeah, I've been showing him around town. Reporter courtesy." He paused, but when I didn't respond he continued. "How come you talked to him and not me?"

"Thought he might know something that would help me."

"Help you do what?" he asked.

This was turning into a soap opera. "My gut tells me Michael didn't do it. And don't ask me why, I don't know."

"Is he your boyfriend?"

I regret to say that I exploded. "What the hell is it with you people? Why ask me that just because I think he's not a murderer?"

"Maybe," he said, evenly, "it's because you and your aunt are about the only people in town who say that out loud. Why don't you tell me why you think that? What do you know?"

"I don't know anything. It just seems that he would be really stupid to set it up that way. He was the only one in the house before I got there." I could hear the scratching of his pencil, and was horrified. "Are we, like, on the record?"

"You didn't say we weren't," he said, very businesslike. I hung up, and didn't answer the phone when it rang again. I put my head on the table. *When will I ever learn?*

CHAPTER TEN

I WAS DEFINITELY GOING to the hearing, and Aunt Madge said she was, too. She even got someone to let the dogs out and told her non-court-attending guests, as she called them, that there would be no afternoon tea. Instead, she arranged for them to go to Java Jolt, her treat, should they want to. Both couples were more than seventy. I did not envision them as Java Jolt customers, but Mr. Hammond, who was visiting from Virginia, said that he'd been going there every day to email his grandson. *Go figure.*

Miller County is the smallest county in New Jersey, and its courthouse is sized accordingly. The judge's bench was raised, but not as high as in TV courtrooms. There were two small tables in front of the judge's bench, each with three chairs. The jury box was so small it barely held the twelve empty chairs. Idly I wondered what would happen if a juror were obese.

The probable cause hearing started at 1 p.m., and we had arrived in the courtroom at twelve-forty-five. We got two of the last seats on the six rows of public benches. I recognized a number of the people as having been at the Riordan house after the funeral, and I wondered if they were there to support Michael or glare at him. No Jennifer Stenner, however. Larry and Honey Riordan sat directly behind the table that I assumed would be for Michael and his attorney, who walked into the courtroom shortly after one o'clock.

Unfortunately, we did not get the last two seats, and Mrs. Jasper sat down on the bench next to me.

I groaned inwardly. At least I would not have to listen to her during the hearing.

"Shame about the article," she said.

I turned to face Aunt Madge, who looked straight ahead. "What article?" I hissed. Before I could query her more the judge walked out of a back room and people stood.

Judge Kevin Rommer gaveled the crowd to order, reminded everyone that this was not a trial but a probable cause hearing that would provide him with the information he needed about whether the case should go forward, and asked the county's prosecuting attorney to call his first witness. As he called Sgt. Morehouse's name, I glanced at the prosecuting attorney's table. Next to Attorney Martin Small's large briefcase sat Annie Milner, legal pad in front of her. She looked more like I would envision a prosecuting attorney – an expensive suit and erect posture – than the man himself, whose shirt was partially untucked and suit jacket lay carelessly on the back of his chair.

As Small paced in front of him, Sgt. Morehouse recounted Harry Steele's call to 9-1-1, and finding me sitting on the floor of Mrs. Riordan's room, "stunned." I felt Mrs. Jasper's hand on my knee, and ignored her.

The prosecuting attorney then asked Sgt. Morehouse if he had been able to verify an alibi for Michael Riordan at the time of his mother's death. Exactly as Michael had predicted, they discussed that he could have killed her just before he left or made it from his car (which had been seen in the lot even though no one noticed him on the beach) to the house and back easily, before the police located him.

Next Mr. Small asked Sgt. Morehouse how Michael would have gotten in the house without me hearing him. Morehouse noted that Michael could have easily come in a side door near the first-floor laundry room and gone up a back set of stairs. I thought about that; he could have.

"What about an alarm system?" he asked.

"He said he turned it off the night before, so he didn't forget to do it when the appraiser arrived."

Michael's attorney, Winona Mason (whoever met an attorney named Winona?) had few questions for Morehouse. "Mr. Riordan was not at the house when you first arrived?"

"That's correct," he said. "Took us about a half-hour to find him." He added that after driving through Ocean Alley and alerting other local jurisdictions' police to the Mercedes they were looking for, local police had finally come across him in a Dollar General parking lot. This struck me funny. I wondered how many Mercedes parked in that lot.

"Did he say why he was there?" she asked.

"He said that the day before his mother had asked him to pick up some light bulbs, and that's where she told him to go."

No wonder Aunt Madge had liked Ruth Riordan so much. They both knew what Aunt Madge would call "the value of a dollar."

I'm no attorney, but I'd watched enough television to recognize that all of the evidence thus far was circumstantial. Morehouse had said that the only fingerprints on the door to the room were Michael and Ruth Riordan's and mine. The maid had cleaned the day before, so all sets of fingerprints were fairly fresh. At least ten people turned to look at me, and I resisted the urge to stick out my tongue.

When the medical examiner took the stand Aunt Madge shifted in her seat. She did not like anything remotely grisly. I wasn't too sympathetic at the moment, still somewhat annoyed that she had not mentioned whatever article Mrs. Jasper had read.

The examiner noted that the time of death would have been "within an hour, maybe less" of the time I found Mrs. Riordan. He based this on body temperature and the fact that rigor mortis had not set in.

Why, Mr. Small asked him, did he think it was strangulation that killed Mrs. Riordan rather than natural causes? The medical examiner went into great detail about what causes asphyxia – spasms (such as from asthma), obstruction (such as a piece of food or other 'foreign body' that will not go down), or compression, which means someone gets a good grip on your windpipe and does not let go until you are history. These are my summaries, of course. Other methods of compression can include someone holding a pillow over your face, but this was not the method used, in his opinion.

He thought the cause of death was strangulation by compression. If she had been smothered, say by a pillow, there would have smudging of her nightly moisturizer. In addition, there was "just the slightest imprint of a finger" on her throat. He believed someone had blocked her windpipe just long enough to deprive her brain of oxygen. Eventually her heart stopped beating.

None of this added to Michael as a murderer, as far as I could tell. Besides, her covers had not seemed mussed to me. Wouldn't it be normal for her to have fought an attacker, and wouldn't the bed have been rumpled? Wouldn't I have heard something? I now wished they had asked me to be a witness. I'd ask them some questions.

As if he read my mind, the prosecuting attorney asked the examiner why the finger imprint was not deeper, or had not left a larger bruise. He attributed this to the fact that Mrs. Riordan had been drugged with probably thirty milligrams of cyclobenzaprine, a muscle relaxer; this was three times the normal dose. It was also the same prescription muscle relaxer that was in Michael Riordan's bathroom. He occasionally took it for back spasms. The judge rapped his gavel to silence the buzz in the courtroom. I looked at Michael, and he looked as surprised as anyone else.

In the medical examiner's opinion, the muscle relaxer made Mrs. Riordan's breathing very shallow. Perhaps the killer had even hoped the pills would kill her.

Michael's attorney asked the medical examiner if he could prove this medicine specifically came from Michael's supply of pills. He could not. That was her only question. Michael had said he was paying this woman a lot of money. *What the hell for?*

To my surprise, the next witness called was Mrs. Jasper. No wonder she had on such a new-looking green suit, complete with cream trim and earrings of cream and green. The outfit would be worthy of an elderly Jennifer.

As with the other witnesses, she was sworn in and said she would tell the truth. Idly, I wondered if Mr. Small would be able to get her to shut up. He began by asking her whether Michael Riordan had been estranged from his mother since his marriage. Mason objected, and the prosecuting attorney told the judge that Mrs. Jasper's comments would provide 'direct information' about the status of Mr. Riordan's relationship with his mother. The judge allowed the question.

With, in my opinion, the sincerity of someone hawking diet pills, Mrs. Jasper relayed the hurt that Ruth Riordan had felt when her son (no mention of the jealous wife) stopped calling and visiting very often. She knew all about Mrs. Riordan's pain because she was her best friend. There was some rustling in the courtroom, and I sensed that there were those in the group who did not think Ruth Riordan would have characterized the relationship this way.

When Mr. Small was done, Michael's attorney asked Mrs. Jasper to explain how she had met Mrs. Riordan, and the kinds of things they did together. Winona Mason pressed with questions until it was clear that the two women had met through their church and that most of their interactions were through the church Social Services Committee.

"Did you have any social interactions with Mrs. Riordan other than at church?" Mason pressed.

"I was always invited to her New Year's Day open house, of course."

"And how many other people were there?"

Mrs. Jasper shrugged. "I'm not sure, maybe twenty or thirty."

"I think it was more like seventy-five, Mrs. Jasper."

She was nonplussed. "Well, not all at once."

There were titters, and the judge rapped his gavel without saying anything.

Michael's attorney continued, "It sounds to me, Mrs. Jasper, as if you considered yourself a better friend to Mrs. Riordan than she considered you."

"Objection," said the prosecuting attorney.

"On what grounds?" asked the judge.

He looked at Annie Milner, and she seemed to mouth something to him. "Relevance," Martin Small said.

Winona Mason pointed out that if the prosecuting attorney was presenting Mrs. Jasper as an expert on the relationship between Mrs. Riordan and her son it was important to know the true nature of the friendship between the two women.

"Overruled," said the judge.

"She asked me to help redecorate her den," Mrs. Jasper said.

"She asked, or you offered?" asked Mason.

Mrs. Jasper paused. "I honestly don't remember."

This seemed to satisfy Winona Mason, and she sat down. I felt a small grain of sympathy for Mrs. Jasper. She believed she was Ruth Riordan's best friend because she wanted to be that person. She was shaking slightly as she sat back down.

Next Mr. Small called the attorney who had redrawn Mrs. Riordan's will after the divorce. Porter Harrison was, there's no other word for it, portly. He was one of those men who seemed to think that if he wore a very large vest over his very large stomach that the proportion of the latter might not be as obvious. Wrong. His chins jiggled as he talked, and every now and then his glasses slid down his nose and he pushed them back.

Harrison recounted that prior to the divorce Mrs. Riordan had planned to divide her property equally between husband and son. She had also had each man as equal beneficiaries in her life insurance policy.

After the divorce, the will had been revised to leave all to Michael except for $20,000 to her maid of ten years and ten percent of the net worth of the estate to be divided among various local charities, specifically, the local Red Cross, Hospice, and First Presbyterian Church, with special instructions that the money go to the latter's social services work. Mrs. Jasper nodded firmly and leaned over to me. "I asked her to do that."

I ignored her. Mrs. Riordan had been generous to her maid. I liked that.

"While the will had not been recently revised," the prosecuting attorney continued, "I believe there had been discussion of revisions."

"Not that I'm aware of," replied the attorney.

Though I could only see Mr. Small's profile, his irritation was obvious. "Mr. Harrison, I believe you are aware that Mrs. Riordan planned to leave her house to the Ocean Alley Arts Council."

"No," he replied patiently. "She planned to deed it to them prior to her death. She did not intend for her home to become part of the estate."

"And now this is up to her heirs?" Mr. Small asked.

"Yes," said Mr. Harrison, nodding all his chins.

"And what would happen if Michael Riordan were found to be the cause of his mother's death, other than in an accident?" Mr. Small asked.

"Mrs. Riordan, of course, had no provision for that, but the State of New Jersey would not permit him to inherit."

"Who would get it?"

"Barring lawsuits from others who felt they were entitled, his portion of the estate would probably be divided among the other beneficiaries, primarily the three charities, since she designated a specific amount for her maid."

Despite their mission to help those who are dying, I couldn't quite see the Hospice organization actually planning Mrs. Riordan's death. I stifled a giggle and Aunt Madge gave me a reproving look.

The prosecuting attorney had no other questions. Winona Mason asked Mr. Harrison if he knew if Mrs. Riordan had planned any further changes in her will, and he said he did not know of any. "So, as far as you know, she had no plans to take Michael Riordan out of her will, or reduce his share of what would ultimately comprise the estate?" she asked. He did not know of any such plans.

Mason had only one more question. "If Mrs. Riordan died when Michael Riordan was still married to his wife Darla, from whom he is now legally separated, would his wife be entitled to a share of the estate?"

Mr. Harrison shrugged. "A lot of those decisions are resolved in negotiation between the attorneys of the two parties seeking a divorce." He hesitated. "She would of course have a better chance of securing some of it prior to the divorce rather than afterwards." There was again a buzz in the courtroom, but it died as the judge picked up his gavel. He didn't even have to use it.

The prosecuting attorney's next witness was Elmira Washington, which seemed to surprise a lot of people. "Mrs. Washington, would you describe the encounter you saw between Mrs. Riordan and her son Michael in Newhart's Restaurant a few nights before she died?"

She looked decidedly uncomfortable. I noticed that Mrs. Jasper leaned forward in her seat, anxious to hear.

"Well, I'm not sure encounter is the right word..."

"Just tell us what you saw," Mr. Small said.

"They were talking."

"Just talking?" Impatience was creeping into the prosecuting attorney's voice.

"It looked as if they were arguing." She looked quickly at Michael and then away.

Exasperation oozed from Small's every pore. "Mrs. Washington, you used the word 'fight' when you first discussed this with my office."

"Argument, fight. What's the difference?"

"As you described the event," he continued, his voice even, "You said it appeared Mrs. Riordan was..." he turned around and Annie handed him some papers. He consulted them and read, "Mrs. Riordan looked as if she was really upset with Michael. Like she was kind of mad about something." He looked at Mrs. Washington. "Those were your exact words."

I saw Michael's attorney lean over and say something to him and he nodded.

"I might have..." she rearranged herself in the witness chair, "I mean, it was noisy in there. I didn't exactly hear what they were saying."

There was true fury in the prosecuting attorney's posture when he said he had no more questions for Mrs. Washington. Winona smiled at her as she approached the witness stand. "Kind of nerve-wracking to be up here, isn't it?" she asked.

"It surely is," Mrs. Washington nodded and smiled weakly.

"Tell me, Mrs. Washington, I infer that you did not hear what Mrs. Riordan and her son were discussing that evening in the restaurant. Is that true?" Winona asked.

"Not the words, no." No smile now.

"Then how do you know it was an argument?" Winona asked.

"The expressions on their faces," was the prompt reply.

After several more questions it was apparent that Elmira Washington could have seen a discussion about local politics or whether it would snow by Christmas. My guess was that she wanted to appear in the know and had not expected to have to take her story to the witness stand. She had the decency to look embarrassed as she stepped down.

But still, what if they had been arguing? I didn't like where this train of thought was heading, and decided to ignore it, at least for the moment.

The prosecuting attorney's final witness was Roger Handley, another vice-president from USA Energy Distributors. He seemed to try to catch Michael's eye, but Michael stared at some notes on a pad in front of him. Mr. Small asked Handley to describe the business Michael helped found, and he said that it had been formed to buy energy from a variety of sources, generally companies that had an excess supply, and resell to utilities in the West.

"So," Mr. Small said, "you were formed after the legislation to deregulate the energy industry in 1992?"

"That's correct. We didn't form until after California deregulated, which was several years later."

"Would you say your firm has been successful?"

"Some years have been better than others. We were somewhat caught up in the last big energy crisis that hit the west, especially California." My sense was that Handley was hedging a bit. As I recalled, it was the consumers who got shafted during those brownout and blackout times, not the energy companies.

The prosecuting attorney did not pick up on this. Instead, he switched to Michael's relationship with the firm. "I believe you fired Mr. Riordan, did you not?"

Handley reddened. "Absolutely not."

"How would you characterize his departure from the firm?" he persisted.

"First, it was simply a disagreement among the founding partners. Second, he hasn't left yet."

"Just a disagreement?" Mr. Small acted as if he were puzzled. This was probably the most attention he'd ever had from the media, and he was milking it for all it was worth. "But this disagreement was going to cost Michael Riordan about $200,000 per year in salary and some nice profit sharing, was it not?"

"Yes."

"And why is he not off the payroll yet?"

Handley really didn't seem to like this question. "Because, because of his mother's illness and his impending divorce."

"So," the prosecuting attorney said, "you would call yourselves a 'family friendly' company, would you?"

Handley said, "You can call it what you want, sir."

"When will he be leaving the company?"

"In the near future."

"And at that point," the prosecuting attorney continued, "he will lose that salary and any share of the profits?"

"Yes."

"Is his silver Mercedes a company car?"

"No." Handley was really going for the mono-syllabic answers now. I couldn't understand why he looked so uncomfortable.

"Is it paid for?" Mr. Small asked.

"You'd have to ask him."

The prosecuting attorney actually smiled at the row of reporters sitting near the front of the courtroom, "I already know there is a substantial note on the car."

Winona Mason had no questions. This whole business about USA Energy Distributors was pretty boring to me. Who cared what his company did?

Now it was Michael's lawyer's turn to call witnesses. First she called the local pharmacist and, after noting Michael had had his own prescription filled in Texas, asked the pharmacist how often he filled prescriptions for cyclobenzaprine. He said it varied from summer to winter, because of course there were so many more people in Ocean Alley during the summer. In the end, he characterized it as a very common drug for back spasms, strained muscles in other parts of the body, and even headaches that were caused by tension in the neck. The prosecuting attorney had no questions.

Ms. Mason's next witness was Madge Richards. I almost tripped her on her way past me, for not telling me. Aunt Madge did not characterize herself as Ruth Riordan's best friend, but said one of the reasons they were fond of each other was because they both enjoyed people but "not talking about people," so they could spend time together without gossiping. I blinked back tears. *How could I have even thought about tripping this dear woman?* Especially in a court room.

Then Mason asked Aunt Madge to talk about recent changes in the relationship between mother and son. "I wouldn't actually characterize the relationship as changing, just evolving to spend more time together again." When asked, Aunt Madge said that Ruth Riordan had been very sad when her son's wife did not want to spend time in Ocean Alley and did not want Michael to do so, either. However, she said, Michael had always made it clear to Ruth that he loved her and his father very much.

It was Larry Riordan's turn to dab his eyes.

Winona Mason's final witness was Michael himself. He answered very directly that he had not killed his mother, and said he missed her very much.

"Were you and your mother arguing in Newton's Restaurant, Michael?" she asked.

"We were having a discussion about when I would finish up with my firm. She favored sooner rather than later." He paused. "I was trying to find a nice way to tell her it was none of her business." There was some brief murmuring and the judge banged his gavel without saying anything.

"Why," she asked, "do you believe that the police and prosecuting attorney have accused you of this crime?"

"Because they haven't had a murder here in many years, and don't have the faintest idea how to investigate one."

This did not appear to be the answer his attorney had coached him to give, as she turned crimson.

CHAPTER ELEVEN

IT WAS JUST AS WELL that Aunt Madge had not shown me the *Ocean Alley Press* article before the hearing, as I might have gone after George Winters in the courtroom and it could have reflected badly on Harry's business, to say nothing of Michael's defense.

The gist of the article was that Michael and I were "close friends from high school" and the implication was clear—I was in cahoots with him to murder his mother before the house, assessed for tax purposes at almost $400,000, was deeded to the Arts Council. The article also noted that my former husband was a confessed embezzler who had raided our personal funds as well, and implied that I thus had a motive (the almighty dollar) for helping Michael. *Perhaps I should rethink hanging up on reporters.*

The only real good news was that after we were back at Cozy Corner, Joel Kenner told me he had a better understanding of why I thought Michael might be innocent. "Really," he said, "it's all pretty circumstantial."

"Too bad you wrote that first article before you knew much about what the police were going on, isn't it?" He walked away without comment. Oh well, no one in Houston knows me.

I wondered if George Winters would see it as Kenner did. In truth, it only mattered what the judge thought. He said he would issue his ruling in about one week as to whether the case should go to trial.

THE NEXT MORNING I was in the county Register of Deeds Office in the court house looking up recent home sales in the popsicle district when who should come in but Winters himself. "You know, you really have a knack for pissing people off."

I assumed he was talking about Kenner, but all I did was shrug. "We all have our special talents." Then, I couldn't resist. "I see that innuendo is one of yours." He left.

The house I was appraising that morning had had two separate additions, done under different owners, neither of whom appeared to take special pride in how the additions blended with the original exterior. While the bright purple paint with lavender trim obviously appealed to whoever had offered the contract, it did little to hide the architectural hodge-podge.

The interior was nicely done. Wallpaper can hide a world of blemishes. However, when I got to the large great room off the kitchen in the back of the house, the first of the two additions, I sensed a definite downward slope. I would have to take careful measurements. This did not bode well for the seller's asking price.

Back in the office, I relayed my thoughts to Harry, and said I was concerned that I wouldn't be able to support the price. This especially troubled me because it was Lester Argrow's sale, and I had hoped he would get over his past funk with Harry and bring us more business. He was very popular with the popsicle district crowd and there were a lot of sales there.

I spent much of the afternoon embellishing the value of some of the house's better features—a hot tub in the new master bedroom (second addition), maintenance-free lawn (read gravel) and hardwood floors in the living room and dining room (original to the house, in need of refinishing). Harry's attitude was that if the house appeared structurally sound, I should merely mention the slope and see what I could do to reach the $154,000 selling price.

Eventually I got the numbers to work without totally compromising my integrity. I wouldn't buy the sucker for $120,000. Who was I kidding? Thanks to Robby, I couldn't get a loan for $10,000.

It was a lot of work for $200, almost all day. I reminded myself that a lot of people make minimum wage, but it didn't help much. When you've had a beautiful apartment and the ability to eat out at the best restaurants without considering the impact on your budget, it's hard to go home to a single room and a budget that doesn't include too much dining out. Thank goodness I like pasta and chocolate.

I had my car since I'd been all over town that day, and I pulled into Aunt Madge's next to a shiny Toyota sedan. It still had new tags, though the sticker had been taken out of the window and was in the back seat. Turned over, so I couldn't read the price. I hadn't realized Aunt Madge was getting a new guest.

Michael Riordan was sitting on the couch in Aunt Madge's great room with Jazz on his lap and Mister Rogers and Miss Piggy at his feet.

"How did you get her to stay off the fridge?" I asked as I sat across from him.

He grinned. "Your aunt had a theory that you were transmitting your fear about the dogs eating Jazz to dear old Jazz here. Since I have no such trepidations, Madge brought her down to me, and we've been sitting here for about half an hour."

Aunt Madge, animal psychologist. I gave him a half smile. "Where is Aunt Madge?"

"She insisted on going to the market to get some butter." He nodded to a paper bag on the counter. "I brought a couple dozen crabs."

"Aren't you supposed to be in jail or something?"

"I suppose that could still happen, but after today I think it's less likely." He shrugged. "I wanted to celebrate, and since my dad's already gone and half the town won't talk to me, I came over here."

"I dunno, I think Aunt Madge scored you a couple of points."

He nodded. "That's why it's only half."

I realized my ridiculous verbal sparring was a product of nerves, and vowed to stop. "Is that your new car?"

"I ordered it a couple of weeks ago."

"Cheaper payments?" I grinned.

"That prosecuting attorney is really a bastard." He placed Jazz on the seat next to him, and she didn't seem inclined to run. Mister Rogers and Miss Piggy were lying on the floor below her. "I did make a point of telling your twin brother George about it, in case he cares to mention that I've reduced expenses."

I let that pass.

"By the way," he added, "Kenner thinks you're a real jerk."

"He wrote a biased story. All he did was talk to Winters, and maybe one of the cops. All those people in Houston probably think you killed her."

At that direct reference to his mother, his face grew somber. "Somebody knows who did it."

I nodded. "I bet if we talked about it more, we could figure out…"

He shook his head, and his expression could only be described as dangerous. "I told you…"

"I know, that's why you pay your lawyer all that money. Frankly, she didn't impress me one bit."

"If you keep this up, I'm taking my crabs back."

I like crab meat a lot, but I hate to pick through the crab looking for it. Many people say they don't like eating crabs because it's tiresome or they get little cuts from the sharp shell, but I think of all that poking around for meat as a major invasion of the crab's privacy. However, all that aside, I decided I'd rather spend time with Michael than have him leave. He was growing on me.

I hadn't realized I'd been quiet for at least several seconds, long for me if I was trying to get my way, and flushed. Luckily he couldn't read my mind. "I'll give it a rest." For now, I thought.

Aunt Madge returned with a pound of butter and I teased her about clogging her arteries.

"I know. But there's just no substitute for real butter when you have crab."

She instructed me to place newspaper on the table, which I knew was the only way to go when you shell crabs, and told me she'd moved the nut crackers and picks to a lower drawer. I found them and poured three large tumblers of ice water while she warmed the butter and transferred it to an old fondue pot to keep it melted.

Michael was sitting on the floor with Jazz in his lap. He would occasionally lift her to one of the dogs, she would smell them and they her, and he would gently put her back in his lap. However, when Aunt Madge called him to the table she did not want to be left on the couch but ran to a chair and jumped from there to the top of a bookcase. Now that the dogs had had a good sniff of her, they did not follow.

"Did you hear any more from my favorite cop about the guy who was bothering you?" Michael asked as he dug into his second crab.

So, we can talk about my problems but not his? "Not a word. I figure if Pedone doesn't want to be found it may take a while."

Aunt Madge cracked a crab. "We don't know a thing about where he's from, so it's hard to tell them where to look."

"I'm sure Robby knows," I said dryly.

"Too true." As she dug crab meat out with a pick she spoke to Michael. "Who do you think gave her those pills?"

He paused in his wrestling with a crab claw and looked at me. Luckily, I did not need to feign innocence. I had not asked her to question Michael.

"I've thought a lot about that, of course. Winona says it's the only really damning thing they've got."

"Were you missing any pills?" she continued.

He shook his head. "Unfortunately, I take them so rarely I can't say. She, Winona, counted the pills left in the bottle and she insists I should remember when I took the ones that are gone, but mostly I can't." He popped the piece of crab in his mouth. "Had 'em almost a year. It's not like I got them the week before...she died."

"Maybe you should try harder," I offered. Not helpful, I guess, as he just looked at me.

"Who else goes in the house?" Aunt Madge asked.

"Of course, I don't know all Mother's friends any more. She occasionally had people over for coffee, and then there was Elsie, the maid. She comes every week. More lately, just to see if Mom's OK."

"So, have Winona ask everyone your mom knew."

He seemed to be tiring of the questions, as his voice assumed the tone one reserves for talking to cantankerous children. "Winona wants to, but I told her to wait until after the judge's ruling. If he doesn't think there's enough evidence to go ahead, there's no point in getting people riled up."

"It's a murder charge," Aunt Madge said. "They can reopen it any time they want to. Those old people will die. She should talk to them now."

Since Aunt Madge rarely butted into people's business, he seemed to be considering her point. "I hadn't thought of that."

Aunt Madge could tell he'd had enough, so she asked him how he liked his new car. He clearly preferred this topic.

I looked down and noticed Jazz sitting by my foot. Apparently the smell of crabmeat was enough to get her off the bookcase. The guys were napping on the great room rug. I gave her a piece. Probably because we had company, Aunt Madge did not scold me.

CHAPTER TWELVE

MICHAEL MIGHT NOT want to pursue much before the judge's ruling, but I did. After all, I had been somewhat implicated in Winters' stupid article. I did not sense that Morehouse thought I was involved in Mrs. Riordan's death. That was fortunate, as I had enough problems looking over my shoulder for Pedone all day.

When I checked with Harry on Wednesday, he had no houses, but he had had several calls. Apparently the agents were getting used to working with him and did not hold it against him that his sole stringer was bandied about as a friend of Michael Riordan's. *Thank heavens for small favors.*

My lack of work left me with too much free time to think about my problems – especially the one who wore patent leather shoes – so I decided to focus on Michael's. I decided to talk to Ruth Riordan's friends. I really didn't want to talk to Mrs. Jasper, whom I did not believe was all that close to Ruth anyway. I knew I would have to eventually, and stalled by going to visit Ramona.

Today's quote was, "A collision at sea can ruin your entire day." Thucydides. I stared at this for a few seconds, and decided this was Ramona's way of telling the world to keep things in perspective.

Scoobie was standing near the entrance inspecting the prices on some steno pads. "Hey. Sorry I ran off the other day. I still want to sit and talk."

He seemed preoccupied. "Good, good." He selected a pad. "I'm on a writing binge. Gotta go." He walked toward the cash register.

I had many good memories of hanging out with Scoobie, and felt bad that I'd hurried away from him when we were having coffee. I hoped that wasn't why he was unwilling to talk to me.

I looked for Ramona, and saw her in the back of the store talking to someone in a tie, so I figured he was the manager. As she nodded in response to whatever they were discussing her large hoop earrings bobbed. They finished their conversation, and she came toward me. "I just came by to chat."

She nodded. "That's OK, but we need to look like I'm showing you something." She nodded toward the side wall. "How about the graph paper?"

"Uh, sure. Graph paper?"

"People from Jennifer's office sometimes buy it," she said.

This woman was much smarter than her loose-fitting, greenish, tie-dyed long dress and orange beret let on. "They must have some folks who like to draw to scale when they work."

"Don't you?"

I shook my head. "I do a rough sketch and let the computer figure out the scale when I tell it the measurements."

"What did you want to chat about?" she asked.

"Did you read the article in the paper about the hearing?"

"Every word. It wasn't such convincing evidence, except for the pills."

I told her I agreed and asked her, casually, if Ruth had come into the Purple Cow very often.

"Not too often. Mostly before her big New Year's Day open house. She bought the invitations here, and Roland ordered special napkins for her."

"Roland?" I asked.

She nodded toward the back. "Mr. Purple Cow himself."

"How'd it get that name, anyway?" I asked, allowing myself to be distracted.

"He was trying to think of a name and he heard some kids say that old rhyme. You know." She seemed to sense my perplexity, "I never saw a purple cow, I never hope to see one. But I can tell you anyhow I'd rather see than be one." She looked at me closely. "The rhyme by Gelett Burgess."

I stared at her for several seconds. Obviously, my childhood had missed something. "And that's why he picked the name?"

"Oh, yes. He said he'd always liked the rhyme and he was glad he heard them say it before he picked some silly name, like 'Ocean Alley Office Supplies.'"

Heaven forbid.

There was no getting around it, I'd have to be direct. "So, who would you say Ruth's good friends were?"

"Ooh. You're investigating." She looked thrilled.

I tried to appear nonchalant. "Winters has me tied into this somewhat, so I figure I have a stake in how it comes out."

She nodded. "That wasn't very nice of him. If he were really good he'd know that it's Jennifer who's chasing Michael."

While this interested me, I couldn't let myself get distracted again. "Was Ruth friendly with Jennifer's mother, for instance?"

This got her into some deep thinking. "I don't think so. She liked your Aunt Madge, I know. I saw them Christmas shopping in Lakewood one time."

Aunt Madge went to Lakewood every year to do her shopping, and when my parents still lived there, my mother would meet her at the mall. I had no idea that she'd partnered with Ruth Riordan after my parents moved. The things I don't know.

"Who else?"

"Roland said that Mrs. Jasper said she was her best friend, at the hearing." When I nodded, she added, "I wonder why George Winters didn't interview her before?"

I snorted. "He'd have to talk to her for an hour to get one quote."

"That's true," she sighed. "I have a very hard time waiting on other customers when she comes in here. And she always wants Roland to give her a discount on office supplies. She says they're for the church." Her tone implied she did not think so, but I really didn't care. I already knew about Mrs. Jasper.

"Mrs. Riordan and Mrs. Murphy were friends," she continued. "I remember when the paper interviewed them about the bazaar to benefit the First Prez Social Services Committee. They joked that they were the most Irish people in their church."

I did not recognize Mrs. Murphy's name, and said so.

"She's very short, and she walks with a walker. You don't see her out much, unless her daughter takes her."

I remembered the woman whom I had almost knocked over at the Riordan's after the funeral, and when I described her Ramona felt certain this was she. She was likely to remember me, that was for sure, and Ramona told me she lived in an assisted living facility on the north side of town.

Feeling as if I'd worn out my welcome, especially given Roland's looks in our direction, I bought a mechanical pencil and some refills for it. At least I wouldn't have to sharpen pencils for a while.

MRS. MURPHY WAS DELIGHTFUL. She was definitely in a lot of pain ("just a crushed vertebra, but did not want me to focus on that.

Her eyes teared when I mentioned Ruth Riordan. "She was one of the kindest people I've ever met. She visited me once or twice a month, and there were a lot of people I used to know better who always say they'll come by, but don't."

I said I wished I'd known Ruth and was trying to get a handle on who might have killed her.

She eyed me with some suspicion. "Are you a reporter?"

"No, ma'am. I'm a friend of Michael's, and…"

She interrupted me. "Of course. The girl from the paper."

It was hard not to sigh. What a way to get known in Ocean Alley. "Yes, but we really are just friends." It was not so long ago that I denied this. I mentioned that I was Madge's niece.

"A very hard-working woman. Ruth really liked her." She nodded, as if agreeing with herself. "Ruth would be glad Michael was friends with Madge's niece."

I decided to plunge ahead with my theory. "Can you think of anyone Ruth thought was a friend, but really wasn't?"

She shook her head. "I've thought all week about that. I can't believe anyone would murder her. She never riled anyone."

This might be true, but it was not helpful. I needed her to describe someone who disliked Ruth, or envied her for her money, or something.

"Of course, there was Michael's wife." She frowned. "Even at the wedding, I thought she was a user."

"Of…drugs?" I asked, in surprise.

This made her throw back her head and laugh, which then brought a grimace of pain. "No, not drugs, people. She seemed phony, and it wasn't but a few months after the wedding that she started telling Michael his mother was against her, and he shouldn't visit so much."

I nodded, this was helpful, and she leaned forward. "She might have had a key, you know. Michael had one. She could have copied it." She laughed, and pointed at a large bookshelf full of books, mostly mysteries. "I have an active imagination."

The key was, well, the key. Even with the security system off, someone had to be able to get in the house without breaking a window or jimmying a lock. Michael would not have left a door unlocked, not with his mother in there.

"Can you think of anyone else she knew well enough to give a key to?"

She thought for a moment. "Not really. She was a friendly person, but she didn't have a lot of close friends. She and that jerk husband of hers socialized a lot as a couple, but you know how that is."

I was surprised at her characterization of Larry Riordan (not that he might not be a jerk, but that she would say so), and told her I didn't understand her point.

"When a woman is widowed or divorced, people just don't ask her around as much. Of course," and she seemed a bit bitter, "they keep inviting the men. Even try to fix them up."

I decided not to ask about her own experience, but turned instead to Larry. "Was the break-up not mutual?"

"They had drifted apart some, but a lot of people do after thirty or more years of marriage. I think," she leaned forward onto the walker parked in front of her chair, "that if he hadn't met that young slut he'd have come back by Christmas of that year. Ruth made a huge deal out of Christmas."

Mrs. Murphy was full of surprises. I plowed on. "I can't think of any reason Larry would have for harming her, can you?"

She shook her head vehemently. "They were very civil about everything. Ruth even told him he could bring that Honey-thing to Michael's wedding, but he had the good manners not to."

I stayed a few more minutes and asked her where she had lived in Ocean Alley before coming to what she called the "old folks' home," and she described a house not too far from Aunt Madge's. She said her two daughters still lived there, both divorced. "But," her eyes lit up, "I have wonderful grandchildren. Two boys and a girl."

I admired their photos, which sat in front of the books, and left her on that happy thought. I took a close look in the dining room and reception area as I left. It was all very elegant, and I figured her 'old folks' home' cost a bundle. It hit me that Aunt Madge might eventually need to live in one of these small apartments, and I didn't like the thought.

Mrs. Murphy seemed to have a pretty good grasp on Ruth Riordan's life. I decided not to explore for more friends, but knew I would have to talk to Mrs. Jasper. I decided to wait a day.

WHEN I GOT BACK to Aunt Madge's after my afternoon run there was a message to call Sgt. Morehouse. I looked at her and all she said was, "He didn't offer so I didn't ask."

All he had to say was that they had found Joe Pedone's apartment in Atlantic City, but a neighbor had seen him leave a couple days ago with a suitcase. The woman didn't know which day and didn't really care. "I figure he's going to stay out of the picture until he thinks we've forgotten about him. Which we won't."

In Morehouse's opinion, I shouldn't worry about Pedone. "He knows we're onto him. He's a bully, but nothing in his record says he's stupid."

Maybe, but I'd underestimated the funny-looking guy with the bunions the first time I'd met him, and I had no intention of doing so again. Instead, I asked about Robby. It seemed I should.

"Don't know too much about him," he said.

"You mean you let him go?" I was astounded.

"Of course not. The FBI came for him the next morning. If he helps them, they'll help him."

Though I did not at all like the way Morehouse had treated Michael, I was grateful to him for helping Robby and said so. "You sure know how to pick 'em," he said. Grateful, but I still didn't like Morehouse's supposed humor.

I told Aunt Madge what he'd said, and she remembered to tell me that Michael had called and said he was going to be in Houston for a few days. I was surprised he could leave the state, and felt a sense of loss. I realized that when he finalized the transfer of his mother's house to the arts council, which could be in the next few weeks or so, he'd be gone. What else had I expected?

With this less-than-cheerful thought, I wandered back to the boardwalk in search of Java Jolt coffee. It was almost dinner time, and I tended to go in the morning. I was surprised at the larger number of people there, and more surprised when Lester Argrow waved at me from the back of the shop. I did not associate him with a smoke-free coffee house.

He cheerfully held out a chair and thanked me for the appraisal "of the purple place."

"It's not a matter of thanks," I told him. "I thought it met that value." I then asked him if he'd skied in the great room, and he laughed.

"They should have flattened the soil better before they poured the concrete. I really don't think it'll settle much more." He then changed tacks with the speed of a sailor in a race. "Ramona tells me you're investigating Mrs. Riordan's murder."

I put my forehead on the table and wondered how I could have been so stupid. If Ramona spoke freely to me, whom she hadn't seen in years, she'd talk to her uncle. When I sat up, I realized people at a couple of other tables were looking at us, and I made a face at one of them. The woman looked away, offended.

"That's too strong a word," I spoke in a much lower tone than Lester's. "After George Winters mentioned me in that article the day of the hearing, I got a little more interested in who did it."

His face showed disappointment. "That's too bad. I was gonna offer to help. I always wanted to be a detective."

"Your fax is enough of a weapon. I don't think you'd be a good person to have a gun."

He laughed loudly, again attracting attention. "I haven't shot anything but deer." He grew more somber. "Listen, kid, I know everyone in town. What do you want to know?"

Kid? He probably was a golden opportunity, but what could I ask? I was hitting dead ends. "I guess you never heard anyone say bad things about Mrs. Riordan either."

"You talked to the reverend at her church?" he asked.

"You think he'd say bad things?"

"Nope, but he knew her pretty well. After old Larry left, she spent a lot more time helping at that church."

It was a good suggestion, one I might not have thought of. I insisted on paying for his coffee.

CHAPTER THIRTEEN

REVEREND JAMISON WAS MUCH younger than most ministers I'd met. He was not wearing his black garb, but was in a pair of thin-lined corduroy pants and a green turtleneck. He looked more like a college professor than a minister.

Aunt Madge had called him on my behalf. Heaven only knows how she described me, because he talked to me as if I were a wayward child. Which some would say I had been, but that was quite a while ago.

"I'm just trying to get a sense of her life."

He stared at me, no comment.

"From what Aunt Madge said and what I heard at the hearing, I don't think Michael killed her, and I'd like to know who did."

"Don't you think that's up to the police?" His smile was polite, but I could tell he thought I was poking into something I shouldn't.

"With all due respect, I think they made up their minds pretty quickly."

He digested that. "Ruth was thrilled when her son said he planned to visit for a few weeks. Frankly, though she'd never have said so, I think she was glad his marriage was ending."

"Did you marry them?" Irrelevant, but I was curious.

"I only came two years ago, and they were married before that."

"You probably read that at the hearing Michael's attorney mentioned that his wife would get some of his inheritance if Ruth died before the divorce was final." He nodded. "Did you ever meet her, Darla I mean?"

He shook his head. "From what I gather, most people only saw her at the wedding. If you want more on her, you might talk to Mrs. Jasper. She knows a lot. Or," he hesitated, "talks a lot about things."

Even a man of the cloth felt a need to comment on Mrs. Jasper's loose lips. There was no way around it, I'd have to talk to her sooner rather than later. I thanked him and left. So much for Lester Argrow's detection ideas.

Mrs. Jasper lived just three blocks from the church, in a well-cared-for bungalow. There were pansies in the front yard, with a half-empty bag of mulch next to the pansy bed. The last couple of years, more people have planted pansies in the fall, the thinking is that they would last until there is snow. I never understand why people create more garden work just when they are raking leaves, but I chose to live in an apartment.

Judging from the brown slacks she was wearing and the tennis shoes neatly placed on paper just inside the front door, Mrs. Jasper must have been working in her garden very recently. She welcomed me and offered coffee, which was very gracious considering I hadn't called.

While she was in the kitchen making coffee, I took in her living room. Her small bungalow had been built as a summer cottage. The floors may never have been varnished; in any event, they were now painted a bright white, which matched the wide trim around the windows. The walls were a pale blue and the stuffed furniture – which I judged to be at least fifty years old – had lace doilies where a head would rest. On each of two end tables were large photos of a man I took to be her late husband. All in all, the décor reminded me a lot of Mrs. Jasper; a bit frilly, but serviceable.

She reentered the room, with two steaming mugs of coffee on a small tray. "Of course I know you and Madge don't think Michael killed his dear mother. Wouldn't that be wonderful?" She sat on the edge of her chair, as if waiting for me to outline exactly who had committed the crime and how.

"You knew Ruth Riordan so well, I thought you could help me understand what she had been doing the last couple of days before she died, maybe help me figure out who she'd been spending time with." Mrs. Jasper was the only person I'd talked to who seemed to accept that Michael might be innocent. I should be gratified, but I found even her eagerness to help to be annoying. *I really need to work on my attitude.*

"Hmm. You know she died on a Thursday, right?" She sat up a bit straighter. "Of course you do, you were there. So, you're talking about Wednesday, or even Tuesday."

I nodded. "But if you think the days before that would be helpful, that's fine."

"Of course, Sunday we were all at church. Ruth sat in her usual pew, third back on the left."

I listened without comment for several minutes as she talked about the church service, and when she wore out that topic she said she knew that Ruth and Michael had eaten out Sunday evening, because she had seen Ruth at the grocery store on Monday and she had mentioned this.

She knew nothing of Ruth's schedule Tuesday, but had seen her Wednesday at the beauty parlor. I had visions of Ruth Riordan changing her hair appointment each week in the hope of missing Mrs. Jasper at the beauty shop. I pushed the rude thought out of my mind.

In Mrs. Jasper's opinion, Ruth seemed distracted on Wednesday. She had the impression Ruth and Michael had had a disagreement, but it was just an impression. Mrs. Jasper had asked Ruth about Michael, and she had not had much to say. This was unusual, because since he had arrived home two weeks before that, she had been "bubbling over."

The one piece of information Mrs. Jasper provided that interested me was that she had talked to Ruth Wednesday evening, to be sure she was coming to the Social Services Committee meeting on Thursday morning at eleven o'clock.

"And she sounded fine?" I asked.

"Oh yes. Same as usual." She paused. "I think Michael must have been out. Since he's been back he's been answering the phone." She couldn't remember exactly when she called, between seven and eight p.m., she thought.

I didn't recall Michael saying where he had been the night before his mother died, and wished I had thought to work it into a conversation previously.

As penance for asking my questions, I had to listen to more than twenty minutes of Mrs. Jasper talking about First Presbyterian's work with the local food pantry and with teen mothers. I considered both very worthy causes, but I wanted to focus on Ruth Riordan. I managed to sidestep her request that I volunteer at the food pantry by saying I was not sure how long I would stay in Ocean Alley.

AFTER EATING DINNER WITH AUNT MADGE and walking the guys, on the well-trafficked street rather than the boardwalk, I sat down to make a list of what I knew and what I needed to learn more about. I did this sitting at the kitchen table while Aunt Madge watched a rerun of Happy Days. She was not pleased about my sleuthing now that I had broadened it to interviews.

What I knew was:
Ruth Riordan had no obvious enemies.
She seemed to have been alone at least some of the night before she died.
She had intended to go to the next day's committee meeting (or at least said she did).
Aunt Madge doesn't think Michael killed his mother.
Everyone in Ocean Alley thinks Mrs. Jasper talks too much.
Darla had a motive.
Michael did not.

What I needed to know was:
Did Michael really fight with his mother?
Did Michael think his mother was alone Wednesday night?
If she was, where was Michael?
Could anyone besides Michael and the maid have had a key to the house?
Why would anyone want to kill such a nice woman?
Where was Darla Riordan Wednesday night and Thursday morning (and how in the hell would I find that out)?
How angry would Michael be if he found out what I was doing?
Why was Michael in Houston?

These last two questions did not directly relate to Mrs. Riordan's murder, but they interested me.

I was trying to remember what Darla looked like (I could remember the suit), when I recalled that she had been with Jennifer Stenner. Maybe

Jennifer knew more about Darla's life, or would at least be willing to talk to me more about it than Michael would.

There was no realistic pretense for calling her. There was always, "I'm thinking of falling for Michael Riordan (at least until the next time he really ticks me off). What are your intentions?" Somehow I thought that would close more doors than open. I wanted to stay away from talking about the appraisal business. If she got under my skin it would be too tempting to say that people were coming to Harry because they didn't like her style.

Jennifer had been homecoming queen, or maybe she was on the queen's court. She was probably working on the reunion. Did I want to pretend that I wanted to go to that? No. Did I want to talk to her about Darla?

THE NEXT MORNING I CALLED Jennifer's office. It seemed the receptionist was gone for quite a while before she returned to tell me that Ms. Stenner could see me at two-thirty. She never asked why I was coming.

I told Harry where I was going and why, because I didn't want someone to tell him I'd been seen going into Jennifer's office. He might think I was trying to get work from her.

When he gave me a short lecture on leaving police work to the police, I assumed Aunt Madge was the one who had told him about my other inquiries around town. However, he let me know it was Reverend Jamison. "I want you to know you are the first young person he has met whom he hasn't immediately invited to church."

Rather than being offended I was practical. "He probably didn't want the roof to fall in."

Harry just raised an eyebrow at me as he handed me a file. "Looks as if your friend Lester was pleased with your work."

More money! I grabbed the file it eagerly, and saw that it was only a few houses away from the purple popsicle house. "I remember this one. His sign was in front of it and what grass there was is a foot high."

Harry nodded. "It's vacant, but he has a buyer. Should make it a short job. He left the key here."

Empty houses are much easier than those crammed with furniture or, worse, lots of little kids. I had the small house examined in an hour and was at the courthouse looking for comps when I saw Lester Argrow in the hallway. I hid behind a pile of ledgers, but it was too late.

"I was just thinkin' about you," he said, approaching as rapidly as a train and stopping abruptly barely a foot from me. "You know who you should really talk to is the maid. Maids know everything."

It was a good idea, but I wished he would lower his voice. "I think I've heard her name, but I can't..."

"Elsie." He pulled a piece of rumpled paper from the pocket of his over-long suit. "Elsie Hammer. Want me to go with you?"

I demurred, but he insisted. For this he did lower his voice. "It's not a very nice neighborhood. But, it's a good place for a bargain, if you know what I mean."

Good old Lester, always thinking about his commissions. I decided that I wouldn't mind his company, and even let him drive. This was a mistake, as his car reeked of cigar smoke. I couldn't imagine a real estate agent driving customers around in it. But not many agents meet their customers in Burger King.

Elsie Hammer's house was almost as far south in Ocean Alley as you could get. From a real estate perspective, the neighborhood could at best be called locationally challenged. Unlike the house next to hers, Elsie's had neatly trimmed grass and all shutters were in place. They were real shutters, the kind you could close during strong storms, not just decorative pieces of wood or aluminum.

Neither of us knew Elsie, though I had seen her at the Riordan's after the funeral, so we first introduced ourselves. I could tell my name meant something to her; she would, of course, have read any articles about Mrs. Riordan's murder. She invited us in without further comment.

I launched into my reason for being there, with Lester interrupting me repeatedly. He might have a good sense of humor, but he had no sense of politeness. "Anyway, Ms. Hammer, I wondered if you could think of anyone who visited Mrs. Riordan the last day you cleaned for her."

"Mister Michael was there, but you don't mean him, I guess."

"Yeah," Lester butted in, "we mean somebody else."

"There was no one else there during the day, but Mrs. Jasper called. I sort of thought she was coming that night." This surprised me, as Mrs. Jasper had only mentioned calling.

"I don't think she went? She mentioned to me that she called Ruth that Wednesday evening."

Elsie nodded. "That's possible. Mrs. Riordan got tired easily after she got sick. She could have told Mrs. Jasper to call first, and then said not to come."

The phone rang and she went to the far side of the small living room to answer it. "So, whaddya think?" Lester asked, in nothing less than a stage whisper.

I glanced at Elsie, who appeared somewhat upset by the call, and was writing something on the pad of paper next to the phone. "I think if you keep acting like a TV private eye we'll get thrown out of here." I used a normal tone of voice.

Elsie rejoined us, sitting even more stiffly than she had previously. "Is everything all right?" I asked.

"Fine," she responded, very quickly. "Just my husband, he's having…car trouble."

As a practiced fibber in my younger days, I knew she was being less than truthful, but it really was none of my business.

Lester then asked Elsie if she owned the house and wanted to sell, and I spent several minutes being embarrassed at having brought him. I finally stood. "I think we've taken up a lot of your time."

"Unfortunately, I have too much time." She hesitated, then asked, "Does your aunt ever need help at the Cozy Corner?"

"Gee, right now she does it herself, but I'll mention that you asked. I expect if Mrs. Riordan liked having you around she would, too."

As the door shut, Lester turned to me. "That went very well, don't you think?"

I didn't punch him.

AFTER LUNCH I HEADED to Jennifer's office. I had avoided having lunch with Lester by saying that I had promised to help Aunt Madge change some sheets at the B&B. This was not true. She says the way she keeps fit is by keeping busy, so pretty much all she ever lets me do is weed the small yard, take out the trash, and water the flower boxes on her porch. I told her about Elsie's interest in employment, but Aunt Madge didn't seem to share it.

It was warm for early November. Before I left for Jennifer's office I changed into a straight blue skirt and a red, short-sleeved knit top with a dark blue necklace, and low heels. I rarely wore skirts in Ocean Alley, a hold-over from thinking of it only as a place for fun. Since I noticed Jennifer had dressed formally at the funeral, I was trying to look like one of her 'crowd.' I hate it when I get into people-pleasing, but I told myself this was a good cause.

Jennifer kept me waiting for fifteen minutes, which I could have predicted. Her outer office was small. Appraisers don't have many customers who need to visit their offices. The furnishings were Shaker design, but rest of the décor was not nearly so plain. Above a small credenza was a print of a Thomas Kincaid painting, with a small cottage and lots of pink and yellow foliage. Every chair had pink and yellow pillows. I doubted her father had used the same decorating scheme.

Eventually, her receptionist led me to Jennifer's office, which was decorated in the same colors. I had expected her to be wearing a formal business suit and was surprised that she had on a sleek plum-colored skirt and silk blouse. A long scarf of plum and blue appeared to have been carelessly wrapped around the blouse collar and then slung around her neck, but I figured she had spent time to achieve the look. It suddenly hit me that she might not have planned to be an appraiser in a small town. She was dressed for a job in Manhattan, preferably one in fashion.

Jennifer greeted me coolly and offered coffee, which I refused. After a minute of small talk about changes I noticed in Ocean Alley now that I was living here again, I told her I was interested in learning about the reunion. Her entire demeanor changed. "I should have talked to you about it. I didn't think you would be interested."

I told her how much I'd enjoyed my junior year here (retch), and said I was looking forward to seeing everyone. She launched into plans for this major event—"the tenth is the first one a lot of people come back to, almost nobody goes to the fifth"—and said she thought there would be about eighty people attending.

"You were homecoming queen, weren't you?" I asked.

Her expression clouded a bit, then cleared. "I lost by two votes. Of course, I'm not supposed to know how close the vote was, but the principal counted the votes and he always liked me."

It must have been a fun evening, in any event."

She laughed. "Much more fun than college homecomings."

She asked if I would like to help with the planning, and I said I'd be delighted. *How do I get myself into these things?* I took out my calendar and penciled in a planning meeting for Sunday evening. *As if.*

That done, I plowed into my planned approach to Darla. "I wanted to compliment you on spending time with Darla Riordan after Mrs. Riordan's funeral. That was very gracious of you."

"I'd seen her at the funeral home, and no one was talking to her." She paused, "I sort of didn't want to, because I thought Michael might think I was taking her side in the divorce stuff."

"I didn't realize you knew Darla," I continued.

"I didn't know her well. I had lunch with her several times when she and Ruth were planning the wedding. She didn't visit much after that." She frowned. "I never understood that."

"Neither does Aunt Madge." I wasn't going to pretend I had any knowledge of Darla's psyche.

Then, the hook. "Is she still in Houston? Michael is down there for a few days."

Her eyes literally widened. I thought that was only in books. "Oh, he is?" She changed to moderate indifference. "She's still there. A couple of times she said it was a really miserable climate, and that no one there has any fashion sense. She just went there because of Michael's company. She wants to move to Manhattan."

That would put Darla Riordan a little too close for my comfort. "I heard some talk after the hearing." This seemed to interest her. "I guess the DA's case didn't look too strong to some people, and they were saying Darla had more of a motive than Michael did."

She waved her hand. "That's silly. She's going to get a lot of money from the divorce. It would hardly be worth killing for more."

"Oh, sure," I wondered how much money she would say was worth killing for.

"Besides, she flew to the funeral from Paris. Didn't Michael tell you she'd been over there shopping?"

That explained the exquisite suit. "No." I couldn't resist. "We rarely talk about her."

Jennifer's attitude was slightly frosty after that comment, but she warmed up again when I said I'd see her Sunday.

CHAPTER FOURTEEN

I KNEW A LITTLE MORE, but while it seemed to rule out Darla from personally killing Mrs. Riordan, it was of no obvious help in learning who did kill her mother-in-law. Impatiently, I put aside my list of "known and unknown" information. Why should I spend time on it when Michael had mentally turned everything over to his lawyer? *Because you think he's a fool to do that, that's why.* More important, because Aunt Madge believed him, and she would be distressed if her good friend's son had to go to trial for murder. Most important because I didn't want any more snide innuendos about me in the local paper.

I picked up the list again. In court the lawyer had said that the only beneficiaries besides Michael had been the three charities and Elsie. Idly I wondered why Elsie was so anxious to find more work if she stood to inherit $20,000 in the fairly near future. Admittedly, it was not enough to live on very long, but it would more than take the sting out of a few weeks with fewer work hours. I didn't know anything about her life other than that she had a husband whose car had a problem. I frowned. I should probably see if there was a reason for Elsie to want that $20,000 now rather than later.

But there was not much I could check into now. It was Saturday morning and the dogs and I could be trotting along the boardwalk. I looked at Jazz, who was sitting in a chair near the window, basking in the morning sunbeam. "You want to come ride on Mister Rogers' back?" I asked her. Since she did not reply, I left her there.

The temperature was not going to reach forty degrees, the first really bone-chilling day of the fall. Naturally, the dogs ignored the elements in favor of several seagulls, and spent half an hour trying to catch them. The birds could easily have flown far away, so I gathered they were playing with the dogs as much as the dogs were playing with them.

Unfortunately, Miss Piggy decided to follow one rather large gull into the water. She came out fast enough when she found out how cold it was, but she was still a mess. I'd have a job cleaning her up before I could take her into the house. To arm myself for the task, I stopped at Java Jolt for some strong coffee.

Michael was sitting at a table with a steaming mug and a scowl. The latter seemed to relate to something he was reading in a newspaper spread in front of him.

"Hey," I stepped to the take-out counter. "You're back." I winced inwardly. He obviously knew that.

"Yeah, got in last night."

He went back to the paper and I paid for my coffee and left, figuring he was still pretty angry with me about the Kenner article. He'd been friendlier the night we had crabs, but he'd just been in Houston, so people had probably talked to him about the story.

I let Mr. Rogers into the house and attached Miss Piggy's leash to the stair rail at the side entrance to the B&B. As I wrestled with her and a towel outside Cozy Corner, Michael's Toyota pulled up. Miss Piggy tried to get loose from me to greet him, and I lunged at her.

"Are you trying to clean her or dirty yourself?" he asked.

Miss Piggy tried to sit on me, which meant we both sat on the blacktop. "Very funny. Next time I'll let her get to you."

"OK, I won't needle you when you can aim a dirty dog at me." He stooped next to her and picked up the other towel. "Give me your paw," he said sternly. She obliged, and immediately sat still.

"That's so...so..." I began.

"Irritating?" he asked, with what could only be called a wicked grin.

When I nodded, he continued. "Same as the deal with Jazz. She's picking up on your nerves."

His certainty about this was even more irritating, but I was still glad to see him. "Are you over being angry with me?"

He glanced at me as he cleaned another paw. "Depends. What were you up to when I was gone?"

I sidestepped that by blaming my visit to Elsie on Lester, implying that he had waylaid me in the Register of Deeds Office and would have gone to see her alone if I had not agreed to accompany him.

"Lester Argrow?" He frowned. "What does he care?"

"I, uh, guess it's because I told Ramona I didn't think you did it, and he thinks you were respectful to your parents in high school." At his raised eyebrow, I added, "And he talked to Elsie about selling her house."

He frowned. "Ramona repeats everything you tell her, in case you didn't know that." He stood, and I realized Miss Piggy was as clean as she was going to get without a visit to the dog groomer.

"Thanks." I took Miss Piggy's leash. "You coming in?"

"Yeah. What did she say?"

"She...Oh, Elsie. We, Lester, asked her who'd been around the day before your mom died, and if she knew if anyone was coming over Wednesday night." Mister Rogers was barking in the kitchen, and Aunt Madge opened the door to the kitchen to let us in. I let Miss Piggy off the leash and he gave her a good smell.

"I'm asking Jolie about her detective work," he said as he gave Aunt Madge a kiss on the cheek.

"And I was afraid you wouldn't like that," she said.

He raised an eyebrow at me again, and I ignored the apparent question there. "Anyway, Elsie thought Mrs. Jasper was going to come over Wednesday night, but Mrs. Jasper only told me she called." Damn! I hadn't planned on telling him who else I talked to.

"You talked to Mrs. Jasper, too?"

Thunderclouds were gathering on the Riordan horizon. "You know how she is. She was in Harry's office, and she talked to me."

"Don't I know her style." He grimaced as he took the cup of tea Aunt Madge handed him.

"Do you know if Mrs. Jasper was there?" I pressed.

He shrugged. "I knew she was supposed to come, so I went to the movies by myself. Mother was in bed when I got back, and I didn't...have a chance to talk to her again." He looked away.

"Hmm." Aunt Madge said. "I suppose if Henriette had been there she would have been letting people know she was the last person to see Ruth alive."

It made perfect sense, of course. "That sounds like a very catty thing for a person to say, if she says she doesn't like to gossip," I teased.

"It's true," Aunt Madge and Michael said together, and they both laughed.

Michael's expression quickly changed. "It will all be moot when the judge issues his ruling. Could be any day now."

Thinking I would divert to a safer topic, I asked, "How was Houston?"

"Not good. I have some difficult decisions to make about the business." He paused. "The good news is Kenner did another article, and he talked about the flaws in the DA's case."

His look said to change the topic, so I did. "Jennifer asked me to help on reunion planning."

"And you told her no, right." He stated it as a given rather than a question.

"I said I'd go to a meeting Sunday, but that doesn't mean I will." I looked away as he gave me a hard stare. "It's the first time she talked to me that she wasn't snotty. I figured I'd be polite."

"You'd hate it. It's all the people who've stayed here because they had no choices."

"Wait a minute," Aunt Madge said.

That caught him up short. "You like it here," he said quickly, "And you have a business. People like Jennifer and her crowd had it made here as kids and by the time they realized they should have left it was too late."

I was staring at him, and he met my gaze almost defiantly. "So," I asked, "does that mean you think someone would be crazy to come back here?"

"You're twisting my words." He was impatient now.

Apparently sensing his mood, Aunt Madge asked, "When will the house transfer be final? I know a few people on the Arts Council, and they are so grateful that you will do as Ruth planned."

"In a month. I hate to think of it. There's so much to do." He ran his fingers through his hair and suddenly looked very tired.

"Do you need some help?" Aunt Madge asked. "It'll take a while to go through things, you know."

"Elsie needs some work," I added.

"I was volunteering our time, dear, not finding ways for Michael to spend money," she said.

I shrugged, and grinned at Michael. "I guess since Aunt Madge found me paying work I can find ways to make you Elsie's donor."

"Gee," Michael said, ignoring my humor, "When I told Elsie she didn't need to come for a while, I wasn't thinking about her income going down."

"I'm sure there's plenty Elsie can do for you," Aunt Madge continued, "but you will need a lot of help going through family things, and that might be a better job for friends."

Before I had a chance to say anything else, she and Michael had arranged for us to go to the Riordan's Sunday afternoon to help Michael go through his mother's clothes and jewelry and such.

SUNDAY MORNING I TOOK the dogs to the beach while Aunt Madge went to church. I was as much looking for Scoobie as I was getting exercise for me and the guys, and I was rewarded by seeing him in Java Jolt, sitting near the window. Since the guys had had a good run, I figured it was safe to tie them to a lamp post at the edge of the boardwalk.

"Hey," I slid into the chair across from him. He had his steno pad open, but wasn't actively writing. It looked as if he had filled half the pad.

"Yo, Jolie." He raised his cup as if toasting me.

I had forgotten that he had often used that greeting, putting emphasis on the 'yo' and the 'lee.'

"Sorry I was kind of short with you the other day. I had some demons I had to get out."

"It's okay." I nodded to his pad. "Did you get the little devils into your book?"

"Mostly." He gestured to the coffee thermoses. "Get your battery acid and come back."

I winked at Joe Regan as I put my coffee money in the honor bowl and returned to the table. Scoobie was studying his words.

"The thing is," he said, "I've filled about twenty of these pads, and I still have wild thoughts puttering around in my head." His smile didn't pack a lot of joy.

I was uncertain what to say. I remembered that when Robby first started going to Gamblers Anonymous he grumbled about the fact that some of the others stressed writing down his thoughts. He had gone so far as to question when 'journal' became a verb, which was one of the few times I was able to laugh with him about what was going on. I've never been one for writing much.

"I know some people who swear by putting your thoughts on paper to help think more clearly." Well, I didn't, but Robby did. Wherever he was.

He shrugged. "Yeah, but they probably have a better idea where they want to go with what they're thinking about."

I snorted. "I wouldn't know. I'm more into the 'ignore it and it'll go away' gig."

"Take this," he said, and began to read.

I'm still rehearsing arguments
We never even had
And even when I let me win
I end up feeling bad
Conversations
I've rehearsed so many times
We'll never get 'em right
Concerning
What I'll say when
You say what I know
Will start a fight
Argument Infinite
With no clear goal insight

He pointed to the last word, to be sure I knew he wasn't talking about visibility.

"Wow." My inarticulateness contrasted with his eloquence.

"Is that a good wow or a that-really-sucks kind of wow?" He stared at me intently, and I felt my eyes fill with tears.

"It's a, a, 'I think I've been there' kind of wow," I almost whispered.

"I'm sorry, I didn't mean…"

"No, your poem is wonderful." I dabbed at my eyes. I could almost sense Joe Regan looking at me, and felt embarrassed. But I wasn't embarrassed at Scoobie seeing my tears. *What does that mean?*

"Here you are," I struggled for words. "Trying to get at what's gone on in your life, and I'm sitting here, Miss Preppy," I gestured at my fashionable sweats, "just pretending everything is okay when it really stinks."

He grinned. "It's not always a bad defense mechanism." He grew more serious. "As long as you don't let it go on too long."

"But, enough about me, what do you think about me?" I needed to let the smart ass in me take charge.

He shook his head, but still smiled. "You did that all of eleventh grade, you know."

"What?"

"You know," he said. And I did. If anyone got too close for my comfort zone, which was quite small at that point, I deflected with humor or sarcasm. With Scoobie, usually humor.

I picked up my coffee cup with both hands. I wasn't actually shaking, but no sense making Joe get out the Java Jolt mop.

"You're right. And I guess your poem gets at me now because I argued with Robby so much about his gambling." I grimaced. "Once I caught onto it, dummy that I am."

"Not dumb," he said. "People who don't have an addiction or compulsion don't suspect, or understand."

"Did I do something wrong?"

He was shaking his head at me.

"What if I'd, like, been more understanding…" I stopped as his head-shaking grew more vigorous.

"Your husband was at the point of embezzling from his company." I inwardly cursed George Winters for his thoroughness.

He lowered his voice. "And if I remember the article, he looted your joint money. Who wouldn't be angry?" He paused. "And, it looked to me on the boardwalk the other night that he pissed off someone besides you."

He didn't ask about Pedone, but I volunteered the story. "So," I concluded, "I don't know where Robby is or if I'll ever see him again."

His head had been bent in concentration as he listened to me, and now he looked at me directly. "That'll make it hard for you to address some of the issues you have about what he did."

I smiled wanly. "What are you, a counselor?"

"No." He was quite definite. "Given my history," he grinned, "I've been around a lot of them. Have you, uh, talked to anybody?"

"Nope. Too much to do."

"When you're ready, you will." He shrugged. "Or maybe you won't want to."

"We need a more pleasant topic."

"I'm used to all this stuff, I guess," he said. "OK. What else do you want to talk about?"

"Why does it have to be up to me?"

"Uh oh," he said, glancing out the window. "Those are your dogs, right?"

I turned to look out the window, groaned, pulled on my slicker and was out the door in two seconds. Miss Piggy had climbed onto the bench next to the light post and Mister Rogers was lying under it. She was reaching down with her paw, trying to hit him. Several people were watching. As I walked out I heard a woman say, "She really whacked him last time, maybe we should call someone."

"They're fine," I walked over and started to untie them. "Sometimes they act like cats. They must have grown up with them."

I bent down to entice Mister Rogers to come out from under the bench, and he licked my face, from chin to forehead. "Ugh." He had sand on his tongue. It was hard to guess what he'd been licking off the boardwalk.

"Don't you know about your own dogs?" the woman asked.

I looked up at her as I wiped my face. She was about forty-five and wearing clothes that could only be described as dowdy. I assumed the two young boys with her were her children, so I did not tell her to mind her own business. "They're adopted."

She was still standing there as I separated the dogs' leashes, which had of course become intertwined. "I think it's safe for you to continue your walk." I said this as nicely as I could.

"Humph. I never tie up my dogs outside a store." She turned and walked down the boardwalk, with the two boys craning their necks to watch me.

When she was out of hearing distance, I mumbled, "At least I don't look like one."

"Now, now," Scoobie said, but with laughter in his voice. He had come outside, coffee cup in hand. Miss Piggy jumped up on me and I pulled dog treats from the pocket of my now-dirty slicker and gave her one. "I see the dogs really have you trained," he observed.

"Very funny." I sighed as I looked at the slicker. "I guess I should be going."

"Yeah. Don't want the dogs to get bored." He laughed as he watched me walk away.

CHAPTER FIFTEEN

I WAS NOT IN THE BEST MOOD as Aunt Madge and I drove to the Riordan house. Thoughts of Robby swirled in my mind, every now and then mixed with some about Michael and Scoobie. I'd been separated less than a month, and I was mildly interested in two men. What's wrong with me?

There was no smart retort to this question, so I turned my attention to Aunt Madge, who was driving. "How long will we be part of this circus?"

"If you want, I can take you back." Her tone was sharp, and it surprised me.

"I don't mind helping," I said, chastened.

She relaxed. "You were moody at lunch."

"Yeah, lots of demons in my head."

"You can always join me for church."

I detected a glimmer of amusement. "Thanks, but no."

We drove in silence for a couple moments before I remembered to ask a question that had kept retreating to the back of my mind. "Do you suppose Elmira really saw Michael and his mother arguing?"

Aunt Madge frowned slightly. "Doubtful it was more than a talk about Michael's business or her treatments. She told me Michael wanted her to go someplace like the Mayo Clinic for more aggressive treatment, and Ruth wanted to stay here."

That made sense to me. Anything that made Elmira seem foolish was fine with me. Still, if the discussion was more heated, it was the only piece of the puzzle that could show Michael as less than a doting son. I had to force my expression to relax as we approached the house.

MICHAEL GREETED US at the door and offered coffee. Aunt Madge declined, but since I'd had little of my Java Jolt cup, I accepted. "The hardest part for me," he said, "will be mother's closet, so I figured if we started there I wouldn't mind the rest of it as much."

Aunt Madge complimented him on tackling the toughest part first, and I concentrated on not spilling my coffee as we climbed the stairs.

The walk-in closet was huge, and packed with clothes, shoes, handbags, and more. There was a rack along the back wall for belts and another for scarves. Many of the clothes were housed in garment bags, and a top shelf, which would not be reachable without some sort of stool, held hats, scarves, sweaters, and a couple small overnight bags.

"The funny thing is," Michael said as he watched us eyeing the contents, "Mother didn't spend that much on clothes. She just never threw anything away."

"It could well come back in style," Aunt Madge said.

Michael and I exchanged an amused glance and I thought again that Aunt Madge and Ruth Riordan were well-paired as friends. "Especially if it involves flared pants."

"You're being a twit," Aunt Madge said, simply. "I suggest we have a couple different sorting categories." While I looked at her with my usual respect for her organized mind, she outlined her idea that we have some for the church thrift shop, some for Goodwill (the ones not now in style or more worn), and a few of her better things for Michael.

"I'm really not into cross-dressing," he said.

"You've been with my niece too much." You may have children someday, and it would be nice for them to see a couple of your mother's lovely outfits."

While Michael did not look as if he agreed with this, I knew he wouldn't argue with Aunt Madge. "There's also her costume jewelry. She had some good stuff, which I'll keep for my kids," he nodded at Aunt Madge, "but she didn't go into buying a lot of gold and gems. She had a lot of pretty decent costume stuff."

Aunt Madge nodded while I craned my head, trying to figure out how to get to the top shelves. Michael must have followed my gaze, because he said, "A couple times a year she has Elsie bring in the stepstool from the kitchen, and they change summer stuff for winter, or something like that." He seemed to realize he was talking about his mother in the present tense, and looked away.

With her usual efficiency, Aunt Madge assigned Michael to get the step stool and told me to pull the jewelry stand into the bedroom and start going through it. She began flipping through the clothes, occasionally pulling out a pants suit or dress.

I inched the jewelry stand out of the closet by making it 'walk' on its legs, and Michael lifted it the rest of the way from the walk-in closet into the bedroom when he returned with the stepstool. I half-listened to them talk as they went through things and carried clothes into the bedroom and laid them on the bed in different piles.

Aunt Madge had probably assigned me to the jewelry because she remembered the times Renée or I had gotten into her much smaller jewelry box and tried on the clip earrings and long necklaces that she favored. Naturally, I was the only one who ever broke anything.

It didn't take me long to figure out that almost every necklace had its specific pair of earrings, and I tried to match them. Fortunately, she wasn't into bracelets or rings, so this process was not as complex as it could have been. She easily had forty pairs of earrings. Unfortunately, she was also into clip-ons, so as much as I liked a few of them, I could not ask Michael if I could have a pair or two. Here you are, sorting through a dead woman's jewelry, thinking of yourself.

"Jolie." Michael stood right next to me and I felt myself flush.

"Having a tough time matching colors?" he asked, seemingly amused at my blush.

"Nope. What's up?" I tried to sound professional, as if closet sorting was my occupation.

He held out a round, blue earring that looked as if the small bauble could have been a sapphire. "This was on the floor. You probably have the mate."

I took it. "Haven't seen it. Funny." I turned it over. "If it's a real sapphire it would be a shame to lose the other one."

He shrugged. "Not that it matters now." I winced as he turned away.

I went back to work, glad that it was Aunt Madge working in the close quarters of the closet with Michael. As I sorted and placed sets into the plastic bags I had asked Michael to get from the kitchen, I tried to think of reasons to ask him to do something with me. He said he'd gone to a movie the night before his mother died, so he must like them.

Michael ordered Chinese food, and when it was delivered we went to the kitchen to eat. By that time, I had graduated to folding sweaters, checking the boxes of shoes to see which were the most worn, and going through the dresser drawers to sort summer tops and nightgowns. It was amazing that sorting clothes could get you so tired.

I half-listened as Michael and Aunt Madge talked about tackling the kitchen next, followed by guest bedrooms. Aunt Madge was outlining a timetable for the next week, figuring they could do a couple hours a day. The den would be last, as that's where Michael spent most of his time.

It was such a short while ago that I had sorted through the apartment I'd shared with Robby for six years. A major wave of sadness swept over me.

"Jolie?" I realized this was probably the second time that Aunt Madge had said my name. "Are you okay?"

"Just having a brain fart." I smiled, probably too brightly.

Michael glanced at his watch as Aunt Madge continued. "Are you good for another hour?"

"Sure." Suddenly, I would have preferred to go home and hug Jazz and play with the dogs. "Oh, the dogs. Don't they…"

"Goodness, it's been four hours." Aunt Madge stood. "I can go and come back."

Michael shook his head. "I'm more tired than I expected to be. Why don't you head home, and I'll bring Jolie in a few minutes."

My thoughts swirled as he and Aunt Madge said their goodbyes and he walked her to the door. I was putting the empty food boxes into the trash when he came back into the kitchen.

"So, Gentil," he walked close to me. "You already think I'm kind of arrogant and like to get my own way, right?"

I knew I was flushing and wished I could control it. "And your point would be…?"

His voice was huskier as he pulled me toward him. "Here's what I want now." He pulled me to him and his kiss was long and passionate.

I faced him and stood on my toes as he leaned into me, pushing the small of my back into him. I returned his kiss with the same passion, wondering wildly if I'd thrown away my diaphragm. Then I forgot about everything.

He pulled away first, breathing ragged, and his eyes met mine. "If we don't stop now, I might not want to."

Who said I did? "What are you scared of?" I was fighting for breath.

He relaxed his grip and then swatted me gently on my bottom cheeks. "I'm not scared of anyone but that damn judge."

Reality rushed back. "Now that's a good birth control device." I tried to keep my tone light.

He took my hand and led me to the living room where we plopped on the sofa. "You're a pain in the ass, Jolie, but I like you. I'm just not sure we should rush into anything."

I nodded, realizing he was being a gentleman. Damn it all. "Yeah, we've both been through a lot. So," I had to grin, "have you got any timeframes or sorting methods in mind for this?"

I AWOKE THE NEXT MORNING in a good mood, happy to know someone found me attractive. I wasn't sure what I wanted in the long run, but the prospect of having fun in bed with someone I liked was very appealing. My nose itched and I opened my eyes to see Jazz's tail. "Soon you may not be my only bedmate, you know." She meowed and jumped down, certain that she had my attention, and began pawing the door.

I snuck down the back stairs and fed Jazz in the kitchen while Aunt Madge carried a new thermos of coffee into the guest dining room. Jazz was now willing to be on the floor when the guys were in the room, but if they approached her she took off for the bookcase or for a slide under the sofa.

As she ate I glanced out the sliding glass door. Winter was knocking at the door, as my father used to say. Most of the leaves were off the trees, and I knew that the light wind was a cold one. The sky was overcast, and I thought I remembered that it was supposed to rain later.

If Harry had work for me, I hoped I could get it done in the morning. Otherwise I'd have to dig out some rubber-soled shoes, and I had no idea which box they were in in the closet. I hummed as I showered and dressed. Maybe my life wasn't going to stay in the toilet after all.

WHEN I GOT TO THE OFFICE, Harry had just gotten a call from Lester Argrow, but I could not appraise that house until tomorrow. Lester also thought he had a prospective buyer for another house, who would pay cash. While there was obviously no appraisal required because there was no mortgage, the buyer wanted an objective opinion, as Lester put it, on the value of the house.

"Your buddy Lester said he tried to talk the guy out of getting the appraisal, told the buyer it was a waste of money." Harry chuckled. "I don't think Lester ever thinks about what he's about to say before it pops out."

"I'm certainly not a waste of anyone's money," I informed Harry, who regarded me with an amused expression.

"Feeling your oats?" he asked.

"Just in a good mood." I offered no explanation. Just then the doorbell bonged and the phone rang. I was closer to the door, and immediately wished I had gone for the phone option. Mrs. Jasper waved at me through the pane of glass.

"Come in, won't you?" I wished I had an appraisal. Maybe I could say I had to go to the courthouse.

"Phone's for you, Jolie. It's Jennifer Stenner." Harry did not seem happy about that.

I picked it up and he turned to Mrs. Jasper. "Hey, Jennifer."

"We missed you yesterday," she said.

It took me a couple seconds, and then I remembered the reunion planning meeting. "I should have called. Michael asked Aunt Madge and me to help him sort through some of his mom's things." There was no response. "Jennifer?"

"Of course," she said sweetly, "that would take priority."

"I am sorry," I lied. "I just completely forgot once that came up."

She told me the next meeting was the following Sunday and we hung up. I didn't write it down. When I turned, Mrs. Jasper was at my elbow, and I quickly stepped back.

"You went through Ruth's things?" She appeared more angry than upset. "I told Michael I would help him."

"It was, uh, spur of the moment. He stopped by to see Aunt Madge, and she offered."

She turned and headed for the door. "I'll let you know more later about how we used your donation, Mr. Steele."

As the door shut behind her I turned to Harry. "I did not have anything to do with that."

He shrugged. "I guess she's having trouble adjusting to her friend's death."

I looked at the door, making sure she was out of earshot. "I hope she doesn't bother Michael."

Harry picked up the file on the bungalow I would appraise the next day. "This one is right on the beach. You'll have to look for water marks around the base. And ask them if they put up that vinyl siding in the last few years. I think that area had some flooding a couple years ago, and it might be hiding some water stains."

I DROVE SLOWLY toward the Cozy Corner. Lester Argrow was still our biggest customer, but in terms of dollars he probably had the least sales volume of all the local firms. I wished I could think of new ways to market Steele Appraisals.

Almost on a whim, I turned around and walked toward the Purple Cow. Maybe Ramona could order some magnetic signs for me to put on my car.

Today the white board in front of the store said "Why is it called tourist season if we can't shoot at them?" George Carlin.

I was laughing as I entered the store, and barely had a chance to step out of Ramona's way as she stormed out the door and began to erase the board. She did not look like her usual tranquil self.

I followed her out and watched her write, probably rewrite, her day's slogan. "People are lonely because they build walls instead of bridges." Joseph Fort Newton. This definitely had nothing to do with shooting tourists.

She turned to face me. "It's at least once a week now. It's always something insulting or crude." She walked back into the store and I followed. I had unfortunately missed the crude ones.

Ramona put her marker in a cup that held pencils and pens, and turned to face me. Her expression switched to her usual serene self. "Can I help you with something?"

Still trying to hide my own smile, I asked her about the magnetic signs and she pulled a book off a shelf behind the cash register and began to describe the options. It wasn't too expensive. For seventy-five I could get two small signs that said "Steele Appraisals" and the phone number. I decided to do it without asking Harry, and ordered them.

As she wrote the order, she asked. "A man was asking about you the other day. Did he find you?"

"Someone from high school?"

She shook her head as she wrote. "No. He was from a bigger city, I think."

"Ramona," I waited until she looked up at me, her glasses forward on her nose. "That's really not the kind of description that can help me figure out who you mean."

She went back to her writing. "He was probably a few years older than us and he had patent leather shoes."

Patent shoes? Why was that familiar? *Joe Pedone.* "Did he have black hair, not too tall?"

"That sounds about right." She finished writing the order.

"When was this?"

"Mmm. Let's see, he liked my Shakespeare quote, you know, 'To thine own self be true,' so that was, maybe, last Thursday."

"Did he say why he was looking for me?"

She thought about that for a moment. "I guess not. He just said he knew you."

As I walked out, I was more worried than I'd been since the night on the boardwalk. I headed for the police station.

AFTER TALKING TO SERGEANT Morehouse for what seemed like an eternity, I turned the car toward the Cozy Corner. My mind was playing two tapes almost simultaneously. I was finally really worried about Pedone, but I couldn't think of anything more I could do to protect myself than tell Sgt. Morehouse and take precautions like looking into the back seat of my car before getting in it.

The other issue swirling in my brain, of course, had to do with Michael Riordan's guilt or innocence. If Darla was in Paris, the only other person to benefit financially besides Michael was the maid, Elsie. She hardly seemed a logical suspect. Although...Jennifer Stenner had said that the money Darla would gain if Mrs. Riordan died before the divorce was "hardly worth killing for." Who was to say what Elsie deemed worth killing for?

AFTER LOOKING THROUGH the library's indexes of several years of the *Ocean Alley Press*, my neck was stiff and my stomach growling. The indexes had seemed the logical place to start looking for less-than-complimentary references to Elsie Hammer. The only mention was her photo as one of a group of volunteers at St. Anthony's church's bazaar. Wait. They called her 'Mrs. Hammer.' That made me think I should look for Mr. Hammer. Maybe there was more to him than just car trouble.

I changed my search of the index for the name 'Hammer' without the name Elsie and almost immediately found Mr. Paul Hammer, who had been arrested three years ago for a drunk driving offense. It also mentioned that he was cited for "driving while barred," which meant that he had lost his license for a prior offense. I looked to see if the article gave his address, but it didn't, so I could not tell if he lived where Elsie did.

However, two articles about arrests the next year did give his address, and it was the same as Elsie's. One arrest was for public intoxication and the other for attempted burglary at a house near theirs. I thought about this. There would be fines to pay. I could look that up in court records. Other records at the old courthouse might also tell me if there were serious financial problems, such as a bankruptcy or possibly a court-ordered lien on the house.

I put the microfilm I'd been using back in the drawer and considered what to do next. I could look up the court records the next time I was looking up comps. Or, I could do it now.

AT THE COURTHOUSE I asked for help in looking up judgments against individuals. "Why do you want to know?" asked an older woman with bluish permed hair.

"Maybe I'm doing research for an upcoming trial," I was trying to be civil.

"No you aren't. You're Madge Richards' niece." She peered out me over the top of her half glasses. "You're in some kind of trouble."

"I'm not in trouble! George Winters just writes articles that make it look that way!"

She literally sniffed. "You young people always want to blame someone else."

I almost said something about her salary being paid with my tax dollars, but stopped myself. "It doesn't matter why I want to know. Just show me how to look up the information." She stared at me. "Please," I added.

She told me there was a computer for use by the public in the Clerk of Court's Office down the hall. "Instructions are next to it." She turned her back on me and walked back to her desk.

I fumed as I walked down the hall. *In some kind of trouble.* How I would love to make trouble for George Winters.

There was only one person in front of me, and I practiced patience as I waited. On the walls were photographs of the courthouse, including one of the fire that Uncle Gordon's grandmother had stopped from spreading to the records storage area.

The woman ahead of me left and I stepped up to the computer. A small sign said, "No Internet Access from this computer." *So much for taking a peek at my email.* The instructions were clear, and I did a search for Paul Hammer's name. I had expected it to pop up, but not nine times. He was a busy man.

Mr. Hammer had been arrested four times for driving under the influence, and had lost his license after the third time. He had two burglary convictions, three arrests for public intoxication, and one for lewdness on the beach. As I recalled, this usually meant relieving oneself on the sand. The fines for the second and third drunk driving arrests had been $1,000; for the fourth it was $2,500 and thirty days in the county jail. This was one expensive husband. I can relate to that.

I didn't bother to look up the other fines. Assuming Mr. Hammer's job, if he had one, did not pay much more than Elsie's housecleaning work, his brushes with the law could easily have put them in dire financial straits. Elsie could well have needed the money, but would she have killed for it?

I must have looked puzzled, because the woman behind the counter was looking at me. "Can I help you?" she asked.

She looked as if she meant it. "Would I be able to find out if someone had been served a foreclosure notice on their home?"

If she thought my question odd, she didn't show it. "I can show you if there is a lien."

She came through the swinging half-door and I moved aside. Fingers flying on the keys, she pulled up one screen and then several more, finally ending at a place where I could key in a name. She smiled. "I'll let you take over from here."

"Thanks." *She's worth my tax dollars.*

I keyed in Paul Hammer's name, and found nothing. However, Elsie's name showed a foreclosure notice had been issued just four weeks ago and the bank had placed a lien on the property. I stared at the information for almost a full minute. *She must have used mortgage money to pay his fines, or maybe he was running up other bills. Now they were coming after her house.* She was a better wife than I was. I still resented paying the retainer for Robby's lawyer.

WHEN I GOT BACK TO COZY CORNER I took the portable phone to my room and called Sgt. Morehouse. He wasn't there, and when he called me back a few minute later he was most definitely annoyed at my question about whether he had looked into Paul Hammer as a suspect. When I started to outline my reasons he stopped me.

"I know who he is, and I know his wife had a key to the house."

"And...?" I asked, letting my question hang there.

"And I'm really trying to find a nice way to tell you it's not your business. Besides, the case is with the county's Office of the Prosecuting Attorney and their investigators are doing most of the follow-up work now. You mighta noticed there was a probable cause hearing already."

I deflected his sarcasm with my own. "I did notice. But whether the prosecutor's information came from your office or theirs, it still didn't make a lot of sense to me." He hung up.

CHAPTER SIXTEEN

I DIDN'T HAVE an appraisal until the next day. Aunt Madge and I headed for Michael's. I debated telling her about Elsie or her husband's potential motive, and decided against it. Besides, it might not be Elsie. She might not even have known of the upcoming inheritance until the will was read. I definitely wasn't going to tell Aunt Madge that Joe Pedone had made another appearance in Ocean Alley. There was no point in getting her worried, too.

Aunt Madge and I were sitting amid a kitchen table piled with pots, pans, and plastic storage containers when the doorbell rang and Michael, who had been going through a credenza in the dining room, went to answer it.

Although I couldn't hear what she was saying, I recognized Mrs. Jasper's voice. Aunt Madge gave a low groan, and I grinned. "Maybe," I offered, "You can get her to match the lids for the plastic containers." She frowned at me.

A moment later Michael entered, looking irritated, with Mrs. Jasper close behind him. "I was just telling Michael that he should have called me. I so want to help." She wore a huge smile and a pearl gray pants suit and rose knit top, with an elegant gray handbag. "I even wore pants, so I can get down on the floor."

I almost suggested the basement floor, but said nothing.

"Hello, Henriette." Aunt Madge gestured that she should sit down and gave her the pile of lids to match with the many assorted plastic dishes of all shapes and sizes. I glanced at Michael who nodded toward the dining room, so I excused myself and followed. I was pretty sure Aunt Madge gave me the evil eye, something new for her.

"She said you told her we were doing this," he said as he picked up a silver sugar bowl and made as if he were about to throw it at me.

"Jennifer called Harry's office just as she came in. I guess I told Jennifer why I missed her planning meeting on Sunday."

Hearing that, he did look put out. "That would have been a good time for one of your white lies. How am I going to get rid of her? I can't very well throw her out."

"Put her in a room by herself. Maybe one of the guest rooms. She'll get bored and go home." This was, of course, wishful thinking, but it could work.

"Jolie," came Aunt Madge's voice. "Would you warm up the water for tea?"

I gave Michael a glum look. "Even Aunt Madge doesn't want to be left alone with her for three minutes."

When Michael reentered the kitchen a few minutes later, he suggested that Mrs. Jasper might tackle the guest bath upstairs. "A lot of the stuff under the sink can just be pitched, but if it looks pretty new you could take it to the girls in the teen mother program Mom volunteered with."

I was actually sorry she liked this idea. Aunt Madge and I had been responding to her with mostly "ummms" and Mrs. Jasper had looked as if she might like to leave. Now that she felt useful, she'd stay.

Michael looked pretty pleased with himself as he came back down alone. "That'll give us a few minutes of peace."

"I need to pray for patience," Aunt Madge said as she poured the last bit of now cold tea down the kitchen sink and reached for the kettle.

I decided that if I prayed for anything it would be that Mrs. Jasper get laryngitis. However, this proved unnecessary, as ten minutes later we heard her walking briskly down the steps, and she went to the dining room to tell Michael she had forgotten all about having promised to pick up some food pantry donations, and left.

Aunt Madge had bought frozen bread loaves to cook for the four p.m. guest snack, so we left about two o'clock. The guys needed a walk, and I needed a run to de-stress from the latest Joe Pedone sighting. I had asked Michael if he wanted to come, but he had found a box of photos in the credenza and said he wanted to look through them. I thought I hid my disappointment well.

I RAN UP THE boardwalk until it ended at the far north side of town, then slowed to a walk as began the trek back to Java Jolt. The light breeze was from the ocean today, and I breathed in deeply. I love the smell of the ocean in the fall; it somehow seems cleaner than when the weather is warmer. I would probably like it as much in winter, but it is generally too cold to want to take a deep breath.

Even a run on the boardwalk could not put Elsie and Paul Hammer out of my mind. Elsie would have had access to Michael's pills, and she could have used her key to enter the house at any time – assuming she knew the code to turn off the alarm system once she was in. Though I had not paid much attention to her after Mrs. Riordan's funeral, my impression was that she was upset about her employer's death. Maybe she was just an accomplished actor.

Gradually I grew aware of footsteps behind me and remembered Pedone. I looked over my shoulder and saw Scoobie walking with his head down and hands in the pocket of an old wool pea jacket that looked as if it was a Salvation Army reject. I stopped and waited for him. When he came closer I realized he had trimmed his hair and beard. I called to him.

He must have been deep in thought, because he stopped abruptly and at first seemed not to recognize me. When he did, he gave his most charming smile. "Perfect. Do you have a library card?" he asked.

"For Lakewood," I waited for him to say why this was pertinent to a walk on the boardwalk.

"You could get one here." He was even with me now and we walked together. "They won't let me check out *The Prophet* for a while. You could do it for me."

For a moment his request didn't register, then I realized he meant the book by Khalil Gibran. "Uh, I guess I could. A favorite of yours?"

"If you would indeed behold the spirit of death, open your heart wide unto the body of life. For life and death are one, even as the river and the sea are one." He grinned. "Thus speaks the Prophet."

The Scoobie I remembered could not have told you who Gibran was when we were in high school. My father liked the Lebanese-American poet, so I would have recognized his name, but certainly could not have quoted him, then or now.

"So, did Gibran replace John Lennon as your philosopher of choice?"

"You know, they aren't all that different. *Life is what happens to you while you're busy making other plans.*" When I said nothing, he asked, "John Lennon too heavy for you?"

We turned from the boardwalk onto Sea View, to walk the two blocks to the library. "Not too heavy. Not 'too' anything. Just…different from the Scoobie I used to know."

"Everyone changes." His tone lightened. "For example, I bet you haven't been on the roof of the school since you've been back."

I had to laugh at that. Scoobie had been in detention for stuffing the ballot box for the student government election (his candidate had been Mickey Mouse), and he wanted a distraction.

"You know," I told him, "if you had opened the window a little wider, I could have gotten Minnie and Goofy into your detention, too." I had two small plastic toys attached to a long string and was angling to get them into the classroom through the window.

"You're the one who made all that noise walking on the roof," he said.

"Who knew there was all that gravel up there?" I had been lucky I wasn't caught. The back of the west wing of the school was a berm, and I had just made it down the earthen hill when the head custodian came out the side door. Apparently the detention monitor, an older history teacher named Mrs. Hamilton, had thought the black Minnie Mouse that I had gotten into the window was a large spider. I had wondered what the screaming was all about.

Scoobie started laughing so hard he sat on the pavement. I grew aware of curious stares, and a couple disapproving ones from people coming out of the hardware store, so I sat next to him. "What? What's so funny?"

"Spider," he gasped.

I waited for his laughing to wind down, and said, "We should have known she was half-blind. Remember how she kept pointing to the Philippines and insisting those islands were Japan?" That sent him into another spasm, and I became aware of the cold pavement under my butt.

I stood and extended a hand to him. He took it, and when he stood he grabbed me in a hug that was tight and close. I was so surprised I relaxed into him. When he pulled back, I saw tears in his eyes. "Where have you been the last ten years, Jolie Gentil?"

"In another dimension," I said, softly.

He let go and said, "Me, too."

We walked the rest of the way to the library without speaking.

I had not been in the library since eleventh grade, and would not have recognized it if I'd been brought in blindfolded and told to guess my location when the blindfold was removed. No more drab colors. The card catalogs that had lined the wall had been replaced by walls of vivid orange and yellow and a group of computers in the middle of the room. Each one was occupied.

Each one was occupied.

The woman at the checkout desk eyed Scoobie as he left me and went into the stacks. When her gaze turned to me, she smiled and I recognized her as a classmate, the only black girl on the cheerleading squad. I had no clue as to her name.

"Well, Jolie Gentil. Everyone knows you're back in town." She laughed. "Still hanging around with Scoobie."

Thank goodness for nametags. "Daphne. It's been a long time." I paused. "I may be causing some trouble. He wants me to get a card so I can take out…"

"The Prophet," she finished. "It's required reading for Senior Honors English at the high school, so I know there will be kids who want it. Otherwise, I just keep letting him check it out."

"I wonder if he'd let me buy him one?"

She shook her head. "He has to have that particular copy."

Scoobie emerged from the stacks, his eyes bright. "How about if I buy the library a copy?" I asked quietly.

"That would be good," Daphne said. "Scoobie, you are so ornery.". She smiled slightly at him as she said it and handed me the brief application for a card.

He grinned, and teased her about being too strict as I wrote out my name and address. "Hey, Daphne. It says I need to show you something with my local address."

She gave a low hoot. "Girl, everyone in town knows you're back."

As we turned to go, I felt a wave of sadness. I hadn't realized Scoobie had so many quirks. Maybe he really was sick or something.

Elmira Washington came through the door, nearly bumping into me. I took a second to feel glad that she had been embarrassed in court, since I still resented that she had told Harry (and surely others) about my life's spiral in Lakewood.

"Daphne," she said, very excited, "Judge Rommer is going to announce his findings about Ruth's son going to trial."

"When?" I asked.

She recognized me and stiffened slightly. "In a few minutes."

"Come on, Scoobie." I grabbed his arm and almost pulled him from the library as he stuffed the book in his knapsack.

"You're going to the courthouse?" He said it as if it were a dirty word.

I slowed. "Oh, yeah. Not your favorite place?"

He shook his head. "On the other hand, since they won't be talking about me, I suppose it won't be so bad." He grinned, but grew more serious when he saw my face. "What is it about this guy? He wouldn't have given you, or me, the time of day in school."

That was definitely the question of the hour. All I said was, "I just don't think he did it, and I don't like to see anyone get railroaded." I looked down at my burgundy sweats and realized I was not dressed for court. I could only imagine what my hair looked like.

As we approached the courthouse I saw the local TV station crew setting up. Their cameras wouldn't be allowed in the courtroom, but they would try to grab people on the way in or out. I made sure we steered clear of them as we climbed the steps.

"It's way before eight-thirty," Scoobie said. "You should call your aunt."

So, he remembered Aunt Madge's sleep schedule. "You're right." I pulled my phone from my purse, but there was no answer at Cozy Corner. "I can't believe they just scheduled this at the spur of the moment," I fumed.

Scoobie stared around the courtroom as we sat. "Definitely better from this side of the witness stand," he said.

Aunt Madge squeezed in next to him. "Henriette Jasper just called to tell me." She nodded at me, then looked at Scoobie. "And how are you, Adam?"

"Not bad. You still make the best muffins in town?"

Her worried expression softened. "Thanks. You can stop by every now and then."

I couldn't see Michael anywhere and assumed he would come in with good old Winona. The smell of rotting food reached me and my eyes traveled to Scoobie's knapsack. I hadn't picked up on it when we were outside. "What the hell is in there?"

"Could be anything. I haven't cleaned it out for a couple days."

"Don't eat it, dear," Aunt Madge said absently as she scanned the growing crowd.

"Hot times in Ocean Alley," Scoobie said to me in a low voice.

He was right. Murders were rare, that of a wealthy woman more so. George Winters slid into a seat behind what would be the defense table. I wished for Scoobie's old squirt gun. I'd put grape soda in it. Winter's rumpled gray suit would look even worse.

Prosecuting Attorney Small and a couple staff members walked out, and he didn't look pleased. I took that as a good sign. I strained to look for Annie Milner, but she wasn't there. A moment later Michael and Winona Mason came out of a side door. He scanned the room and started to smile when he saw me. His expression froze at the sight of Scoobie, and he nodded before he sat down.

"All rise," said a bailiff, and Judge Rommer entered and sat at the bench. After again explaining that the purpose of the probable cause hearing had been to determine if the evidence supported going to trial, Judge Rommer said he found it to be "entirely circumstantial" and that a motive was "lacking." There was a major rumble of conversation that died as he used his gavel. Michael lowered his head and then raised it to look at the judge.

"Mr. Riordan." Michael stood. "The case against you can be reopened if the prosecuting attorney finds additional evidence." There was a brief buzz from onlookers and he cleared his throat and it quieted. "However, from where I sit, it looks as if the police and Mr. Small should be exploring other avenues."

I felt a huge wave of relief and didn't listen as the judge made a few more comments. Aunt Madge reached over and touched my shoulder and blew me an air kiss.

"Lucky stiff," Scoobie murmured.

When the judge rose to leave I expected Michael to turn to us, but he walked through the same door he had entered, ignoring calls from George Winters.

CHAPTER SEVENTEEN

NO MICHAEL ALL AFTERNOON. I needn't have rushed through my shower or shaved my legs. Aunt Madge figured he had a lot of calls to make, and she was probably right. I prowled around the house and finally settled in Aunt Madge's sitting room with a book. I promptly fell asleep.

In my dream I was on a ship trying to find a pier to tie to in Ocean Alley. I was in Uncle Gordon's old dory, which was painted bright red. The boat started to shake and I sat up suddenly. Michael grinned at me. "I hope you were dreaming about me."

I shook my head to clear it. "Indirectly." I held up my arms and he knelt down for a quiet hug. He smelled like the brisk sea breeze, and I could have sat there for an hour. The popping of a champagne cork jarred us after a few seconds, and Michael stood.

"I would have opened that, Madge," he said.

She looked at us both. "It's my pleasure." She held up the bottle. "Our guest brought celebratory alcohol."

I laughed and swung off the couch. Jazz was zooming around the floor, batting the cork, and Mister Rogers and Miss Piggy appeared to be agonizing on the porch because they were not included.

Aunt Madge poured and Michael handed me a glass. When we each had one, he raised his. "To the American system of justice, which only cost me my reputation and almost $20,000."

I almost spit into my champagne. "Wow." I recovered in time to take a sip. "Do you get it back?"

"No way." He seemed bitter, and I didn't blame him.

"We need to focus on gratitude," Aunt Madge said.

From anyone else it would have sounded patronizing, or at least corny.

"It's hard for me, Madge, but I'll work on it," Michael said quietly. Then he took a long gulp of champagne.

We moved to the couch and Aunt Madge let the guys in. "Stay down!" she commanded, and they walked rapidly around the room and settled at her feet as she sat across from Michael and me. I looked around and saw that Jazz had jumped on the back of the sofa and sat next to Michael.

"So," I felt a need to break the silence. "What's next now that you're footloose and fancy free?" I wanted him to say something about going over to his place, and not to sort his mother's belongings.

"I'm not free yet," he looked moodily at the dogs. "I've got to go to Washington."

"Washington!" Aunt Madge and I said in unison.

"My firm seems to have inflated some oil prices when we passed costs to customers in California. We're being investigated by some federal energy regulators and maybe a congressional committee."

Several seconds passed before Aunt Madge said, "Were you involved?"

"Not knowingly," he said. "And I think the investigators believe that."

"Why?" I regretted the speed of my question as soon as the word was out of my mouth.

"Because, Ms. Detective, my bank account did not inflate at the rate of my partners'."

"Thank heavens for small favors," Aunt Madge said.

"Yeah, less for Darla to get." He finished his champagne.

"When do you go?" I asked.

I saw the amusement in his eyes, and figured he knew why I asked. "Not for a couple days."

The phone rang and I jumped. As Aunt Madge got up to answer it he slipped his arm around me and leaned close. "Any reason you're so jumpy?"

His breath was warm on my temple and he kissed me lightly. Warmth spread through me and I felt my nipples tighten. "Must be the change in your legal status." I didn't want to be a smart ass, but it is my most familiar behavior.

"Jolie," Aunt Madge held out the phone. "It's Sgt. Morehouse."

"What does he want?" Michael asked, in a harsh tone.

Aunt Madge's face asked the same question as I took the phone.

"Ms. Gentil," he began, "You didn't happen to call the station early this afternoon, did you?"

"Absolutely not."

He sighed. "I figured it wasn't you."

"Why do you ask?"

"Can't tell you that. Might be nothing." He said goodbye and hung up without giving me a chance to say anything else.

"He's just trying to harass you," Michael said when I explained what the sergeant had asked. I wasn't sure I agreed with him, but chose not to pick a fight.

"Why don't you two go out," Aunt Madge suggested.

The phone rang again and she smiled as she listened and handed it to Michael.

He took it with a questioning look, and then his face lit up. "Dad."

Aunt Madge and I walked back toward the couch. "I think he's in town."

My heart sank. *Are we never going to get a break?*

Michael hung up and turned to us. "I can't believe he did that. I called him this morning to say the judge was going to announce his findings, and he got in his car and drove straight to the airport. I wondered why I couldn't get him this afternoon."

"That's great," I didn't mean it.

"And the best thing is that Honey doesn't get here until tomorrow."

"Keep an eye on your mom's knick-knacks." I clapped my hand over my mouth.

He shook his head. "You don't have to tell me she's a gold digger." He turned to Aunt Madge. "I can't thank you enough."

She waved a hand. "You just did. Your mother would be proud."

When he bent to give me a kiss I thought his eyes looked misty.

THOUGH I HAD AN APPRAISAL TO do the next day, I was slow to get up. I was happy, wasn't I? As I fed Jazz I told myself I was just impatient at having to wait to spend time, quality time I told myself, with Michael.

It was well past guest breakfast time so I padded around the kitchen in my slippers and bathrobe. Aunt Madge must be at the grocery store. I had finally figured that she went each day as a way of seeing people.

The phone rang and I was surprised to hear Scoobie's voice. "Could you, like, come bail me out?"

In the background, I heard Sgt. Morehouse say, "I told you, you aren't under arrest."

"You want me to come down there?" I asked him.

"Yeah."

I dressed without showering and drove the short distance to the police station. The desk clerk seemed to be expecting me and ushered me into Sgt. Morehouse's very small office. A visibly upset Scoobie sat in the chair next to his desk, his foot tapping fast and his eyes anxious.

"What's up?" I wasn't sure who to ask, so I looked at both of them.

"He thinks I did it!" Scoobie shouted.

"No, I don't," Morehouse yelled. "Put a cork in it for one minute!"

"Both of you, calm down." I used my best Aunt Madge voice. They stared at me. "You start." I pointed at Sgt. Morehouse.

"I got this call yesterday, and this woman with a funny voice says I should look for Scoobie if I wanted Ruth Riordan's murderer."

"Wrong!" Scoobie said.

"Lemme finish," Morehouse growled. "She said to check his knapsack and I'd find some rare coins that had been in the house."

"Your basic circumstantial evidence," Scoobie said.

Morehouse looked like he would like to gag him. "I know that," he snapped. "I found Scoobie this morning at Java Jolt, and the coins were in his knapsack."

"Along with some other great-smelling stuff," I smiled to Scoobie.

"Nah, I tossed the old crab cakes before that." He seemed to be getting calmer.

"All I'm asking," Morehouse said, "Is that you think where you were with that knapsack."

"That's all?" Scoobie asked.

"That's what I been trying to tell you for half a damn hour," Morehouse said.

Scoobie thought about this. "Well, I was at the courthouse yesterday, with Jolie."

"And the library before that." I added, and he nodded. "And after the courthouse?"

"The library, and the diner near it, and then the library again." He thought some more. "Then back to where I sleep."

"Still at the place on F Street?" Morehouse asked. When Scoobie nodded, he continued. "And you had the knapsack with you the entire time?"

"Heck no. I always leave it at my table in the library when I go to the diner." I must have looked at him oddly, because he added, "It's near the reference desk. Nobody bothers my stuff."

Morehouse sighed. "Anyone could have dropped them in there."

"I'm glad you don't think it's Scoobie," I said, quietly. "How do you even know the coins were from Mrs. Riordan's house?"

"Michael and his father are coming down later this morning, but they checked and a small bag of silver dollars from the 1800s was missing from a cabinet in the den."

"Which I didn't take," Scoobie said.

"I think," Morehouse glared at him, "that whoever killed her took them in case their frame of Michael didn't work." He shrugged. "Or maybe they wanted a memento. Some weirdoes do that."

"So, Scoobie can leave?" I asked.

Sgt. Morehouse nodded at him. "Just do me a favor and think if you saw anyone near the knapsack." He paused. "And try not to let it get to you. You been having a good couple years."

Scoobie didn't say anything, but picked up his knapsack and walked out.

"Thanks," I said quietly to Morehouse.

"I'll say it again," he said with a hint of a smile. "You sure know how to pick 'em."

I hurried from his office, wanting to catch up to Scoobie, and bumped into Larry Riordan, with Michael behind him, his head turned and eyes on Scoobie as he walked out of the station.

"Miss Richards, is it?" Larry asked.

"It's Jolie Gentil. I'm Madge Richards' niece," I extended a hand, reluctantly accepting that I'd have to find Scoobie in a few minutes.

"Jolie, were you here with that loser?" Michael asked, frowning.

"He called me. He was upset." I was angry at his characterization of Scoobie, but tried not to let it show.

"He may have killed my mother you know," he said, voice rising.

"He didn't. Ask Sgt. Morehouse."

"Why were you sitting with him in the courtroom yesterday, anyway?" he asked.

Larry Riordan shifted slightly, and I sensed his discomfort. "Because he's my friend."

"Your friend? He's a pothead. He hasn't done anything with his life." Michael's face was red.

"He, he writes beautiful poetry. And you're, you're arrogant as hell!" I nearly ran out of the station.

I DROVE AROUND for quite a while, checking the library and Java Jolt before I gave up on finding Scoobie. *When would I ever learn?*

I went by Harry's to pick up the material about the house I was to appraise. My anger was so close to the surface that I almost snapped at Harry. *Men are such jerks.*

"You don't look as happy as I thought you would, after the judge's ruling yesterday." He started to say something else and stopped.

"I'm sorry." I almost sighed the response. "Just a lot on my mind, and I'm a little worried about Scoobie."

He nodded. "I don't really know him of course, just see him around town." He fiddled with a file on his desk. "He's lucky to have you for a friend."

I sensed he wanted to say something else. "And…"

"You've had a lot going on in your life lately." He looked at me very directly. "It might be tempting to help Scoobie in some way, but you know he has to find his own path."

With a brief nod, I picked up the appraisal file from his desk and managed to thank him for caring.

ELSIE HAMMER'S HOUSE was half a block from the house I was appraising, and I glanced at it as I drew close. An unkempt looking man of indeterminate age walked out the side door. I slowed a bit and watched him light a cigarette and walk toward the pickup truck in the driveway. I frowned. Didn't Paul Hammer have his driving license revoked? A voice in the back of my brain chimed in. Is this really any of your business?

A couple houses down I pulled over and looked in the rear view mirror. Sure enough, the pickup pulled out of the driveway with a man at the wheel. I told myself it didn't have to be Paul Hammer, though if anyone met the stereotype of a disheveled drunk it was he. I busied myself with my purse as he drove by, then for reasons unknown even to me I waited for him to drive a block down the street and followed him. He drove around the block and made his way toward the center of Ocean Alley and pulled into the Burger King parking lot.

I sat at a traffic light. See Jolie, not everyone's up to no good. But no sooner had I chastised myself than he walked across the street, toward the building on the opposite corner – the Sandpiper Bar and Grill. He tripped as he got to the curb and almost stumbled. He seemed to have had a good start on his drinking. For a couple seconds I wondered why he had parked at Burger King, then realized the police probably knew his truck and if they saw it on the street near a bar they'd look for him inside.

I didn't even think of minding my own business as I got to the next red light. My cell phone was in the side pocket of my purse. "Nuts, I don't have a phone book." Under my seat was the Lakewood phone directory, a good resource for any realtor working there to have at hand, but useless in Ocean Alley. I debated whether I wanted to call 9-1-1; I didn't. The Purple Cow was two doors down, so I headed there.

Roland looked up as the door chimed, and a quick frown creased his brow and left as he nodded at me. I nodded back. "I'm not here to bug Ramona."

"Can I help you with something?" he asked.

"May I use your phone book?"

He walked the few steps to the counter and pulled it out. "You need a phone?"

I started to say no, but changed my mind. Maybe I didn't want my name showing up on the Police Department caller ID. "If you don't mind."

He walked about a dozen feet away and began to straighten a table of discounted goods.

Morehouse took about five minutes to get on the line. I figured he was hoping I'd go away. Once I began to say where I had seen a man I assumed was Paul Hammer he interrupted me and got off the phone. Since I was in the Purple Cow, I stayed on the phone for the several minutes he was gone; otherwise I would have hung up. If he didn't want to hear about someone driving with a suspended license did I really care? Of course you care. *The next car he hits could be Aunt Madge's.*

"Sorry to keep you waiting, Jolie. I wanted to get someone over to the Sandpiper right away."

Gulp. "No problem. "I guess I don't know anything more…"

"If it comes to it, would you be willing to tell Martin Small or his people what you saw?"

My stomach did a back flip. "Umm, I guess so," I straightened my shoulders. "Of course. He could hurt someone."

"How the hell did you notice him, anyway? I wouldn't think you knew him."

I embellished a bit, telling him I was driving by Elsie's house and saw him stumble as he got into the truck, which got my attention. I could almost see him roll his eyes. There was a slight pause. "I'd hate to think you were sticking your nose someplace it didn't belong."

"I'm not spying on Elsie, if that's what you mean. You can ask Harry if he just gave me a house to appraise a block from the Hammer's." He either believed me or was tired of me, because he thanked me and hung up with his usual style, which meant no goodbye.

When I turned to thank Roland for the use of his phone he was only about three feet from me, and I jumped. "Sorry," he said. "I wanted to tell you that you did a good thing. Paul Hammer is one evil man."

"I don't really know him, just heard he had a lot of DUIs and lost his license."

"That's not the half of it." He walked behind the counter and put the phone back on a shelf under the cash register. "My wife and I went to high school with Elsie and Paul. He gets more like his old man every year." Seeing the question on my face, he added, "He skipped a lot of school and stuff like that, but nothing more. But the older he gets the more he drinks. My wife thinks maybe he hits Elsie sometimes."

"Good God." Though I did not consider my life to be protected from the real world (especially in the last few weeks), I had never actually met someone who beat his wife. *Not that I know of.*

"So, does Elsie not have anywhere else to go…?"

"She's had offers." He glanced around. "I shouldn't really say, but my wife works in the ER. I know they talked to her a couple times when she came in." He shrugged. "Nancy, my wife, says Elsie is always emphatic that she fell or something."

I thought about how stressed Elsie looked the day Lester and I barged in on her. Sounded as if Paul Hammer was a lot more trouble than a flat tire would indicate. I shook my head slightly. "I hope I didn't buy her more trouble."

Roland looked puzzled for a minute, then caught on. "Oh, if he's pi.. irritated if he gets arrested." He thought for a moment. "I'll ask Nancy to give her a call. Maybe invite Elsie out for supper."

A customer came in, and I left. I knew I did the right thing, but if it meant Elsie got a black eye, or worse, it would be awful.

I was still feeling heartsick about Elsie's situation as I pulled into the driveway of the Cape Cod house on the west edge of town, facing the beach. I concentrated on an attitude adjustment as I stepped out of the car, and promptly stumbled on a child-size green football. "Sorry," a woman called from the back doorway, which faced the driveway. "I didn't quite get finished picking up the yard."

I glanced around at the toys that littered it, and heard shouts of play from the front. "It's okay," I limped forward. "We really only look at the house itself, not stuff that's around."

She hovered by me until I found a polite way to tell her she was driving me nuts. The house had a lived-in look that spoke of an active family rather than poor housekeeping or neglect. As I was measuring the dining room a naked boy of about two ran through, followed by an older sister, clutching a diaper. "Come on, Randy," was all she said, and I sensed this was a regular routine.

Though it was a difficult house to measure, I didn't mind, and even found myself relaxing. By the time I left it was hard not to laugh at Randy as he ran out the back door, again buck naked. "Don't worry, he'll be in real soon, it's cold," the mom said as she reached for a hooded sweatshirt hanging on a hook and stepped into the yard after me.

When Lester appeared at the Register of Deeds Office as I researched for comps, I remembered he probably looked for me on the days he knew I was appraising one of his sales. Crafty guy.

"Did you hear the latest?" he asked.

"Depends on what it is."

"I heard they're questioning that pothead, Scrubbie, about Ruth Riordan's murder."

"It's Scoobie, and the police asked him to help with some information, that's all." I forced myself to think about the information I was writing rather than my desire to scream at Lester.

He pushed up the sleeve of his suit so he could reach into his pocket for a handkerchief and blew his nose loudly. "How do you know that?"

"You know what they say about that little bird." The weak smile I gave him was the best I could do. Before he could ask anything else I said, "I hear you have a cash sale coming up."

"Yeah, I love those. Get my commission really fast." He blew his nose again, emitting a loud, squeaky sound.

Such a gentleman.

"Harry tells me I can do the appraisal tomorrow." I shut the ledger I was looking in and closed my own notebook.

"Yeah, but not until late afternoon. It's vacant, and it's supposed to rain. The buyer wants you to see if any water seeps in anywhere."

I DROVE AROUND FOR ANOTHER half hour and then parked and headed for the boardwalk. I had no idea where Scoobie's "permanent half-way house" was on F Street, and probably wouldn't have gone there anyway. After walking up and down the boardwalk for an hour and peering into Java Jolt twice, I gave up and headed back to the Purple Cow, my local news source.

This time I actually liked what was on the white board. "The greatest part of our happiness or misery depends on our disposition and not on our circumstances." Martha Washington.

"That would be a good quote for Scoobie," I said, as Ramona walked up.

"He thought so, too," she replied.

"He was here? When?"

The feathers on the top of her brown felt hat looked as if they would fall off as she tilted her head back, seemingly deep in thought. "Oh, maybe an hour ago."

"Did he seem, um, normal?" I asked.

She shrugged. "For Scoobie. He said you helped him at the police station."

"He wasn't in trouble. I guess he was just mad that Sgt. Morehouse hauled him down there."

She nodded. "He gets upset sometimes." She leaned closer. "I think the pot used to calm him, but he swore off it. I told him that was good. It's supposed to lower a man's sperm count, you know."

Because Roland wasn't around, I didn't buy anything. I gathered he hadn't mentioned my phone call to Morehouse, or Ramona would have asked me about it. She promised to tell Scoobie I was looking for him, and I headed back to Aunt Madge's.

Her car was gone, but Scoobie sat on the porch, collar of his pea jacket up around his ears, writing in his steno pad. The late afternoon temperature had fallen to about forty degrees, and he was glad to be invited in for a cup of tea.

"I've been writing. Want to read it?" I turned up the kettle and sat next to him at the kitchen table.

You ask
What is this
That you call soul?
It is the stuff
That makes me whole
Not just me
No
But rather
Uniquely me
And it is not for sale
It used to be

"That looks like a good beginning," I was never certain what to say about poetry.

"It might be the whole thing," he said.

We sipped our tea in silence until I said, "You seem to be feeling better about Morehouse."

"I'm not, but I reminded myself I can't do anything about it." He kept studying the poem, and then said, "Whatever happened to that guy from the boardwalk?"

"He seems to be still around. Ramona said he was asking about me."

"Ramona. She's always on my side."

I thought that was an odd thing to say, but decided he meant she was supportive.

"If he's around, you should be careful." He drank more tea. "And the other man, he was your husband?"

I thought Scoobie knew this, and decided he was just checking up on my safety. "Robby'll be my ex-husband eventually. He...well, you know he flushed a lot of money down the toilets that masquerade as slot machines at the Atlantic City casinos. I guess he borrowed money from the wrong people."

He drank the last of his tea and stood. "Hope you didn't mind that I called this morning."

"Nope." I grinned. "I won't say 'any time.'"

He hoisted his knapsack. "You call me if that guy bothers you."

"Thanks." I walked him to the door and was touched when he kissed me on the cheek as he left.

CHAPTER EIGHTEEN

EVEN THOUGH THE APPRAISAL was not until afternoon I was up early. I'd been thinking about Elsie Hammer as I fell asleep, and my sleep was fitful. When I got downstairs, Mister Rogers was running through the great room, ears flapping behind him, making circles around the couch. I let him into the back yard and looked at Miss Piggy, who only yawned.

As I walked into the kitchen area I saw the cause of his consternation. A mound of chewed plastic, formerly a bowl, sat in the middle of the floor. Aunt Madge hadn't been kidding about their affinity for prunes. I made Miss Piggy get up and was ushering her out the door when Aunt Madge came out of her bedroom, dressed for the day. I held up the remains of the bowl.

"Drat. I must not have shut the door to the pantry completely." She took the bowl and threw it in the trash and began to make coffee, muttering to herself about the trouble the dogs caused.

I pulled out two mugs for us and began to thumb through the paper. Yesterday's paper had reported on the judge's finding, and today's had a caustic editorial about how the prosecuting attorney had based the case against Michael on "pretty flimsy" evidence. It urged the police to solve the murder quickly, for the sake of the family and the tourist trade. At least they had put family before tourism.

"I'm going back to Ruth's today, probably for the last time. Can you help?" Aunt Madge asked. When I hesitated, Aunt Madge added, "Michael won't be there. He's leaving for DC this morning."

"I guess he told you I called him arrogant, huh?"

"Not in so many words, but he didn't ask where you were, and all Larry said was that they had run into you at the police station." She took out the muffin batter she had stored in the freezer. "He's not an easy man to be with, I suppose."

"I'm not always eggs-over-easy either." I thought about it for a moment. "I don't have any business falling for anybody now. It hasn't even been two months."

"It's not a matter of time, just who the person is." She glanced at me. "You'll know if it's right."

"Bottom line is, I'll go," I told her, "But I have to leave by three to do an appraisal."

Before we left a couple hours later I checked the small backyard for signs that the dogs had done their business. From the look of the small mulched flower bed and bricked walkway, they had done a month's worth. I let them in, and they waited patiently on a scatter rug while I wiped their paws.

Aunt Madge and I took separate cars, since I was going to work after we helped at the Riordans'. It looked as if it would drizzle or rain lightly all day. I was glad I'd found my sturdy shoes, as any work I did outside the house I was appraising would involve sandy muck.

AUNT MADGE HADN'T MENTIONED that Larry Riordan would be at the house, but I found him much easier to be around than his son. Honey was another matter. She followed me from room to room as I checked in closets and drawers for anything that looked like a family heirloom or memento Michael might like to keep. He was going to keep these and a few pieces of furniture and have an estate sale company take away the rest of the house's contents.

I thought I'd gotten away from Honey when she went downstairs to have coffee, but I heard her and Larry coming up the stairs. I had spread much of the costume jewelry on the bed, trying to decide what to donate to the Church Thrift Store and what to put in a box for the sale, and was sorry she was going to see it all. Surely she would want something.

Larry had a forlorn look about him, and I recalled that Mrs. Murphy had said she thought he and Ruth might have gotten back together if he hadn't met Honey when he did. I tried to be charitable, remembering that he had lived in this house for many years and it must be hard to see it being picked through and packed.

"Hi, hon," Honey said brightly. "Got your work cut out for you in here, don't you?" She walked to the bed and began surveying the jewelry. "She sure liked rose and purple, didn't she?"

"Pretty much." I picked up the single earring that had been on the closet floor the other day and placed it in the drawer of the bedside table. No point wrapping it up; besides, I might yet find the other one.

"Larry, I noticed some mahogany carved ducks in the den. Were they yours?"

He brightened. "I don't think Michael will mind if I take them. Ruth gave them to me for Christmas a number of years ago."

Honey seemed put out by that comment, so I put her to work packing the jewelry in tissue paper and placing it in shoe boxes that would go to the church thrift store.

I LEFT PROMPTLY AT two-forty-five, and Aunt Madge walked out with me. She had again bought the frozen bread loaves from the store, and I kidded her about becoming a lady of leisure. "Oh, I don't think I'll stop baking bread as long as my fingers can knead it. It's a very satisfying feeling, having your hands in that soft dough."

Lester had given me the key to the house the day before, so I didn't need to stop by his office. However, he had asked that I drop it back there between four and four-thirty p.m. I sensed he was more interested in me than the key, and then chided myself about thinking I was some kind of glamour girl.

The two-story house on G Street was toward the south side of town in an area comprised almost totally of summer rentals. It was clean and furniture-free, so I worked quickly. I finished measuring all of the rooms on the ground floor and then opened the utility closet door in the kitchen to verify that the central air and furnace systems were as young as the owner indicated.

"Surprised?" Joe Pedone asked, as he grabbed my wrist.

He was so quick I didn't even have time to scream. He swung me around and pressed my back to him, clapping his hand to my mouth.

"I was just trying to collect some money. Money rightfully due to my boss," he squeezed harder as he said this, "and you had to go make it personal."

When I tried to pull away he just pressed harder against my ribs, and within a few seconds I found it hard to breathe, even through my nose. *Think, think!* In a self-defense class in college the teacher said never to try to kick a man in the balls, because we were so programmed not to injure men in that area that we might hesitate. No worries there, but I wasn't in a good position to do it.

"You had to go to the police," he hissed in my ear. "You lost me my job. Boss doesn't want troublemakers on the payroll." He pushed my face against the refrigerator and held me there with one hand and a knee jammed in my back as he reached in a drawer next to it and pulled out a pre-cut piece of duct tape and forced it over my mouth. My heart was pounding so hard I wouldn't have gotten out a scream even if I had the breath for it.

He threw me on the floor and reached in his pocket and pulled out a wad of strips of cloth. When he reached down I sat up halfway and tried to push myself away.

"Bitch!" He grabbed my arm and reached for the other one. He may have been short, but he was really strong. As he bent over I kicked him hard in the knee, and when he yelled in pain I did it again. Suddenly he was on the floor, but the kitchen was narrow and he was blocking any escape route.

I tried to pull the duct tape off, but just barely had it loose when he lunged at me again. In an instant I went from overwhelmed with fear to angrier than I could remember feeling. This time I aimed my elbow at his eye and hit him with all the force I could muster.

"Ow! Aagh!" He covered his eye with both hands and I jumped up and ran past him. He was running after me in two seconds and I could hear him breathing hard. I'd never make it outside; it was too hard to breathe and I was winded.

I made a sharp left into the master bedroom and lunged into the bathroom. I almost had the door shut when he rammed it with his shoulder. I braced myself against it, the rubber soles of my shoes giving me traction on the tiled floor. I grabbed at the duct tape, finished yanking it off, and took a deep breath.

I still couldn't scream. I pressed my shoes against the floor. I had to keep him out! *Breathe in. Breathe out.*

"You bastard," I gasped. And I yelled "help" with all my might.

He jumped back from the door and I pushed it shut, turned the bolt and sank to the floor with my head between my knees. I could hear him breathing hard. "Next time. There will be a next time." I heard him run out, and I slumped to my side and began to sob.

It was several minutes before I could stop. If I hadn't needed to wipe my nose on the toilet paper I probably would have lain there crying for twice as long.

Blearily I sat up and took stock. My purse with the mobile phone was in the kitchen, probably on the floor, but I wasn't leaving this room. Pedone might be out there. The window was too high to climb out without standing on a chair, which I didn't have, but I thought I could get it open and yell. For all the good it had done me a couple minutes ago. Almost all the nearby houses were closed for the season. Lucky for me, Pedone didn't know that, which I supposed was why he left. *Or did he really leave?*

I stood and rubbed my ribs. The window was the old casement type with a lever to open it. I tugged for almost a minute and couldn't get the lever to turn. Unfortunately, the window was frosted, so even when I stood on tiptoes and looked out the lower part of the glass I couldn't tell if Pedone was just outside, maybe with a gun. *Don't be ridiculous. This isn't the movies.* Maybe not, but he wasn't rational, that's for sure. I wished I'd had the presence of mind to listen for a car engine right after he left.

"Damn!" I tugged at the window but couldn't force it. My ribs throbbed from him holding me tight. Finally, I realized that if I stayed here long enough, someone would come looking for me. I'd told Aunt Madge I'd probably be back by five; Lester wanted his key. I closed the lid to the toilet and sat on it and rested my head on the sink, and giggled. Thank goodness all the cottages in Ocean Alley now had indoor plumbing. My giggle turned to a sob and I cried for a few more minutes.

"OK, Jolie." I blew my nose and continued talking aloud. "If you keep crying you're going to look like hell when the police get here."

I'd think happy thoughts. *What happy thoughts?* Aloud, I said, "My husband lost all our money and I'm living with my aunt." Aunt Madge's kindly face came into my mind, and I told myself to breathe deeply. *You've got a job. OK, it's one where you find dead bodies and somebody tries to mug you."* Or worse. Harry's thoughtful face came to mind and again I breathed deeply.

Aloud, I said, "At least you're not accused of the murder. And you are alive." That was a big plus. I wasn't Ruth Riordan.

Who killed Ruth Riordan? I mused. Even as disenchanted as I was with Michael, I couldn't believe he did it. Darla had been in Europe. Maybe Darla paid someone to do it. That was pretty melodramatic. Would Paul Hammer really have killed his wife's boss just to get her inheritance a little early? Would he have even known about it? *I bet he'd do it.*

I got back on the floor to lie on my side and closed my eyes. Definitely better than the toilet seat. Who else saw Ruth a lot? Lots of people saw her at church and through its Social Services Committee. They seemed like unlikely candidates.

Mrs. Jasper had an incessant need to talk, but that didn't make her a murderer. *Probably people want to kill her.* I smiled to myself for a second. I should feel sorry for her, she considered Mrs. Riordan her best friend.

Means, motive, and opportunity. Even Aunt Madge knew to think in those terms. I opened my eyes and stared at the beige tiled walls. I wished the prior owners had left a towel in here. I was getting cold. If I had Mrs. Riordan's cash I'd start a fire in the bathtub.

I sat up. Mrs. Riordan's money. What had that lawyer said about the will? Something like, "barring lawsuits from other people," if Michael had killed her the three charities would get the money. And one of those charities was the First Presbyterian social services activity. Mrs. Jasper?

"That's ridiculous." I put my head on the floor again and crossed my arms to stay warmer. Could Mrs. Jasper have done it? She said she hadn't visited the night before I found Mrs. Riordan. But what if she had? Surely Ruth Riordan would not have gone to bed if Mrs. Jasper were there.

I was getting awfully tired now, and my ribs still throbbed.

"Jolie, Jolie!" In my dream, Michael was calling me and he was very angry. And what was that pounding?

I sat up. "Here. I'm here!"

"She's in here, Madge." It was Harry Steele's voice.

It was dark, and I fumbled for the door lock, forgetting that there was a light switch somewhere. The door opened and I nearly fell into Harry, who grabbed me and held me upright as Aunt Madge reached for me.

"He was here." I was sobbing again. "Is he gone?"

"There's no one here, Jolie." Harry's voice was calm, and it helped. When he turned on the light it helped even more.

Aunt Madge patted me on the back like a baby. I pulled back and looked at her, and read the anguish in her face. "I'm so sorry I worried you."

She stroked my hair, tears on her cheeks. "I knew when you weren't home…" Her lip trembled. "And Harry called Lester and he hadn't seen you."

I'd never seen her really cry, and this jarred me into calming down some more. "I'm okay. I kicked him." I gave a short laugh. "And I elbowed him in the eye."

"Come on," Harry said. "Let's get your purse and lock up and go to the police."

I HAD SPENT MORE TIME in the Ocean Alley police station in the last couple weeks than I'd spent in all police stations I'd been in during my entire life combined. Sgt. Morehouse was at home, but someone called him. I figured I was probably at the top of his shit list.

At some point, someone called Lester. This did not make matters easier, but it did shed some light on why Pedone was in the house.

"Jeez, the guy showed me his bank statement. He had the money." Lester was holding his unlit cigar, occasionally putting it between his teeth and then removing it.

"For sure, this guy?" Morehouse had a photo of Pedone, from the looks of it a mug shot from some previous pleasantry.

"Jeez Louise, that's him." Lester began to pace the small conference room. "He came in last week, said he was looking for a place to put some money he'd inherited, thought a rental property would be a good investment."

"I can't believe I suggested you go into appraisal work again," Aunt Madge said.

"Aunt Madge, it's Mother who's the travel agent for guilt trips. Don't send yourself. Besides," I gave her what I hoped was a halfway cheerful grin. "It's probably the safest occupation for me now. He'd never try that again."

Morehouse grunted. "It might be better if you and Harry did a couple together, just for a while."

I almost mouthed off to him, but caught Aunt Madge's eye in time to avoid it.

"We can work something out," Harry said. He winked at me.

Finally, there was nothing more to do, and Morehouse said he would get the state police more involved in looking for Pedone and keep us informed. "I'll call you every day," he said to Aunt Madge.

We trooped out, with Lester still apologizing.

"Relax, Lester, You're the one who lost the sale." This did not cheer him up, but did silence him.

CHAPTER NINETEEN

I REFUSED TO GO TO a doctor, insisting that if my sore ribs were broken it would hurt a lot more. My theory was that the fewer people who knew about Pedone attacking me the better. Good theory, but I hadn't thought about the fact that reporters listen to the police scanner constantly and look at the police blotter each day.

"Local Appraiser Accosted in Vacant House," read the morning headline. It was a short story, and quoted Morehouse saying that they thought I knew the suspect. It made it sound as if I hung around with people who regularly tried to beat me up. Elsie's face came to mind, and I felt a guilty twinge that I had forgotten about her. I should have asked Morehouse if they picked up her husband.

My phone in Lakewood had not rung so much the morning that the article appeared about Robby embezzling from the bank. Some of the callers were Aunt Madge's friends, but some were people I knew. Jennifer Stenner implied it would never happen to anyone from her firm, and I was tempted to tell her I'd hired someone to go after her. Joe Regan offered me free coffee for a week, and Mrs. Jasper wanted to stop by, but Aunt Madge told her I was lying down.

"Didn't you teach your Sunday School classes not to lie?" I asked, as I poured Jazz a small amount of milk.

"Henriette Jasper is the definition of extenuating circumstances."

At about ten-thirty Michael called. He was still in Washington. "This is your arrogant classmate."

My words have a way of coming back to haunt me. "I should probably apologize for that."

"Not necessary. I was out of line."

We were both being very polite. "You were upset; you thought Scoobie might actually have done it."

"I did for a bit. I should have realized he probably couldn't organize all that." I started to say that Scoobie was certainly as smart as we were, and realized it was pointless. We saw Scoobie very differently. "Listen," he continued, "you aren't going to do any more appraisals alone until they arrest this guy, are you?"

"I can usually take care of myself."

"That was obvious." His tone was mocking.

"Michael, did you call to harass me?"

I could hear the amusement in his voice. "Actually, since I'll be hanging around Ocean Alley awhile longer. I was going to offer to ride along the next time you have to do one in a vacant house."

"I guess I'll have humble pie with my coffee."

"Have two helpings," he offered.

I supposed I deserve that. "Listen, I've been meaning to talk to you about something to do with Mrs. Jasper."

He groaned. "I'd rather face a bunch of congressional investigators."

I realized I hadn't asked him about his work in DC, and he said that when he got home he'd pick me up for a trip to Java Jolt to discuss it. He neatly sidestepped Mrs. Jasper, but I had no plans to let go of my idea about her having a possible motive.

That evening Scoobie came over and he and Aunt Madge and I played cards. She wiped both of us out in a game of hearts.

SCOOBIE WAS AT JAVA JOLT when Michael and I arrived there the next day. He said a polite hello and left, and Michael, perhaps reflecting on my anger at his earlier comments, had no comment. He had a lot to say about the accusations about his firm.

"The funny thing is, we weren't one of the companies that withheld energy supplies from California to get higher prices. Of course," he took a sip of coffee, "those firms had to pay a lot of that back."

"Pay back to whom?" I asked.

"Ultimately, consumers." I zoned out somewhat when he described the complexities of making that happen, and tuned in more fully when he started talking about his partners. "Apparently, they figured everyone was paying attention to the California energy crisis, and decided to overcharge for what we sold after that."

"But you weren't in on that."

He nodded. "But I was in charge of all in-house operations, and I hired the auditors every year. It never occurred to me to suspect what was going on, and I guess my partners hid it well enough that the auditors didn't pick up on it."

He shrugged. "Frankly, I'd gotten bored with all of it. If I'd been as involved in things as I should have been, I might have recognized what was going on, at least enough to dig deeper myself or point the auditors toward the mess. When I did start to figure it out, Mom was already sick and I just told my partners I wanted out." He gave a humorless laugh. "Mom being sick made me think about health insurance, so I said all I wanted was a couple weeks or a month to buy some health insurance."

"So that's why you said you were leaving but hadn't stepped down?" I asked.

He nodded. "It was really the chicken-shit approach. Mother urged me to report it, and I didn't want to. Those guys were my friends." He grimaced. "Used to be. That's what we were talking about the night Elmira saw us at Newhart's." He stopped, as if trying not to tear up. "Mother's death made me rethink some things."

"Are you saying these DC investigator types didn't spot all this on their own?"

He took another sip of his coffee. "I heard they had an anonymous tip."

"OK, I won't push."

He raised his eyebrows. "But the bottom line is, the investigators don't believe you were involved in the overcharge stuff, right?" I asked.

"Apparently one of my partners told the government investigators that. If I find out which one, I might offer to let him bunk with me when he gets out of prison."

"Wow." This was way beyond Robby's level of malfeasance. "So, what do you do now?"

"I'll go back to Houston and supervise things until they get sorted out." He looked at me directly. "Want to spend some time in Houston?"

"I...don't know about that." I looked away for a moment, and then back at him. "I'm not sure we have a lot more in common now than we did in high school."

It was his turn to look away. "Maybe," he said, reaching for my hand, "we'd have more in common if we spent more time together."

I felt the same surge of warmth that his touch had prompted in me before, and half of me wanted to pack up Jazz and go with that feeling. The other half figured I might just be back in Ocean Alley a couple months after that. "Maybe."

He slowly released my hand, and his tone was more detached. "Not a very strong maybe."

I shook my head. "It's just, everything, and I mean all the stuff with Robby, too, is just so...new."

"Am I pushing too hard?" A smile played at the corners of his mouth.

"Do you know how not to?"

He shrugged. "Probably not, but I do know some good things are worth waiting for." I must have looked pleased at that, because he added, "But I'm not good at waiting too long."

"Gee, why am I not surprised?" I stirred my coffee, not sure what to say next, so I opted for a complete change of topic. "I wanted to talk to you about Mrs. Jasper."

His gesture was impatient. "You need to give the stuff about my Mother a rest, Jolie."

"I would love to. I just...can't."

"Learn," he said, shortly, and louder than what my Mother would have called an 'inside voice.'

I noted Joe Regan look at us and leaned a bit closer to Michael. "Just hear me out. Please."

He looked at his watch. "I have to leave in ten minutes to take my dad and Honey to the airport. You can have that much time."

"Gee, thanks, sir." Feeling that I should probably not irritate him too much, I launched into my thoughts about why Mrs. Jasper might want a larger share of his Mother's estate, and how she could get it if Michael were guilty of Ruth's murder. He listened, saying nothing.

I plowed on. "She once told me that her work with the church was 'her life.' What if she wanted a lot more money for those causes? What if she did go to the house that night?"

His look was skeptical. "And if that's all true? It doesn't prove," he lowered his voice, "that she murdered Mother. Even if she was there the night before, she would have left. Someone was in there the next morning," his voice tightened. "Someone stopped her breathing." His voice caught and he stopped.

"I know," I used my most gentle tone. "But what if she put something in your mother's tea the night before, and then came back to see if it had killed her?"

His fingers drummed the table. "The key words are 'came back in.' I didn't let her in, and the house was locked."

"But the alarm was off. I'd bet any amount she had a key."

He waved his hand dismissively. "Mother would never have given her one."

"What about when she helped her redo the den?"

He thought about that for a moment. "It just doesn't seem likely."

"But she could have," I persisted. "Maybe to let in a delivery person, or..."

"Jolie, you're grasping," he was getting more irritated.

"We need a way to get her to admit she was there the night before, that's a start."

"Why would she do that?"

"That's where you come in." I had thought about this a lot since my time on the bathroom floor in that little house. "Tell her you want to talk to her about your Mother, you..."

He laughed. "I've spent the time since my Mother's death avoiding her. You want me to call her?"

It took me five more minutes to get him to agree, but in the end, he said he would invite Mrs. Jasper over to take the shoeboxes of costume jewelry to the thrift shop, and ask her if she wanted a couple of pieces for herself. When she was there, he would mention that he had thought she was coming over that night, and ask her about his mother's last evening. Finally, he would say he was collecting any keys neighbors and friends had, so there weren't any outstanding when the Arts Council moved in.

I told Michael I would walk back to Aunt Madge's, and he left to pick up his father and Honey to go to the airport. In honor of convincing him to at least talk to Mrs. Jasper, I selected a chocolate-coated glazed donut and poured a second cup of coffee. Joe Regan grinned at me. "OK, Jolie, one free donut." I stuck out my tongue at him.

It wasn't long before I was aware that people were stealing furtive looks at me from time to time. I considered just standing up and announcing that yes, I was that Jolie Gentil, and no, I did not have a magnet on my back to attract trouble.

AUNT MADGE WAS FURIOUS that Michael had let me walk back to Cozy Corner alone. "What could have gotten into him?"

"Common sense. He knows I'm probably not too much of a target walking from Java Jolt to here in broad daylight." When she jammed a teacup into her dish drainer and didn't say anything, I walked up behind her and hugged her around the waist. "I have a better chance of being arrested for forgetting to take a pooper-scooper when I walk the dogs than of running into Pedone again."

"That's wishful thinking."

It might have been, but it worked for me. I insisted she let me finish the lunch dishes and told her I was going over to Harry's. She didn't argue. Poor Aunt Madge. Her life was a lot simpler before I showed up.

En route to Harry's I saw Scoobie walking along B Street, knapsack on his back, his head bowed against the wind. He accepted my offer of a ride to the library, but did not look too comfortable as he sat beside me in the front seat.

"You mad at me, or something?" I asked.

"Nope. Just wish you'd be more careful."

"Honest, I think that guy was just trying to scare me."

"What guy?" he asked.

Reading the paper was apparently not on Scoobie's to-do list. I explained about Pedone, and he was upset. "You've got to stay away from that guy."

Duh. "I'm not looking for him. Besides, I thought you knew about it. What did you mean about being more careful?"

"I meant about that Riordan guy."

I had to suppress my smile. "He's not as dangerous as he looks."

Scoobie grunted. "His kind never looks dangerous. They just suck the souls out of people around them with their stuck-up attitudes and penny loafers."

I wasn't about to tell him he made no sense, so I played along. "What about the penny loafers?"

"They walk all over you."

I pulled up in front of the library and he got out. Before he shut the door he leaned back in. "You should watch out for the other guy, too."

AS IF TO MAKE UP for sending me to Pedone, Lester had called with two more houses, both occupied, both in the popsicle district. Lester was hot, and interest rates were low. It was a good combination for appraisers.

I couldn't do the houses for another day or two, so I drove by to look at them and then went to the courthouse to research their prior sales and some comps. As I was leaving the Register of Deeds Office, George Winters stopped me.

"What I want to know is, was your life this exciting in Lakewood, or did you just decide to spice it up after you moved here?"

He had his reporter's notebook in his hand, so I nodded toward it and asked, in my most charming voice, "Are we on or off the record?"

He grinned. "We can be off the record."

"Then I'll be happy to tell you what you can do with your question." I shoved open the courthouse door and started down the steps.

"Come on, Jolie. I know we got off on the wrong foot." I kept going. "Okay. I'm sorry I wrote that article that implied you and Riordan were lovers."

"Apology accepted."

"But, since you're my sister and all, I thought I was in the loop."

I stopped, hand on my car door. "Look, I'm sorry I used that name when I called Kenner."

His laugh was more like a whoop. "I love it. You aren't sorry you impersonated a reporter, just sorry you got caught."

"In a nutshell, yes."

As I turned back to open my car door he put his hand on it and opened it. "Listen, who was this guy last night? I mean, I got his name and past record from the police, but why was he after you?"

"My soon-to-be ex-husband owes him some money."

"And so he's after you?" He flipped open his notebook.

I slid into the front seat. "You agreed we were off the record." I smiled as I pulled away, and it really looked as if he was about to throw the notebook at me.

MICHAEL HAD LEFT A message with Aunt Madge saying he'd had an unexpected call from DC and had to go back overnight. This annoyed me, as it meant that he wouldn't be able to talk to Mrs. Jasper for a day or two. Patience is not one of my virtues.

When Aunt Madge was sitting with her guests during their four o'clock tea, I called Mrs. Jasper.

"Jolie, I'm glad you called back," she gushed. "I was so worried when I read about you in the paper."

"Thanks. Listen, I have a favor to ask."

When she assured me she'd be delighted to help, I launched into my rehearsed script. Michael was wrapping up things at the house and wanted her to select a couple pieces of his mother's costume jewelry for herself (this drew a gasp) and then take the rest to the church thrift store. He'd been called away unexpectedly, and I had foolishly left my key to his house inside it and locked the door on the way out earlier today. She had one, didn't she?

There was a long pause before spoke. "A key? No. But..." She stopped again, then continued. "But if Michael hasn't changed the security code on the side door near to the garage, we might be able to use it to get in."

And all this time I had thought only about a key. There was only one door with a keypad. I had noted it during the appraisal, but it hadn't registered as an entry point for the murderer. "That would be great. Shall we meet over there in half an hour?"

When she agreed I was ecstatic. I told Aunt Madge I was heading for Java Jolt and then to the grocery store to pick up some of Jazz's favorite cat food. I felt a slight amount of guilt for lying to her, but not enough to deter me.

I was waiting in the Riordan driveway when Mrs. Jasper pulled up in an older Ford Taurus. She had on a sweat suit and tennis shoes, so I figured she must have scheduled her daily walk for the evening instead of morning.

She got out of the car, smiling. "Good evening. I'm just sorry Michael couldn't be here. When does he come back?"

"Maybe late tomorrow."

The code turned out to be the same. "We have to walk quickly into the house. If we don't push the same security code on the alarm pad inside the kitchen, the alarm will go off."

My heart beat faster. If Michael had changed that code and the alarm sounded, I was screwed. He'd be furious and Mrs. Jasper was sure to tell the story at church, which would mean I'd be in hot water with Aunt Madge, too.

Luckily, the code was unchanged, and we looked around Ruth Riordan's beautiful kitchen, now a mass of packed boxes and empty coffee cups. She sighed. "It's just so sad to see the house this way."

I was too excited for empathy. "The jewelry is in some small boxes in the master bedroom." As we climbed the steps, I hoped Honey hadn't made off with all of it.

Again, my luck held. I was surprised at Mrs. Jasper's eagerness to see what was in them. She looked disappointed when she saw things had been neatly sorted and placed in small plastic bags. "Oh, you've been through it all."

"Yes. Some's going to the estate sale, some to the church thrift shop."

"So, I won't see it all then?" My look must have been puzzled, and she continued. "There were a couple things that especially reminded me of Ruth, but of course anything would be lovely."

"Actually, there's no formal inventory, so you can look through all the boxes." This was going to take forever, and I had what I wanted. I knew she could get in the house.

I was only half-listening as she commented on an occasional piece, and I wandered around the room, glancing out the window into the dusk. We both paused at a sound that seemed to come from downstairs.

"Wind," Mrs. Jasper said, and I nodded.

I was nervous now. *You have no business being in an empty house,* I scolded myself.

"There were some earrings she wore a lot," Mrs. Jasper said, more loudly. "Blue sapphire in the center. I don't see them."

Why did she want those? It means something. "I remember, but I think she must have lost one." I walked over to the bedside table and opened the drawer. The earring was still there, and I pulled it out.

Mrs. Jasper grabbed it from me, a triumphant look on her face. "There you are."

My mind raced. She'd been looking for it. That's why she so wanted to help Michael sort through Ruth's things. It wasn't Ruth's, it was hers. "Did you lose it over here?" I asked.

"Yes. No!" She tried to cover her gaffe. "Where's the other one?"

"There is no other one." I walked closer to her and spoke slowly, looking directly into her eyes. "That wasn't Ruth's earring. It's yours. You lost it here, maybe when you murdered Ruth."

Her face was expressionless, and then she gave me a stilted smile. "You had a difficult time yesterday, Jolie. You aren't thinking clearly."

"Yes, I am. If Ruth was dead and Michael was convicted of her murder, Social Services at the church would get something like one-third of her estate. It would be a lot of money. You would manage that money."

Her eyes studied mine for a moment, and then her voice took on an almost syrupy tone. "You make it sound as if I wanted it for myself. I wouldn't have touched a dime."

I was astounded. She was admitting it. "So you really did it?" In the movies, the sleuth did not sound surprised, but I'd never done this before.

"It shouldn't have been so difficult." She frowned. "I brought over tea bags that night, told her I had just gotten them as a gift and I made the tea It was sassafras, has a strong taste so she wouldn't taste anything I added to it. Those ground-up pills I put in her tea should have slowed down her heart and breathing enough to stop them." Her expression was bitter. "Leave it to Ruth to have such a strong constitution."

"How did you know those pills were there, or was it just a coincidence that you use the same kind of muscle relaxer that Michael had?"

She sniffed. "Ruth was always concerned about Michael, she knew about his back hurting him and never wanted him to lift things for her. She cared a lot more about him than he did about her, I can tell you."

I wasn't about to contradict her, though I thought she was very wrong. When I said nothing, she continued. "I knew he took medicine, so I went into his bathroom one day when I was here to visit with Ruth. I read the label and took a few, and when I looked up the medicine I figured it would work perfectly."

"And when it didn't, how did you know?"

"I came back in when I was sure Ruth would be asleep. Michael came back from the movies earlier than I thought he would, so I went into the closet when he looked in on her. I was going to wait until he went to bed and then help her along, but I fell asleep on the damn closet floor."

"And that's how you lost the earring?" I asked.

"Yes. I didn't notice, of course. And I didn't wake up until morning when he opened the door to look in on her. He almost ruined my plan, but Ruth had told me you were coming, and that Michael was going to leave when you arrived, because he didn't especially like you." She smiled at this.

"How convenient for you."

Her look was almost triumphant. "All I had to do was wait for him to go, and then I could kill her and leave. You work so slowly, I just slipped out the front door when you were in the kitchen."

Her pride in what she had done sickened me, and I sat on the edge of the bed.

"Don't be so wishy-washy. She was going to be dead in a few months anyway. And she wanted Social Services to have some of her money." She smiled. "I just wanted us to have more. You have no idea how many truly needy people there are here." She leaned toward me, as if confiding something important. "And I had to do it before she transferred the house to the arts council. All those people are rich! They don't need this house."

"Mrs. Jasper." I stopped, uncertain what to say. "You need to come to the police with me."

"Nonsense…" she began.

"I got a better idea. Why don't we all go?" Joe Pedone stood in the doorway, gun drawn, and a sick grin across his face.

CHAPTER TWENTY

"WHO ARE YOU?" Mrs. Jasper asked. I took a small amount of pleasure in her frightened expression.

"I'm a real angry guy," he said, in a pleasant tone. His clothes were rumpled, he had a day's beard growth, and his patent leather shoes were dirty. I was pleased to see a purple bruise under one eye. He gestured with the gun. "You ladies can just walk downstairs and I'll follow."

Mrs. Jasper seemed to regain her high opinion of herself. "You can just put that gun away," she said, rising to every inch of her short stature.

My mind seemed fuzzy. He had been following me, and we had not locked the door. *How stupid can you be, Jolie?*

"I could kill you here," he said amiably, "but it's such a pretty house."

Mrs. Jasper looked at me again, fear oozing from her. She had no right to be afraid. She was a murderer, too.

"Where are you taking us?" I needed to stall him, think about what to do.

"For a ride."

Despite his tough-guy talk, I sensed he was no more sure of what he was doing than I was. Unless, of course, his arrest record didn't reflect all of his past work.

"We'll go downstairs." I tried to think of what to do. Maybe if we were in the living room with lights on, someone driving by would see us, and notice his gun.

"You'll go where I say you go." Again he gestured with the gun, and I nodded at Mrs. Jasper to go ahead of me.

When we got to the steps, she said, "I need to use the railing."

I stepped to one side and let her go down on my right. We had gone only a couple steps when I remembered her daily walks and how spry she was. I glanced at her in time to see her arm reach out to push me, but I had no railing to grab.

As I pitched forward, I heard Pedone say, "What the hell are you doing?" In the split second before I actually fell I tried to grab backwards for Pedone, but all I grabbed was air.

Those ads about carpet being soft enough to sleep on are a crock. I landed hard on my shoulder two steps down, and then rolled. Every time I rolled on my right shoulder I gave a squeal.

I landed on the foyer floor, out of breath and sore, but pretty sure I was alive. I could hear someone running down the steps, and then a voice called out. "Police. Drop the gun!"

Gunshots are very loud. I had no idea. There was about a two-second pause after the loud crack of a gun, and someone started tumbling down the steps after me. My mind told me to move, but none of my muscles were inclined to follow directions.

Suddenly, I was aware of someone diving toward me, but not from above, from the hallway nearby. He slid into me and pushed me out of the way, so the body coming down the stairs landed behind us.

"Yo, Jolie," said Scoobie.

I fainted.

I REMEMBER SGT. MOREHOUSE tapping me on the cheek, and me telling him not to call Aunt Madge, but I must have passed out again, because I don't remember anything until a while later, in the emergency room. Of course, he called her.

"Jolie," Scoobie whispered in my ear. "I think your aunt's out there. You probably want to wake up."

"What? Oh. Scoobie." I looked at him intently. "You pushed me."

He grinned. "You can thank me later."

They must have given me something for the pain, because my shoulder didn't feel too bad and I was kind of woozy. I thought I remembered someone saying it had been dislocated and they were 'putting it back.'

"She said she was going to get cat food." Aunt Madge came in from the other side of the curtain, Sgt. Morehouse behind her. She saw I was awake, and frowned at me. No sympathy there. "Young lady, don't you ever lie to me again."

Morehouse had the nerve to chuckle, and she turned on him. "That's not funny." He sobered quickly.

"I was just supposed to see Mrs. Jasper." Aunt Madge actually glared at me. "I know, I should have told you, but you just would have worried."

"I wonder why?" she asked, but her expression was softening as she looked at me. "Why does she have that IV in?" she asked Morehouse.

"Uh..."

He was saved from a response by a no-nonsense woman in a nurse's uniform who flipped back the curtain and entered. "There are too many people in here."

"I'll leave," Morehouse said, and beat it.

"I saved her. I'm staying." Scoobie said.

Aunt Madge lunged at him and hugged him, and when she finally released him she fished in her pocket for a tissue. She turned to the nurse. "What did happen to her?" Ordinarily, I would have objected to being talked about in the third person when I was in the room, but as I wasn't sure what had happened in the last half-hour or so, I kept quiet.

"She was pushed down a flight of steps and dislocated her shoulder, but the doctor has fixed it. We've taken x-rays of her head and neck. There is nothing broken."

"That's a good thing," Scoobie said to me, reassuringly.

"The IV is just for pain medicine and hydration." The woman smiled. "She'll be fine."

I was glad to hear that.

"Who pushed her?" Aunt Madge asked.

"Mrs. Jasper," Scoobie said.

"That's right, she did." I tried to sit up and, reminded of my shoulder, sank back onto the pillow.

"If you'll excuse me, I have other patients." The nurse left.

Aunt Madge sat on a chair next to Scoobie. "Was it an accident?"

"No way," Scoobie said. I was happy to let him tell the story. "They were coming down the steps, in front of the guy with the gun, and..."

"Gun!"

Scoobie was very patient with Aunt Madge. "The man from the boardwalk. The police call him Pedone."

"I told you not to go out alone," Aunt Madge said to me, with her severest frown.

"Yes ma'am," I said, very fast.

"Anyway," Scoobie continued, "they were at the top of the steps when Mrs. Jasper just pushed her. Sgt. Morehouse said this Pedone guy should drop the gun, but he aimed it at the sergeant, and Sgt. Morehouse shot him." Scoobie drew a breath, obviously keyed up. "But just in the arm. I think he's somewhere in the hospital."

I did not like that idea.

"And why were you there, Adam?" Aunt Madge asked.

"I saw Jolie pull out of your driveway, and Pedone followed her. I ran to the police." He frowned. "No one believed me, but Sgt. Morehouse was there, and he came out."

"That's why he called and asked for you," Aunt Madge said, nodding at me.

Bless him, I thought.

"He didn't tell me what he wanted," Aunt Madge continued.

"We drove to Java Jolt, and then he thought of the Riordans'. The garage entrance was open, so we went in." Scoobie stopped and looked thoughtful. "That's about all I know, except that when Pedone started to fall down the steps I figured I should push Jolie out of the way."

"Adam, if you hadn't seen her…" Aunt Madge was crying for real, now.

"Aunt Madge. Really, I'm okay. I promise." I tried to reach for her arm, but she was too far away.

Then she was furious. "You could have been killed! What would I tell your mother?"

"Yeah, now I have to tell her," I realized I was in for one hell of a tongue lashing. It only takes two seconds for my parents to make me feel like I'm five years old.

Sgt. Morehouse came back in. "You're in luck," he said to me.

"This is luck?" I was starting to come to my full senses, which is not always a good thing.

"Mrs. Jasper says you and her were there to look at jewelry, but Pedone said he overheard a conversation between you and her."

Morehouse grinned. "He says he's willing to tell us about it if we take it into consideration when we prosecute him."

I was actually going to be in debt to Pedone. *Who knew?*

"So, what did happen before we saw you?" Morehouse asked.

I told him about my theory, and that Michael had agreed to help me find out if there was any substance to it, but he'd been called out of town and I didn't want to wait for his return. As Aunt Madge made tutting and gasping noises, I relayed everything through arriving at the top of the steps. "It wasn't until after we started down that I kind of wondered why she wanted the railing. She's pretty spry."

Morehouse thought about this. "Probably just gave her better leverage to push you."

"But why?" Aunt Madge asked.

"Jolie would be dead, or so she hoped, and Pedone didn't really have a beef with Jasper. That's my guess, but we may never know. She's insisting they were just there to look at jewelry and crying about Ruth Riordan being her best friend."

"I'm surprised she told me the whole story." I said this as much to myself as the others.

Morehouse shrugged. "I doubt she would have owned up to it if you brought her to me. It would have been her word against yours, and where was the proof?"

"She got me this coat," Scoobie said, and we all turned to look at his second-hand pea jacket. "Why would she do that, and then kill somebody?"

"People are complex," Aunt Madge said, gently. "It's rare you meet someone who is all good or all bad."

"In my book, she's just a plain thug with a motive," Morehouse said. "A pretty sick one," he added.

THE HOSPITAL KEPT ME overnight to monitor my blood pressure and make sure I didn't have a concussion. This was fine by me, as I was having trouble maneuvering my arm in the sling I was supposed to wear for a couple of days. I also figured it would be good to let Aunt Madge have a night to get over being so mad at me.

Contrary to conventional wisdom, the hospital food was not bad, and the next morning I was trying to butter my toast with one hand when the door to the room pushed open. Ramona looked windswept, her long, blonde hair loose and a deep purple cape over her shoulders. "Jolie!" She stood and stared at me.

"Could you do this?" I shoved the toast toward her.

"Okay." She dropped a small notebook on my bed and started to work on the toast. "I was on the boardwalk on the way to my walk, and Joe Regan hollered at me. He had the paper."

George Winters. I hoped he had the decency not to come to the hospital. "Damn." I chewed hungrily on the toast. "So, everybody knows?"

"They know some guy got shot at the Riordans', and you ended up in here." She wiped her hands on my napkin. "But there's not a lot of why. Where was Michael?"

Michael. Aunt Madge's anger was nothing compared to what his was going to be. "He had to go to DC on business."

"Ooh, and you must have a key. That'll fry Jennifer."

I laughed, really laughed. "You can tell her she has nothing to worry about."

This interested her more than the story of what had happened last night. "Really? She'll be glad to hear that." She reached for the small notebook. "Every day I write down the saying I put on the board. Do you want to borrow it?"

"That's so kind." I had enough of them when I read the board. "I might forget it here. Can I read it later, at the store or something?"

"We'll have supper some night." She stood. "I can't be late for work. I'm opening the store."

She bent over and kissed me, and I thanked her for coming. "Maybe you, me and Scoobie."

She pulled the curtain back to let in sunshine, and added, "Roland was in Java Jolt. He said to tell you Elsie Hammer's going to stay with them for a few days, until she finds another place to live." Ramona looked at me, perhaps expecting a comment on how I knew Elsie well enough for Roland to send that message.

"That's good," I said, my mouth full of toast.

AUNT MADGE CAME TO collect me, as she said, about ten a.m. "I was going to come an hour ago, but between the phone and Jazz, I couldn't get out of the house."

"Jazz. What's wrong with her?" This concerned me much more than my shoulder.

"I suppose she's upset because you aren't home. She's been chasing the dogs all over the kitchen and my sitting room."

"Don't you mean the dogs are chasing her?" I asked.

"I wish I did. I can make them stop." She paused in collecting my clothes from a closet. "It took me fifteen minutes to catch her, and then I only did because I opened a can of tuna."

I would have paid to see this, but did not say this aloud. "I'm sorry, Aunt Madge."

"Tuna's cheap."

"No, I mean about worrying you, and all."

She was taking my clothes out of the tiny closet, and turned to face me. "You've always been headstrong. I suppose that's why it's hard for you and your mother sometimes." She paused and then smiled, but there was a wicked twist to it. "But if you do anything like this again, I'll make your mother look docile."

THE FLOWERS FROM MICHAEL arrived in the early afternoon. All the note said was, "You owe me stairway carpeting." Aunt Madge thought this was warped, but I was pleased that he had a sense of humor about what had happened.

Though I didn't think I owned a muscle or joint that wasn't sore, I knew I'd been lucky. As Scoobie said when he visited late in the day, if I'd landed on my head a clam would have more mobility than I did.

I was lying on the couch sipping tea after dinner when Michael arrived. Aunt Madge decided she needed more orange juice for her breakfast guests, which I knew was a lie since there were always extra cans in the freezer.

"You really did it this time, Gentil," Michael said as he settled a few feet from me on the couch. "I have a bullet hole in the wall and crime scene tape all over the place. And I believe I already mentioned the carpet."

"You didn't mention the lack of time in prison if they got interested in you again." I matched his serious tone with my own.

"True. You get some credit for that." He smiled. "What in the hell were you thinking?"

"I'm just not good at waiting. Of course, I thought all I was doing was checking to see if Mrs. Jasper had a key."

"I never use the keypad for the door near the garage; I use the key, since I usually have them out when I get out of the car." He shook his head. "I can't say mother never used the pad, because she obviously gave Mrs. Jasper the code to use it at some point. I can't imagine why."

"Maybe when they were working on the den, or maybe they went in that way once and Mrs. Jasper just watched when your mother used the keypad." I set my teacup on the coffee table. "It's not likely we'll ever know."

At this he grew glum. "I talked to Sgt. Morehouse a couple times today. Other than Pedone's and your testimony, there is not a lot to link her to Mom's death. Not even finger prints on the doorknob. She must have opened it with her skirt or jacket over her fingers."

"She could have even been wearing gloves. Older people get cold more easily." When he looked at me skeptically, I added, "My testimony should be slightly more believable than Pedone's."

"Slightly," he agreed. "It's a lot more than they had to go on with me, and you saw how hard the prosecutor pushed that."

"Scary."

Neither of us said anything for a few moments, and then our eyes met.

"You'd probably hate Houston," he said. When I kept looking at him, he added, "I'm going back there to run the company while my partners stand trial. It'll help our employees keep their jobs, at least for a while."

"Probably too hot and humid for me," I agreed. "I know a B&B where you can have a free room whenever you want to visit Ocean Alley."

"I can probably afford the rate." He stood and then bent over and kissed me lightly. "Thanks for believing in me."

"What are friends for?" I asked.

WITHIN TWO DAYS I WAS raring to get back to work. Despite regular visits from Harry, Scoobie and Ramona, it was boring to sit on the couch and play with Jazz and the guys. Jazz had taken to diving off the bookcase or any table onto Mister Rogers' back, which terrified him. Several time a day I had to coax him from Aunt Madge's bedroom. "You're letting her know it bothers you," I told him. "Just act nonchalant and she'll get tired of it."

"I'm not sure that's within a dog's realm of reasoning," Aunt Madge said, as she kneaded a bowl of afternoon bread.

Later I walked down to the boardwalk to enjoy the fifty-degree weather, rare for this time of year, and sat facing the ocean. When I came here I could not have imagined such an eventful first month. I was trying to get away from the limelight and restore some order to my life. While my life with Aunt Madge had not been as peaceful as I'd planned thus far, I had unmasked a murderer, found a job with a nice boss, and renewed friendships. Not a bad inventory for a little more than a month. Something to build on.

"Yo, Jolie." Scoobie was coming toward me on roller skates.

"Pretty cool. Where'd you get those?"

"Traded some guy for my knapsack." He carried a large plastic grocery store bag that was quite full. "I needed a new one anyway, that one was starting to stink. There's a sale at Wal-Mart. You can give me a ride up there."

"Sure."

He circled me and skated to an easy stop beside my bench and sat next to me. "Read my new poem." He pulled it from his bag.

start of a voyage
the end of our fate?
hearts out of storage
kept safe for a soul mate

"This is beautiful. Umm. Is this the whole thing?"

He shrugged. "I'm not sure. If more comes to me, it won't be."

"If more comes to you. This comes from you, Scoobie." I searched for words. "You're as good as your poetry."

"I may be someday." He stood up. "Who I am now is OK." He grinned. "I'll go stow my stuff, and stop by your aunt's, if it's OK to go to the store now."

I nodded, still thinking about his poem.

As he rose to skate away, Scoobie's plastic bag caught the edge of the bench and its contents spilled. I stooped to help him collect the items, and then sat back on my heels, with a red white-board marker and small sponge eraser in my hands.

"You rewrite Ramona's board?" I asked, amazed.

He grinned as he took them. "Yeah. She really needs to lighten up."

"I never would have guessed you for that."

"You, Ms. Gentil, have a lot to learn."

So I do.

* * * *

Authors appreciate reviews. If you enjoyed Appraisal for Murder, please consider writing on short review, and letting your library know you liked the book. Thanks!

Books in the Jolie Gentil cozy mystery series are:
Appraisal for Murder
Rekindling Motives
When the Carny Comes to Town
Any Port in a Storm
Trouble on the Doorstep
Behind the Walls
Vague Images
Ground to a Halt

Books are in ebook (all formats), paperback, large print, and audio. Your library or bookstore can order copies, or you can purchase them online. For sites that sell the books, go to
www.elaineorr.com/fiction.html/
www.elaineorr.blogspot.com
Follow Elaine on Twitter @elaineorr55

Made in the USA
Middletown, DE
18 May 2015